CHOIR BOY II:
A Time To Reap

To Herbert
I thank God for you. May
he continue to bless you abundantly
Clyde Niv 10.9.11

CHOIR BOY II:
A Time To Reap

C.L. Austin

To order additional copies of this book, contact:
Xlibris Corporation
1-888-795-4274
www.Xlibris.com
Orders@Xlibris.com
101045

Dedicated to Aunt Etta, much love to you.

Chapter 1

"Seeing all those lights, people running around, the noise, not to mention seeing Alicia lying there with blood all over her—it was just too much for me.

"My head was spinning. I was confused and overwhelmed. I had just lost everything, including the person that was very special to me. No, I wasn't running away from anything. I was confused."

"So tell me, Sonny. You said that Alicia was dead at the scene. Are you sure that she was dead? Perhaps your dreams might be trying to tell you something."

"I guess she was. The paramedics covered her head with the sheet. Not only that, but everybody saw that she was dead."

Sonny's therapist tried to be as objective as he could be. "Sonny, sometimes when there is a crime that took place like this one the paramedics will usually cover all of the victim's heads to protect their identity. Now I'm not saying that Alicia wasn't killed. I'm just saying that you can never be sure of something like this. You mentioned that sometime after you arrived home, you had visitors from Las Vegas."

"Yes. Her uncle and aunt came here to let me know about a contract."

"Did they mention anything about a funeral for Alicia?"

Sonny thought for a moment. "Come to think about it you know, they never did."

"So tell me, Sonny. Doesn't it seem sort of strange that they wouldn't mention anything to you about Alicia's funeral, if she indeed died? I mean, really. If you spent as much time with her as you did, they must have felt it necessary to tell you about any impending funeral arrangements. Don't you think?"

It all seemed to make sense to Sonny. He began to wonder if Alicia had actually died.

"Don't try to figure it out right now, Sonny. But here's what I feel you should do. Before our next appointment, decide whether you want to get answers to the questions you have about Alicia. I really think that you need some closure."

"You know what, Dr. Smith? I don't think it's closure that I need."

Rising from his chair, the therapist walked over to a window and looked out. "I know what you're thinking, Sonny, and I agree."

Looking out of the window, Sonny responded, "I don't know if she's dead or not. Why hasn't anyone told me?"

"That I can't tell you, Sonny."

Sonny looked at his watch. "I know it's time for me to go. I'll call you next week and let you know what I've decided."

"You do that, Sonny. Take care of yourself."

As Sonny was headed out of the door, Dr. Smith spoke, "I'm glad that you haven't used since you've been coming to visit me. How long has it been? Three months now?"

Sonny smiled, saying, "Yeah, three months. Thanks, you really helped me a lot."

Sonny left the doctor's office, letting the door close behind him. Outside the elevator, he began to think about the visit from Pearl and DJ while he was standing at the foot of his deceased friend's grave. His mind wandered back.

"Hey, Bro Winston, it sure was a crazy ride, but I made it. I got my name up in lights. I know you would have been proud of me, but you know, there's something bothering me. I met this young lady that I got really close to. We had a great time together. Of course, not all of it was good, but that's life, huh.

Anyway, the strangest thing is that I never really got a chance to know anything about her. Yeah, she was a lot of fun and good-looking, but there were so many things I believe that she intentionally kept from me about herself. Well, I guess, at this point, it really doesn't matter now that she's gone."

Sonny began to brush dried leaves from around the grave marker when he heard a horn blowing. He turned to see who it was and quickly recognized Pearl and DJ as they both got out of the car.

He was glad to see them as he hurried to his feet and ran over to meet them. Giving Pearl a hug and DJ a handshake, he glanced over to the police officer who was with them, along with some guy in a light brown suit and tie.

"Hi, baby, how are you doing?" asked Pearl.

"I'm doing just fine, Ms. Pearl, and how are the two of you doing?"

"Well, I guess about as good as expected."

Sonny's demeanor changed as he began to speak. "I'm so very sorry . . ."

"That's okay, Sonny. We are too. We know you care a lot for Alicia. So do we."

As Sonny reminisced, the ding from the elevator got his attention and he got in.

There was a young African-American woman standing in the corner of the elevator as if she was contemplating whether or not she was going to get off. As the door was closing, she quickly stuck her hand between them, reversing the mechanism, and she hurried out.

Sonny remembered how hard it was for him to see a therapist at first. He pushed the button for the first floor and the door closed. Watching the floors' numbers go down as he descended from floor 7 to 1, he again thought about the conversation that took place at the cemetery.

Ding!

Stepping out of the elevator, it dawned on him that neither Pearl nor DJ spoke of Alicia in the past tense. He thought, *I wonder why?*

Walking out through the double doors, he decided to stop at the library and get on the Internet to get some information about the crime that took place in Las Vegas more than three months ago.

He had to park his vehicle across the street, so before crossing, he pushed his unlock button on the remote control. The car alarm whistled and the door locks popped up.

Sonny really appreciated driving his Denali. Just as always, he cranked up the stereo as he drove off. Going down the street, he listened to his Oldies station.

Tom Joyner rocked Rick James and Sonny sang along. He thought about Alicia when Tina Marie sang her part of Fire and Desire.

The song played until he arrived at the library. Pulling his car into the parking lot and taking a parking ticket, he preceded in driving around until he found a safe place to park.

Not wanting to take any chances of getting bumped by a careless driver, he pulled into the space as close to the curb as he could get and checked the distance between the lines and was satisfied. Inside the library, Sonny found a computer station that was available.

There were always a lot of people at the stations; most of them were college students and homeless people. Even this time, Sonny had to really scan the area because it seemed as if all of the stations were taken.

At his station, Sonny decided to do a Google search. He typed in google.com, then Las Vegas newspapers.

The Web page opened to what he was looking for. He clicked on the Las Vegas Sun. While waiting for the page to open, he heard some squabbling coming from behind him. Turning to look he saw two men fighting over an old coat that was lying on the floor.

One looked like he was in his forties and dressed very well in a light blue shirt and tie. The other was obviously homeless. He was wearing a pair of torn pants over a pair of pants and had on several dirty shirts. He reminded Sonny of some of the guys living in the homeless shelter in Las Vegas.

Apparently, as Sonny could gather from the loud discussion, the homeless guy had laid his coat across the chair where the other guy in the suit was sitting when he had gotten up and went to the bathroom. When he came back, he saw the coat and threw it on the floor.

The homeless man was offended by this. He told the suit guy, "Hey, sir, just because my coat is dirty, doesn't mean you have to throw it on the floor."

The other guy responded, "Man, get away from me. I don't need somebody like you telling me what not to do."

"What do you mean somebody like me? You think you're better than me? Is that what it is?"

It just happened that the guy in the suit was a Caucasian man and the homeless guy was Black.

"Yeah, you and everybody that looks like you."

"Now he's gone too far," said Sonny. He got up and approached the two men.

"I think you owe this man an apology," he said to the white man.

He looked at Sonny and asked, "And who do you think you are?"

"Listen, dude, it doesn't matter who I am, nor does it matter who this man is. You should respect what he is, a human being."

The white man looked into Sonny's eyes, which didn't even blink. He could see that Sonny was not about to put up with his bigotry. Still he didn't pick up the coat. "To hell with you, boy," he said and turned away.

Sonny gave a grimacing smile. "Bustin," he said. He wanted to open up a fresh can of whup ass, but he chilled instead.

"You know what, dude? You've just proven to everybody here that this gentleman, whose coat you threw down on the floor, is the better of you two."

When Sonny turned to pick up the coat, the man whom he defended had already picked it up.

"Thank you, young man. I could've handled him, but . . ."

Sonny interrupted saying, "That's okay. I thought I would step in, besides you remind me of an old friend of mine."

"Well, thanks anyway," said the homeless man. He continued asking, "So what's your name? I don't think I've ever seen you around here."

Sonny looked up at the man and said, "My name is Sonny. Sonny Brooks."

The man began to have an inquisitive look. "Why do I feel that I've heard that name somewhere?" he asked.

"Are you from around here?" asked Sonny.

The man began rubbing his unkempt hair, trying to remember. "No, I'm not. I'm actually from everywhere and nowhere all at the same time. I just get around."

"Well, anyway, I hope you have a good day," said Sonny.

As Sonny was headed back to his computer, the police came in following someone who looked like a library employee. The woman pointed in the direction of the white man in the blue shirt and tie. He was busy on the Internet looking at some pictures.

11

The police approached him from behind and got his attention. "Sir, we need to speak with you."

When he looked up and saw the police, he tried to jump up and run, but they apprehended him. One of the cops grabbed him by his arm and wrestled him to the ground and cuffed his hands behind him.

"Bustin!" said Sonny.

The homeless man who had not yet left saw all that happened, but what really got his attention was when he heard Sonny say, "Bustin."

After the cops took the man outside and put him in the squad car and drove off, the homeless man said to Sonny, "I think I know where I recognize your name."

Sonny looked at him. "Okay, tell me where."

"Have you ever been to Las Vegas?"

"Yes. In fact, I have."

"That's it then. I was in Vegas about three months ago. I was staying at the rescue mission. Now I wasn't sure at first, but when I heard you say that word, um, I think it's Bustin that made me know for sure that you were the one."

Sonny gathered his things and said to the man, "Let's go outside."

He hurried the man out. When they were about fifty feet from the doorway, he stopped and told the man. "I need to talk to you about something very important."

He asked Sonny, "How important is it?"

Sonny knew what he was alluding to. "Where would you like to eat?"

"Well, that all depends on how much money you're willing to spend."

"A number 5 meal deal or a number 6 value meal—those are your choices," said Sonny firmly.

"I'll take the meal deal, the fries are better."

"Fine, let's go."

Sonny forgot to get a coin for the parking lot gate. "Wait here, I'll be back."

When he returned, he made haste getting to the nearest McDonalds.

He pulled up close to the entrance and asked the homeless guy if he wanted to go in.

"Sure, that way I can get refills."

They went inside and approached the counter. There were not many people inside, so they were helped right away. "What can I get you?" asked the cashier.

Sonny started to order for the homeless man but caught himself. He looked at him and said, "You know what? I don't even know your name."

"I'm Simon Jonas, better known as Peter."

"Are you serious?" asked Sonny.

"I'm as serious as a heart attack."

"I wish you wouldn't say that," responded Sonny.

"Say what?"

"That 'heart attack' thing my friend died of a heart attack."

"Well, I'm just saying that's how serious I am about my name being what it is, that's all."

"All right then, Peter Simon, go ahead and order whatever you want."

"I'll have the number 5, and super-size it please."

The cashier took Peter's order and asked Sonny for his. "No, ma'am, I'll just have some tap water."

Sonny paid for the food, and the two went and sat near the exit door close to Sonny's vehicle.

Peter went back to the condiment area and completely loaded his French fry box that he had emptied onto his tray full of ketchup.

Sonny didn't waste any time getting to the questions. "So, Peter, you said that four months ago, you were in Las Vegas. Do you remember hearing or reading about the murders that took place there around that time?"

With his mouth full of fries, he answered, "Yes, I was there and do remember the murders. I also remember that shortly after that took place, you entered the rescue mission."

He paused to take a bite of his sandwich. Then he paused again. "I don't know where my manners are," he said. Setting his sandwich back into its container and closing his eyes, he began to pray.

"Dear God in heaven, I thank you again for feeding me today. Bless this young man for his generosity. In your Son's mighty name, I pray. Amen."

Sonny was not surprised by this at all. He knew that many homeless people were very thankful to God for whatever they received.

"Now where were we? Oh yeah, I was about to eat this burger."

Bustin, thought Sonny.

"Actually," said Sonny, I asked you if you remembered the incident in Vegas four months ago."

"I told you yes, Sonny."

"Well, tell me this. Do you remember anything about a funeral being held for Alicia Highsmith?"

Peter again had his mouth full of fries. Before he swallowed, he took a deep, long sip of soda from his straw.

After swallowing, he thought for a moment and then answered, "You know, Sonny, as I think about it, there was no mention of a funeral at all." He began to devour the rest of his burger.

Sonny was quiet for a couple of minutes. He was not sure what else to ask Peter, who, after he had consumed all of his food, rose up and got a refill on his soda. Returning, he had a question for Sonny.

"Now it's my turn to ask you a question, Sonny."

"Okay, go ahead."

"You don't recognize me at all, do you?"

Sonny studied the man intensely but came up with nothing. "No, I don't recognize you. I never even heard your name before today."

"That's because you only knew me by my alias."

Right there in McDonalds, Peter began revealing himself as he explained to Sonny their previous acquaintance.

"You see, Sonny, I was your drummer, who stood in for your original drummer that got sick the night you were going to perform live with your band for the first time." It became clear to Sonny this person's real identity.

Now Sonny's eyes were opened, and he remembered. "Bustin! Sticks, I remember you."

"There you go with that damned word."

"Well, what do you expect? I thought you were some helpless homeless guy, and here I am feeding you. You owe me an explanation."

"Sure I do. First, my real name is Mathias. Mathias Blackmon. I am a private investigator, and by the way, I paid your drummer to take the night off. The police special drug task force wanted me to go undercover because they had gotten wind of a possible drug operation taking place at Starz."

"You sure had me fooled. You are definitely a master of disguise. So why did you tell me your name was Peter? You even swore to it."

"You know, Sonny, when a person like me is on a case, I have to always keep people in the dark about my identity."

"So how do I know that your real name is Mathias?"

Reaching into his coat pocket, he pulled out his badge and identification card.

"Are you satisfied now?" he asked Sonny.

"I guess so. How did you find me anyway?"

"You are not an easy fellow to find, Sonny."

"Why have you been looking for me?"

"Believe it or not, I've been looking for you for the same reasons you were asking me, or 'Peter' those questions about Alicia Highsmith."

Sonny was curious about how Mathias found him in Saint Louis.

"It wasn't easy. I had to trace every step you made since the time you got involved with Quinton Brown aka Q."

"Quinton. I thought he got his name from his fraternity?"

"Well, he was an Omega, so he used the Q for his name."

Sonny became serious. "So tell me what happened to Alicia. Is she dead?"

"Sonny," said Mathias, wiping excess makeup from around his lips, "I can assure you that Alicia is alive."

"So how is she? Where is she?"

"Well, Sonny, Alicia is in a coma."

Sonny was unsure of his feelings. He was glad to hear that she was alive but certainly not happy to hear that she is comatose.

"So, Mathias, how long has she been in that condition? I mean, I thought she was dead. She looked dead, and the medics had a sheet over her head at the crime scene."

"I'm sure they did, Sonny. That's what they usually do when there's a homicide. Just in case the killer or killers are still in the area. They don't want anyone to know either way."

"What about Q? Was he killed?"

"Yes, he was killed. There were also some other people there that we identified, one of which worked at the hotel that you were staying at."

Sonny was oblivious to all of this. He did not know what the reason was for all of this to happen. Although he remembered that his money was stolen.

"Was he the person who broke into my room and stole my money?"

Mathias had removed all of the makeup from his face, and his true identity was fully revealed. "So do you recognize me now, Sonny?" he asked.

Sonny took a minute to try and recollect his memory. He finally realized who it was sitting with him. "You are the guy who tried to talk to me at the homeless shelter."

"That's very good, Sonny."

"I remember you asking me all kinds of questions about what happened, but I wouldn't talk to you."

"That's right, Sonny. You would not talk to me or anybody else other than that white girl at the shelter. What was her name?"

"Her name was Sam," Sonny answered. He then added, "You didn't answer my question."

"Remind me what it was again."

"My money dude. The guy that was killed at the murder scene. You said he worked at the hotel. Did he steal my money?"

Rubbing his head, which was full of hair, Mathias answered, "It's very possible, Sonny. We found a large sum of money on his person. Alicia also had some cash."

"You don't think Alicia was in on this, do you?" asked Sonny.

"Well, Sonny, we traced her steps back to the hotel that you were staying and talked to the manager. He explained that Alicia had arranged to throw you a big celebration party, after the gig was over at Starz. He also said she paid him in cash."

Sonny was not sure what to think about all this.

"So are you telling me that Alicia was in cahoots with this guy?"

"I'm not telling you that at all. We don't quite know who was involved with what happened beyond the gang that we think was involved. All we know is that there was an apparent drug deal that went bad and left dead bodies all over the place. That night, I actually got side-tracked by what was going on inside the club and missed the major deal."

"How did you miss all of that?"

"Believe it or not, somebody from inside the club tipped me off. I had a person working from the inside. Don't ask who it was. Anyway, he gave me a bad tip. Apparently, he double-crossed me. This guy was very clever."

Sonny was now standing in the restaurant with his hands in his pockets. He became aware of how much trouble he had escaped but wasn't sure if he was clear of any wrongdoing.

"So, Mathias, you came here looking for me. So now you've found me. Now what?"

"Yes, I have, Sonny. Please sit down. There's something of great importance I need to tell you."

Sonny took the same seat that he was in.

"Sonny, there is something that has been bugging me since I've been on this case."

Sonny became very curious. "So what is it?"

"All of the time that you spent with Alicia, did she ever let you in on what was going on?"

"What do you mean 'what was going on,' Mathias?"

"What was going on between her and Q?"

"No. I never even thought about that. From the time I won the big contest, things began to move very fast. The next thing I know is, Alicia is lying on the street, she and Q all shot up."

"Sonny, there is a lot more to the story than you think. I'll tell you what. I'll be here for a couple of days." Mathias pulled his wallet from his breast pocket, removed a card, and handed it to Sonny.

"Here's my card. If you can remember anything that you may have heard Alicia saying to Q, or anything that the two of you talked about, please give me a call."

Sonny took the card and read it. "So you are a private investigator working for the police," Sonny concluded.

"Yes, that's right. I was hired to find out where you were and if you had any information about the drug deal that was on."

Sonny was very confused by all of this. "You know, dude, I don't know a thing about any drug deal, but I would like to know how Alicia is doing."

"Sonny, we have Alicia in protective custody. Even though she's in the hospital, we are not sure if the killing is over. We know that the shooters may still be out there, and they may be looking for you."

Sonny's heart skipped a beat. "How do you know this? Why would anybody be looking for me?"

Again Mathias went into his wallet; this time he pulled out a letter.

"I found this note nailed to the door of Starz nightclub about a week after the killings."

He handed the note to Sonny. He read the note: *We got Q and his freak. We want the choirboy too.*

"What is this supposed to mean, Matthias?"

"That's just it. We don't know, but we thought that perhaps you may be able to help us. Do you know why anybody would be after you, Sonny?"

Thinking about it for a minute, Sonny answered, "I have no idea."

Sonny handed the note back to Mathias. "Okay, I'll call you if I remember anything."

He got up from the table and started to leave.

"I would like to have your cell number, so I can call you with information about Alicia."

Sonny paused. Against his better judgment, he wrote his number on a napkin and gave it to Mathias.

"Where are you going, Sonny?"

"I'm gonna leave here and go home. When I get there, I'm going to pretend as though this conversation never happened. How's that?"

"Just call me, Sonny."

Sonny left the restaurant, got into his vehicle, and drove home. At the restaurant, Mathias was thinking, *He's the only person that can help Alicia. I hope he realizes this.*

Not giving a second thought about the conversation he just left from, on his way home, Sonny listened to the song that Brother

Winston had written. Since he's been home, he began working on a recording at his friend's studio.

He had rearranged the melody and added some more lyrics to what was already a beautifully written song. As he approached his father's house, he could see that RJ was there.

The two of them were getting along, but Sonny knew that RJ was just trying to avoid upsetting his father. Sonny, on the other hand, was trying to avoid RJ.

After parking his car behind RJ's and going into the house, the first person to greet him was Martha; she was in the kitchen preparing supper.

"Hello, Sonny."

"Hi, Mom," he returned the greeting with a kiss on the cheek.

Moments later, RJ entered the kitchen.

"Hey, Sonny."

"Hey," Sonny responded.

Sonny went into the fridge and took out a bottle of water and sat at the kitchen table.

"So, Mom," said RJ, "I just spoke with Tanya, and she said she should be returning back to St. Louis this week, maybe Saturday."

"That's good. Maybe she'll be here for church on Sunday," said Martha.

"Yeah?" said Sonny. He continued, "I haven't seen Tanya since that day we all met her for the first time at church. Man, she was fine!"

"That is my fiancé you're speaking of, Sonny, said R.J."

"Yeah, and does that mean she's not fine? It's a compliment, bro."

"Just watch how you speak about the woman I'm going to marry, okay?"

"Okay, much respect." Sonny then got up from the table and went into the den where his father was watching the evening news.

"Hello, Dad."

"Hi, Son, what do you know?"

Sonny sat on the sofa across from his dad who was sitting in his leather recliner.

"Man, I had some kind of a day. Work was busy and I stopped at the library today."

Sonny intentionally did not tell his father about the therapy sessions; he wanted to keep that private from everybody, since nobody knew about his drug use while he was in Las Vegas.

"What did you stop at the library for, to check out a book?" asked Raleigh.

"No, sir, I wanted to look up some information on the Internet."

Raleigh didn't bother to ask any further questions, as they both quietly watched the news.

Sonny became more than interested when the reporter announced a big story about a con artist being arrested that day at the public library, downtown.

"I was there today when that happened!" said Sonny.

"You don't say," remarked Raleigh.

"Yeah, it was crazy. I was talking to that very person just before the cops came in and grabbed him. It totally messed me up."

Raleigh sat up straight in his chair and asked Sonny, "What were you talking to him about, Son?"

"Believe it or not, I was actually defending a homeless man, whom he was disrespecting."

Raleigh gave Sonny a look of content. "A homeless man, huh?"

"Yes, a homeless man, Dad." Sonny knew that Raleigh had some kind of an aversion toward homeless men.

"Sonny, why do you have to get yourself involved with these kind of people? Haven't you learned your lesson?"

"There you go, Dad. One day you are actually going to live the gospel that you preach. Besides, what would Jesus do?"

From in the kitchen, RJ overheard the conversation and got angry when he heard Sonny speaking to his dad in the tone that he used. He then came into the room.

"Dad, is everything here all right?" he asked.

"Yeah, just fine," answered Raleigh.

"Is that so, Sonny? Is everything all right?" RJ asked.

Just before Sonny could respond, the news came back on. Sonny and Raleigh both became quiet and listened.

After the report was over, RJ asked Sonny again, sternly, "So is everything in here all right?"

From where Sonny was sitting, he looked up at RJ and answered, "Sure. Does it look like something is the matter?"

RJ started to say something, but he was interrupted by his cell phone vibrating. He looked at who was calling and departed from the den. Sonny chuckled slightly. RJ looked back at Sonny, who turned quickly looking the other way.

"Dad, Mom, I have to go. I'll see you tomorrow," RJ said, kissing his mom on the cheek before leaving. She said to him before he walked out of the door, "If that's Tanya, tell her hello for me, please."

"Yes, it's her. I'll tell her."

Martha called to her husband and Sonny that supper was ready. Raleigh joined her in the kitchen, while Sonny stayed in the den watching the latest sports news. Afterward, he joined them.

Sonny took his usual place at the table as did everyone else, and Raleigh gave thanks for the meal. When he finished, he asked Sonny to pass the potatoes.

"Sure, Dad, and can you pass those green beans and pork chops."

Martha sensed that there was something not quite right about Sonny's behavior. He was acting as if he had something to talk about.

Ever since he came back home, she noticed that there was something different about him, but she never brought up the subject. However, she knew something wasn't settled in his heart. *I'm going to talk to him tonight,* she thought.

After dinner, Martha asked Sonny to help her in the kitchen. Raleigh had retired to his study to prepare his sermon for Sunday's service, so this seemed like the perfect time for Martha to talk to Sonny and find out what's been bothering him.

"Those pork chops were good, Ma. They were tender and juicy with a nice blend of spices," said Sonny as he was running water to rinse off the dishes.

"Thank you, baby. I made them a little differently than usual. I put some different seasonings on them. I'm glad you liked them. Your dad seemed to like them as well."

"Yeah, he did. He ate almost three whole pieces." Sonny laughed.

"So tell me, Sonny, what have you been doing since you've been home?"

Hesitating before answering, Sonny wanted to tell his mom about his visits to the therapist but changed his mind.

"Well, Mom, I've been working a whole lot lately. JR put me in charge of scheduling for the entire company. It's a lot harder than it used to be, since we have the Com. Tower. It takes me twice as long as it did him when he was scheduling before the Com. Tower."

"Well, I don't know what it took for RJ to get that contract, but it really helped your dad a lot. I thank God every day that he was able to retire when he did."

Putting away the plates he had just dried, Sonny really felt that he had to mention to his mom what happened today at the library. "Mom, the strangest thing happened to me at the library today."

"You don't say. What was it?"

Before telling the story, he wanted a glass of orange juice, so going to the fridge, he got the juice and filled a glass and sat at the kitchen table. Martha turned on the tea kettle to make some hot tea. The dishes were done, and they both sat at the table.

"So here I was at the library talking to this guy who I thought was a homeless man. He turned out to be a private investigator."

"Why were you talking to a private investigator, Sonny?"

"I didn't know he was, not until he started removing his makeup while we were at McDonalds. There he told me who he was."

"So what did he have to say to you, Sonny?"

Sonny was starting to slump over on the table. It was obvious to his mother that there was something really bothering him. With his head down on the table, Sonny began to speak, but Martha could not make out what he was saying.

"What did you say, boy?"

Sonny then sat straight up again. With his face in his hands, he repeated, "He told me that Alicia is still alive."

"That's what I thought you said."

Martha got up from the table to get a glass of water. After pouring herself a tall glass, she leaned against the stove and took a long drink and then spoke, "What do you think about that, Sonny? Do you believe him?"

That question made Sonny realize that it was about time that he should tell his mom about the therapist that he's been seeing. "Mom, I've been seeing a therapist. It's been about three months now, and he told me that I should find out if Alicia is indeed dead."

"Sonny, if you think that this was something that you couldn't share with me before now, then you were mistaken. I think that it's a good idea that you're seeing someone to talk to. Believe me, I've had my times that I only wished that I had someone to talk to."

Sonny felt relieved that his mom understood, but he feared that his dad wouldn't. Being old-school, Raleigh believed that if there's a problem, you work it out; there's no need in paying some white man to tell all of your business.

"Mom, I just don't know what to do. I don't even know what to believe."

"Well, Sonny, I think this is a 'come to Jesus' moment. When you can't figure out what to do, the Lord has already come up with the answer. Just trust him that he will lead you in the way that you should go, Sonny. I'm not telling you what I heard. I'm telling you what I know." The kettle whistled, and she poured water into her teacup.

After speaking, Martha walked over to Sonny and kissed him on the cheek. "Talk to God about it. He knows." She then left him alone in the kitchen.

He got up, put the remainder of the orange juice back into the fridge, and went out to the back yard. Looking up into the sky, Sonny gazed at the stars. It was a beautiful and clear night. *Sure are a lot of stars out tonight,* he thought.

He began to think about Alicia. The stars reminded him of the first night at Starz. He could see her smile and the curves of her body. Suddenly, he saw a shooting star streaking across the sky and fading away. "Ah, I don't know what to believe. All I know is that I'm tired." He turned and entered the house and headed for the stairs saying "good night" to Martha, who was sitting in her favorite chair, knitting.

Upstairs in his room, Sonny undressed, put on a robe, and went to take a shower. With the warm water running down his body, he became totally relaxed. After drying off, he knelt down beside his bed and had a talk with the Lord.

"Lord, I thank you for all that you are and all that I've been able to do today. Right now, God, I need some help. Please tell me what to do concerning Alicia. It's very important to me. Thank you. Amen."

After praying and climbing into bed, he quickly fell asleep.

The smell of sausage and the sound of gospel music rising up through the ceiling and into Sonny's room welcomed him to a bright and shiny Saturday morning.

Rising from his pillow and inhaling the aroma of breakfast, he slowly got out of bed and put on his jeans and T-shirt and headed to the bathroom.

Downstairs in the kitchen, Martha was stirring a pot of grits so that they could be smooth and creamy. Raleigh was sitting at the table, drinking coffee and reading the morning paper. Sonny soon joined them.

"Good morning," he said.

"Good morning," Martha returned the greeting.

"Hey, Son," said Raleigh.

Sonny poured himself a glass of orange juice and sat at the table across from his dad. Looking at the back of the newspaper, he read the headline, "Con man arrested at City Library."

"So, Dad, did you read the article about the man who was arrested at the library?"

"Yeah, I read it. I'm glad he was caught." That was all Raleigh had to say about that.

"The food is done. You can put the paper down now so you can eat." Martha sat a plate of grits, scrambled eggs, sausage, and toast in front of Raleigh. Sonny got up from the table and made his own plate. Martha sat down with her food and asked Raleigh to give thanks.

Placing his paper on the empty seat beside him, Raleigh thanked God for the food.

"Amen," said both Martha and Sonny.

While eating their breakfast, Sonny's cell phone rang. He had forgotten that it was in his pocket.

"Didn't I tell you not to bring that cell phone to the table, Sonny?" barked Raleigh.

"My bad, Dad. I forgot that it was in my pocket." Sonny rose from the table and went into the den.

He didn't recognize the number, and it had an unfamiliar area code. "Hello, this is Sonny."

"Hello, Sonny, I hope that I didn't awaken you."

"No, not at all. I was actually eating breakfast."

"Well, this won't take too long, I promise you. My name is Malcolm Floyd. I am with the *Las Vegas Sun* press. The reason I'm calling is that I am doing a story on the popularity that people like you gave to karaoke."

Sonny was surprised that this person wanted to talk to him, but he was also cautious.

"Tell me, Mr. Floyd."

"Malcolm."

"Okay, Malcolm. Tell me this. Why do you want to talk to me? I'm not in Vegas anymore. Aren't there other people there that you can talk to?"

"That's very interesting, Sonny. The reason I want to talk to you is because not long ago, you were the biggest karaoke singer in the country, and I also know that you won a huge recording contract, that you have yet to accept."

"Yes, that's true, but I've decided not to go back to Vegas. That wouldn't be good for me."

"Listen, Sonny, I understand that you may have some reservations about who I am. I assure you that I am totally legitimate. Now I don't want you to decide now about this. Give me a couple of minutes, and I'll send you an e-mail with more information."

"So you want my e-mail address so you can send me some info, is that right?" questioned Sonny.

"Yes, that's correct. Listen, it's not like I can steal your identity by your Web address. I really want to do this story. It could mean something big for you and for me."

Sonny softened up his defenses. "Okay, Malcolm, I'll give you my e-mail. Are you ready?"

"Go for it."

"Sbrooks@hotmail.com."

"Thank you, Sonny. I will send you something as soon as I can. You will not regret this if you decide to work with me."

"We'll see. Just send me something, and I'll look it over."

Something dawned on Sonny, that he should ask Malcolm. "Malcolm, how did you get my number?"

"Well, Sonny, like I said, I work for the paper. I did my homework and found DJ. He wouldn't tell me where you live, but he gave me your number."

"So now you somewhat know where I live, right?"

"You're a smart man, Sonny."

"Just send me the e-mail, and I'll give you a callback once I've looked it over."

"Thank you, Sonny. You have a good day."

Sonny hung up the phone and went back to the kitchen.

"Who were you talking to?" asked Martha.

He didn't want to say anything about the call with his father there, so he didn't answer.

Raleigh recognized Sonny's disposition, that it was one of annoyance. Sonny sat down and finished his breakfast. Raleigh had completed his meal and excused himself from the table.

"I've got work to do at the church this morning, baby. I'll be out for about an hour."

"Okay, baby, I'll see you later."

Raleigh gave Martha a kiss and said good-bye.

"Goodbye baby. Don't forget to call when you get there."

"Bye, Dad. See you later."

Raleigh waved a hand to Sonny as he exited through the back door.

Sonny was headed to his room, when Martha halted him. "Wait, boy. You didn't answer my question."

Sonny was trying to get away, but he knew he'd better answer his mother. He went back to the kitchen and sat at the table. "Mom, you won't believe this, but that call was from Las Vegas."

"Is that right?"

"Yes, it was some guy named Malcolm Floyd. He says that he works for the *Las Vegas Sun* press, and he is doing a story on the interest of karaoke, so he contacted me."

"Are you going to talk to him?"

"I'm not sure. I have to check him out first. I was just on my way upstairs to my computer to Google his name. If he is who he says he is, then maybe I will talk to him."

"You be careful, Sonny. Don't do anything that will upset your daddy."

"Mom, that's the last thing that I want to do, but I have my own problems, and there are so many questions I need to have answered."

Martha looked upon her son in wonderment. She had come to see how much he has matured over the last year. However, she realized that he was still very naive.

"Sonny, I need you to think hard and long about any decision you make, especially if it means you going back to Vegas."

"Well, Mom, you don't have to worry about that. I'm not even thinking about going back there. If I decide to talk with this guy, it'll have to be over the phone."

Martha gave him a smile. "Okay, Sonny. Just do what I say. Think hard and long."

Sonny got up from the table and headed upstairs to his computer. Martha knew in her heart that Sonny was not telling her the truth.

Sonny was very anxious to find out whom if this Malcolm Floyd was legitimate. Several names for Malcolm Floyd appeared on the screen. Scrolling down about halfway, he finally came to what he was looking for: *Floyd Malcolm, Las Vegas Sun press.* Sonny clicked there and waited for the next page to open.

"There it is. Malcolm Floyd, beat writer for the *Vegas Sun* press."

After reading a few inserts about him, Sonny was convinced that at least there is a person named Malcolm Floyd, with that paper.

He then went to his e-mail. The page opened, and he scanned the list looking for something worthwhile. He stopped when he came to a mail from *mfloyd@vegas.sunpress.org*

Sonny opened it. There was an attachment that he also opened. When it finally downloaded, the Web page was full of color and a scene of the Vegas skyline. It brought back memories to Sonny.

Scrolling down the page, he clicked on the link with Malcolm's name on it. Another page opened that had all the information on it that Malcolm said it would have. Sonny read the entire page and all of the links.

After reading, he reclined back in his chair and relaxed. He was thinking about the possibility of doing an interview and what questions would be asked.

What if he asks me about Alicia's death? he thought. As he was deep in thought, he heard the doorbell downstairs ring. He listened to hear who it might be.

He heard his mom's shout of delight, and decided to go see for himself who was at the door. Standing at the bottom of the stairs, he saw a woman's backside with RJ standing next to her. Martha was giving the woman a hug. Right away, Sonny supposed it to be Tanya.

Martha did not see Sonny standing at the bottom of the stairs as she called him to come down. "Sonny . . ."

"Yes, Mom, I'm right here."

She looked up and let her embrace go. "Sonny, Tanya is here."

"So I see. Hello, Tanya," he said.

Tanya turned to greet Sonny. As she did, Sonny was suddenly struck by the resemblance she had of Alicia.

"Hello, Sonny. It's so good to see you."

Sonny was so taken by seeing her that he could hardly speak. "Oh yes, I mean, sure is. Hey, it's good seeing you too, um, Tanya."

"What's the matter with you, Sonny? You act like you've just seen a ghost," said RJ.

"No not at all. Bustin!" he said.

Chapter 2

At Mercy Hospital in Las Vegas, Detective Riley of the Las Vegas police was getting information on Alicia to determine how soon they should transport her to a more secure room. They were informed that it may be dangerous for her to stay where she was now.

"Well, I would think that by my patient being comatose, there should not be any problem moving her to a different room. As long as we can monitor her without any interference, I'm okay with that."

"That's fine, Doctor. All we need to do is get you to sign these forms for our records, and we will assist you in any way we can to make the move."

The doctor signed the forms and informed the head nurse of the floor about the situation.

"Good, it looks like everything is in place. The only thing I have to make sure of is that, you understand that this is a highly sensitive matter. We need to constantly monitor every person that comes near her and this room. In fact, the entire floor needs to be monitored 24-7."

"We will do all we can to accommodate you, sir. Our people here understand these matters fully. We've been here before."

In Alicia's room, the nurse on duty was taking some vitals when something strange happened. Just as she was about to tighten the wrap, Alicia whispered something.

It was ever so slight that the nurse barely heard it. However, she was sure that she heard Alicia say something. The nurse made sure to document Alicia's activity. After everything was done, she left the room.

Inside, whatever was going on in Alicia's mind was causing her motor sensors to react; very small, yet substantial movements were happening.

This type of activity would be vital to her recovery. She had taken a bullet to the head that lodged in her brain, damaging her cerebellum, which controls her movement. After the surgery to remove the bullet was completed, she slipped into a coma, which was a slight possibility of happening.

The doctors expected the coma to last maybe a couple of days, but it had been over three months. They were not sure when she would come out of it or what condition she would be in, when she does.

Minutes later, Detective Riley and three other officers, along with the hospital staff, entered Alicia's room to transfer her to a more secure area. With bandages around her head, Detective Riley commented on how peaceful she looked.

"Why would anybody want to do more harm to this woman? She looks like she wouldn't hurt a fly."

"Well, Detective, obviously she's gotten herself into something that required killing, everything, including flies and all witnesses," said one of the officers.

"Yeah, you can never judge a book by its cover," remarked Riley.

After getting her secured in the bed so that she could be moved, the doctor wanted to be sure that the police knew exactly which room they were taking her to. After confirming the charts, he and everyone else were satisfied, and they transferred Alicia without incident.

"There is one person that we need to inform about the move," said the doctor.

"Yes, and who might that be?" asked the detective.

"Her next of kin, I believe her name is Pearl."

"I will have to have her last name, Doctor."

"Sure, I'll get the nurse to give you that information. I only know her as Pearl."

"So is Pearl married?"

"I believe that she is. The nurse can give you that information as well."

Detective Riley looked at the doctor with amazement. "What do you actually know about your patient, Doctor?"

"Unfortunately, not a whole lot I've recently took this patient, and I haven't had the time to familiarize myself much. The only reason I know who her next of kin is because she visits the patient quite often."

"I need to make sure that the only person who comes and visits this patient is related or accompanied by Pearl. We can't take any chances. We need the cooperation of every person working on this floor, because we will not have an officer here around the clock. With this economy, the way it is, we just can't afford giving the overtime."

"I assure you, detective, that we will do all we can to help. Our patient is important to us as well as our reputation. So we won't let this patient or you down. I give you my word."

After assigning an officer to stand by for the next couple of hours, Riley was confident with the instructions given and departed.

As he was leaving the hospital, Aunt Pearl was coming to visit Alicia.

"Hello," she said, passing by.

Detective Riley stopped and looked back, but kept walking never returning the greeting.

As Pearl was about to pass by the information desk, the woman on duty stopped her.

"Ms. Pearl," she called out.

Pearl stopped by. "Hi Beverly, how are you doing today?"

"I'm doing fine how about you?"

"Well, I'm hanging in there."

"In case you're going to see Alicia, she's been moved to another room."

"She has? Why didn't anybody let me know?"

"I really don't know, Ms. Pearl. In fact, did you see that man you just passed?"

"Yeah, I saw him. He didn't speak."

"Did you tell him off, Ms. Pearl? Because I know you don't play that rude stuff."

"No, I didn't, but I started to."

"Anyway," said Beverly, "he was the one who requested that Alicia be moved to another room."

Pearl was curious as to why the police wanted to move Alicia. "What floor is she on now?"

Beverly became somber.

"What's the matter with you, Bev?" asked Pearl.

"I'm sorry, but I wasn't told what floor she was on for security reasons."

"Security reasons?" Pearl was angry.

"Why am I the last one to know about this? Call the doctor. I need to get some answers, and he better tell me where the hell they moved Alicia to."

The information desk telephone began to ring. "Mercy Hospital. How may I direct your call, please?"

"This is Detective Riley. By any chance, is the aunt of Alicia Highsmith there? I need to speak with her if she is."

"Detective, you know that it is against our policy to confirm or deny the presence of any visitor."

"Yes, I know what the rules are. Just tell me if she's there."

"Yes, she's here. In fact, you walked by her on your way out."

"Yeah, after I got to my car. I sort of thought that was her, so I decided to call.

Pearl, who was standing right there, asked, "Is that for me? Give me that phone."

She reached over the desk and grabbed the phone from Beverly.

"Hello, this is Pearl. Who is this?"

"Hello, Pearl, I'm Detective Riley from the—"

Pearl interrupted, "I know where you're from. Why did you move my niece?"

"Ms. Pearl, please calm down. I will explain everything."

Pearl calmed down and said, "Okay, I'm ready. Start explaining."

"As you may not know, there has been a private investigator on the case of the homicides that took place involving Alicia Highsmith. At first, we thought that it was a closed case until just two days ago, a letter was found at the establishment known as Starz. This letter indicated to us that there may be others out there looking to even a score or something with a young man called 'Choirboy.' We don't know who this Choirboy is, so we decided to tighten security around Alicia."

Pearl was concerned for Sonny, but she wanted more information. "Why didn't you call me before you moved Alicia?"

"That isn't the way we operate. To insure that security is tight, we couldn't let you know until now. This is why I'm calling you, to let you know what's going on."

"Okay, that's all fine and good. So tell me what floor Alicia is on."

"Sure. She's on the fourth floor. When you arrive, talk to the nurse on duty. She'll direct you from there. I'm sorry for the inconvenience, but it's for the safety of your niece."

"Thank you, Detective, but you have to understand. I'm all Alicia's got, so I have to know what's going on concerning her."

"No need to explain, Ms. Pearl."

"Well, thank you anyway."

"You're welcome. Good-bye." They both hung up simultaneously.

"Thank you, Bev, for letting me use the phone," said Pearl as she made her way to the elevator. It was a long walk to the east elevators. Making her way through the corridors, passing by the different shops, she decided to stop and get some fresh flowers.

Entering the flower shop, where they also sold newspapers, Pearl gazed down at the *Las Vegas Sun* press. There was an article on the front page that grabbed her attention.

Police investigation of multiple homicides is taking shape. She picked up the paper and read a couple of sentences.

Today, the Las Vegas Police, working with a private investigator, uncovered evidence that there may still be surviving participants following the mass murder three months ago. An unidentified investigator reported that he is following leads that may lead to possible arrests.

"I sure hope they catch the people responsible," thought Pearl aloud.

"Pardon me?" said a male patron standing near.

"Oh, nothing, I was just thinking out loud."

Pearl looked the man over and noticed that he was well dressed in an expensive-looking suit and tie. "Are you a minister?" she asked him.

"Yes, ma'am, I am a minister."

"Well, you sure do look the part."

"Thank you. I'm actually on my way to work."

"Do you work here?"

"No, I work at the mall, at a men's clothing store."

With a smile, Pearl said, "I bet you have all of the young ladies chasing after you, especially since you're not married."

"You are very observant. No, I'm not married, and, yes, I get a few invitations."

Pearl turned her attention to the flowers.

"So you're obviously here to see someone. May I ask who?" said the young man.

"I'm here to visit my niece, and who are you here to see?" she asked.

"No one actually I always stop here on Saturdays to buy flowers. What I do is give them to the lady at the information desk and have her to give them to the person that gets the least amount of visitors. Just to let them know that there is someone out there who cares, even though you may not know who they are."

"That is so nice of you. What a ministry!"

"I'll tell you what. You take these and give them to your niece."

"No, I have money."

"It's okay. I've got a feeling that your niece fits the description."

"Are you sure?" asked Pearl.

"Yes, I am. Here take them. I insist."

Pearl reluctantly took the flowers.

"Tell me, young man, what's your name?"

"I'm Reverend Astin."

"Well, thank you so very much, Reverend Astin."

"You're welcome, and have a blessed day."

Pearl watched as he walked out of the shop. *What a wonderful man!* she thought.

Making her way up to Alicia's room, Pearl could not get her mind off the minister who gave her the flowers. Boarding the elevator, she was privileged to be the lone rider.

She never liked riding the elevator with strangers. It always seemed so awkward how people would look up at the numbers while just standing there. No one really wanted to be social and say something to the other person.

She made it to the fourth floor, and the door opened. To her pleasure, there was no one boarding; that situation was just as awkward to her. It wasn't too far to the nurses' station, as she could see it from the elevator.

It was a different kind of floor. There were hardly any patients in any of the rooms. It didn't even smell like a hospital on this floor. There was kind of a neutral smell, like going into an empty house. No paint, no food, no anything, just neutral.

There was nobody at the nurses' station. Then somebody came out of a room.

"May I help you, please?" said the nurse. Pearl sensed that the nurse wasn't really asking to help; it was more like: What are you doing here?

"I'm here to see my niece, Alicia Highsmith. She was down here from the sixth floor."

The police officer, who was sitting nearby, overheard Pearl and came to assist the nurse.

"So you are Alicia's aunt, Pearl?" he asked.

"Yes, I am. May I see her?"

"Yes, but I'm going to have to ask you to leave your purse with me."

"Whatever," said Pearl and dropped her purse on the floor beside the officer.

She took the flowers inside and sat them on the windowsill. Turning her attention to Alicia, she spoke to her comatose niece. "Hi, baby. I got these flowers from a very nice gentleman named Reverend Astin."

Pearl sat down in a chair next to the bed. Alicia just lay there oblivious to her aunt and anything else going on around her.

Pearl realized that she left something in her purse, so she went back out to retrieve what she needed. The officer was outside the room flirting with the nurse on duty. Pearl gave him a look of disgust and turned her nose up at him. "You should be more concerned about your weight," she murmured.

He turned and faced her but said nothing. Back in Alicia's room, she opened the book that she brought with her. She felt that if she couldn't talk with Alicia, the least that she could do was read to her.

After getting herself comfortable, Pearl began reading quietly.

Back at the Brooks' home, RJ was curious about his brother's awkwardness. "So what seems to be the problem, Sonny?" asked RJ.

Sonny was not sure what the problem was. All he knew was that Tanya looked a lot like Alicia. "No problem at all. I'm just glad to see Tanya made it back. After all, I haven't seen her since the day we all met her in church."

"Oh yeah, that was the first and last time we seen each other, Sonny, and I remember everything about that day. You were so funny." Tanya reached out and gave Sonny a hug. RJ watched as the two embraced.

A couple of seconds and they released. Sonny was trying to figure out why Tanya resembled Alicia so much.

"Well, Sonny, I have to get going, but I'm sure we'll have time to get acquainted. Perhaps we can have lunch one day."

"Sure, Sonny, you can join me and Tanya for lunch," responded RJ.

"Well, I am very busy these days, Tanya—"

Tanya interrupted, "Well, if you're too busy today, then maybe tomorrow?"

"Sure, tomorrow sounds like a good idea. We all can go out after church."

"Absolutely not," said Martha. "We will have dinner right here tomorrow. You kids can save your money and enjoy a good home-cooked meal. Besides, Tanya probably hasn't had one in a while."

"You are so right, Mother Brooks. I could use a home-cooked meal. I've been eating so much restaurant food, I feel like I should own one."

"Well, you can just keep your money and put it in church tomorrow," said Martha.

They all began to laugh. Sonny decided that this would be the perfect time for him to depart, because he had to go to the studio.

"Well, Tanya, it's good seeing you again, but I have to get going. Maybe we all can get together later if RJ isn't too busy."

"So where do you have to go on a Saturday morning, Sonny?" Tanya asked.

Before Sonny could answer, RJ spoke up, "He's probably going to his makeshift studio to fool around."

Usually, RJ's indifference toward Sonny's passion wouldn't bother Sonny, but this time it did.

"You know, RJ, if you would stop being such a hater, then maybe you could come down to the studio and see just what we're doing there."

Martha didn't want to get in between her sons, so she excused herself. "I guess this is where I get to go clean the kitchen now. Tanya, I'm glad you're home. I hope you can stay a while." She hugged Tanya and gave RJ a hard stare as she went to the kitchen.

By this time, Sonny had slipped out, leaving RJ and Tanya standing there in the living room. Acting as though nothing had just taken place, RJ attempted to put his arms around Tanya, but she halted him by holding up her hand between them.

"What was that, RJ?"

"What are you talking about?"

"You know exactly what I'm talking about. You just totally dissed Sonny in front of me, like his feelings didn't matter," she said angrily.

"Tanya, I didn't mean anything by that. Sonny knows this. You're just overreacting."

"You know what, RJ? I'm going to pretend that I didn't hear you just said that, but I want you to know one thing. If your attitude doesn't change concerning your brother, you may be sorry about it later."

"What do you mean by that, Tanya?"

"Oh, don't tell me that you don't know what the Word says."

"I have no Idea what you are talking about, Tanya."

"Remember this, RJ. You reap what you sow, and there will be a time for reaping one day."

RJ realized that he had no argument against what Tanya just said, so he began to backpedal. "Yes, Tanya, you're absolutely right. I really was out of line. I'm sorry, okay?"

Tanya was very much in love with RJ therefore, it didn't take much from him to win her forgiveness. She placed her arms around his neck and pulled him close.

"You know, RJ, it's been several whole months since we've been together. I think that we have some getting reacquainting to do."

"That sounds like a very good idea, future Mrs. Brooks."

They began kissing so passionately that they didn't hear Martha entering the room.

"Excuse me. That is done in this house by only me and the man that I sleep with."

Quickly Tanya and RJ released one another. Tanya felt embarrassed, while RJ felt cheated.

"Mom, why didn't you just act like you didn't notice?"

"Excuse me, RJ. This is my house, so if you have some business to take care of, I would suggest that you go to your own apartment."

After saying her piece, Martha continued on doing whatever it was that she was doing, leaving Tanya and RJ alone again.

Turning his attention back to Tanya, he tried to kiss her again, but Tanya stopped him.

"Didn't you hear what your mom said, RJ?"

He removed her hand from his chin and said, "Yeah, I heard."

Tanya backed away and picked up her purse. "Let's go," she said.

"Go where?"

Tanya looked at RJ, shaking her head in disbelief.

While in the car, Tanya asked RJ what he's been doing over the last few months. "So I'm sure you've been busy working as always, haven't you?"

"For sure. This business keeps me on my toes," replied RJ.

They were making small talk while going to RJ's place, when Tanya's stomach began to growl with hunger.

"Was that you, Tanya?"

"Yes, I'm starving."

"Where do you want to eat? There's this new restaurant just around the corner that we can go to, unless you have somewhere else in mind."

"Believe it or not, RJ, I have been craving barbecue ribs since forever. Can we go to the Rib Ranch?"

"That sounds good, but don't you think it's a little early for ribs?"

"Only if they're not open. So can we go by and see?"

"The Rib Ranch is all the way on the other side of town, Tanya. I don't want to drive that far if the place is closed."

Tanya was getting very irritated by RJ's resistance, mostly because she was so hungry.

"Why are you acting this way, RJ?" she asked angrily.

"Tanya, I just don't feel like driving all the way over there for ribs. Besides, this restaurant that just opened has a pretty good menu. We can get ribs later."

Tanya acquiesced.

"That's fine then. Since you don't want to get ribs now, let's go to this new place. What's the place called?"

"It's called *Gateway Grill.* A good friend of mine is the owner."

"So that's the real reason you don't want to take me to the ranch, isn't it?"

"Well, that's part of it, Tanya. The other reason is that my friend and I have been talking about me becoming part owner."

Tanya became suspicious. She wanted to know why he had not told her about this before.

"So tell me, RJ, why haven't I heard anything about this? How long has this plan of yours and your friend been in the works?"

"I'm sorry that I didn't mention it to you in our conversations over the phone, but I wanted to be sure that it was going to happen before I mentioned it to anybody."

"Your father doesn't even know about this?"

"No, he doesn't. I don't have to tell him everything that's going on in my life, Tanya."

They were just about to pull into the parking lot when RJ's cell phone rang. He parked the car and then answered. He could see that it was the owner of the restaurant. "Hey, Max, what's happening?"

"Didn't you see me? I just left the restaurant," said Max.

"No, I didn't."

"My fiancée."

"We'll be here for a while."

"Okay, then I'll see you soon."

"Good-bye."

"Good-bye."

"I guess you know that was Max."

Tanya's stomach growled again. "Can we hurry in and get something to eat?" she said.

When the two of them approached the entrance, they were met by a young man who was standing outside the restaurant. He looked ragged, dirty and was carrying a medium-sized plastic bag.

Stopping RJ and Tanya before they entered, he began begging. "Excuse me, sir. I see, you and the lady are going into eat. Can you spare some change, so that I can get something to eat?"

At first, RJ was appalled by the beggar, and then he realized that he should get back into good graces with Tanya, by trying to impress her.

Reaching into his pocket and pulling out a wad of cash, he fingered through the bills and handed the man two singles. "Here you go, partner. This ought to hold you until your next meal."

Tanya could not believe that RJ only gave the man two dollars. She didn't say anything to RJ but spoke to the beggar instead.

"So when was the last time you had anything to eat?" she asked him.

"Oh, I think since yesterday morning, ma'am."

She looked at him with compassion. "Have you ever eaten in here?"

The young guy looked over at RJ. "No, I haven't. They actually won't let me in because I never have any money."

"Well, you keep that money and come on in here with us. By the way, what's your name?"

The young man looked at RJ, who seemed perturbed, and then over at Tanya, answering, "I'm LaRon Diggins."

"Pleased to meet you, LaRon. My name is Tanya, and this is—"

Before Tanya could finish, RJ interrupted, "Raleigh Brooks is my name."

"Why are you being so formal, RJ? LaRon, everybody calls him RJ."

"RJ, so you are Raleigh Brooks Junior then?" asked LaRon.

"That's very good, LaRon," remarked Tanya with a slight laugh.

Inside, the hostess greeted them and presumptuously said, "Just the two of you today."

Tanya was not so pleased with the hostess' disregard of LaRon, since he was standing right there as they were all talking and entered together.

"Excuse me, but can't you see there are three of us here?"

"Well, I didn't know . . . and you didn't ask, either did you?"

"So you need a place for three then?" asked the hostess.

"A table please," responded Tanya angrily.

All the while, as this was unfolding, LaRon was trying to figure out why Tanya was being so kind to him. He could see that RJ was not pleased with his company.

They were seated, and a waitress came over to bring them water. "Can I get you something other than water to drink?" she asked.

Tanya looked over at LaRon, who was sitting across from her, and told him to get whatever he wanted. RJ sat back in his chair, making it very obvious that he didn't appreciate what Tanya was doing.

"I'll have some coffee, please," said LaRon.

"I think I'll have coffee too," said Tanya.

"Make it three," said RJ.

"Coffee for three," said the waitress while handing out the menus. "I'll be right back with your coffee."

LaRon got busy looking at the menu. RJ took advantage to say something to Tanya. Discreetly, he leaned toward Tanya, saying, "What are you doing?"

She didn't respond, but she did give him a frown.

"Tanya, I'm talking to you," he said quietly.

With her eyes still on the menu, she lifted up her right hand, palm facing outward just inches from his face.

Before he could say anything else, the waitress came back with a decanter, filling each of the coffee cups, and then sat the decanter on the table. This really got to RJ.

You mean I have to share the same pot with . . . Ugh! he thought.

The look of disgust on his face told the story, and Tanya read it well. RJ quickly tried to masquerade his feelings by smiling sheepishly.

"Are you ready to order?" asked the waitress.

Tanya closed her menu and asked LaRon if he decided yet.

"Yes, I have."

"So you go ahead, LaRon."

Looking up at the waitress, then back down at his menu, he asked if he could have extra onions with his Western omelet.

"Yes, we can put extra onions on that. What kind of bread would you like?"

"Whole wheat bread, please."

"Would you like anything else with that?"

"May I have some grape jelly?"

"Sure."

"Is that all?"

"Yes, I think so."

After giving his order, he took four packets of sugar from the canister, situated them evenly in his hand, and tore all packets open simultaneously and poured them into his coffee. Then he took the cream and poured enough into his coffee to change its color to a very light brown.

During that time, Tanya was ordering her meal while RJ continued looking at the menu.

"So what have you decided on, sir?"

"I'll have a cinnamon raisin bagel, please, with just a touch of butter."

Before RJ could hand his menu back to the waitress, he noticed that she was refilling LaRon's coffee. He hadn't even touched his yet.

While waiting on their food, there was absolute silence between the three of them. The only person who seemed to be interested in anything at all was LaRon; he was now on his third cup of coffee.

"Boy, you drink a lot of coffee to be so young," said Tanya.

"Yeah, I know, but when coffee is sometimes the only thing there is to put in your stomach to keep from starving, you get an appreciation for it."

"So tell me, LaRon, how old are you?"

"I'm twenty-six years old."

"Where do you live?"

"Well, I actually stay at the shelter during the night, so I guess I'm homeless."

RJ chimed in on that note, "So how did you become homeless?"

"Well, I had a home, before I went into the army back in 2002."

"What happened?" asked Tanya.

"I lived with my girlfriend. She was pregnant, so I went into the military. I had to do something. I wasn't working at the time. So it was the only thing I could think of doing. After boot camp, I came home to find my girl was living with another guy."

"Oh my goodness! That must have been tough," said Tanya.

"Yeah, it was."

"Did you and your girlfriend talk this thing out? I mean, she was pregnant with your baby."

"Yes, we did, Ms. Tanya, but she didn't want to have anything to do with me. So after my leave time was up, I went to Fort Lee, Virginia, for training. From there, I had orders to go to Iraq, so I had to give the army the name of my next of kin. So the only person that I could name was my girlfriend."

RJ was sort of perplexed, by LaRon naming his girlfriend as the next of kin. "So why didn't you name your mother or father or a sibling?"

"My mother died in 1998, and I never knew my father. I don't have any brothers or sisters and no grandparents. The only grandparent I actually knew was my grandmother, and she died before my mother. So I had nobody else."

"That's really sad," said Tanya.

"Yeah, I guess you never really know when you're going to be alone in this world, but I've made the most of it until I returned from Iraq. Then I realized just how lonely I was. I didn't have anywhere to go, and my ex-girlfriend was nowhere to be found. I don't even know if I have a son or a daughter. I was so depressed. I found a job and got an apartment, and lost both, because I started using drugs."

Tanya was speechless; she sat there nearly in tears. RJ, on the other hand, became very judgmental. In his mind, he believed that most homeless people were just drug users and irresponsible. To him, this validated his beliefs.

"So basically, you're telling us that you became homeless because you couldn't deal with your problems and decided to use drugs, is that it?"

43

Both Tanya and LaRon were surprised by RJ's attitude. LaRon took offence.

"Hell no, man, I'm not saying that at all."

RJ remarked, "So I guess it's the government's fault that you are homeless. That seems to be what all you people think."

Tanya was finding it hard to believe what was coming out of RJ's mouth.

"That's not fair, RJ—"

LaRon interrupted, "That's okay. I can speak for myself. Listen, sir, I don't know what you mean by 'you people,' but I can tell you this. I have never blamed anybody for my situation. I don't really owe you an explanation about me. The problem you have is that since you laid your eyes on me, I knew what you were thinking.

"How I wanted to be wrong about you, but you are no different than the people who feel like they have to give a handout to a homeless person to validate themselves!"

"Then you feel like we owe you some kind of an explanation in return?"

"Yes, I was hungry, and thank God, Ms. Tanya insisted that I accept the invitation to come in here."

LaRon paused for a moment when the waitress brought their food to the table. After she filled his cup and departed, he started where he left off.

"If doing this for me makes you feel better as a person, I'm glad for you, but don't think for one moment that doing this for me makes you better than me."

Tanya was really pleased that LaRon had given RJ the business. However, she could see in RJ's face that he was livid.

"So, LaRon, I think that you are very ungrateful of my generosity—"

LaRon interrupted, "Stop right there. I'll show you how ungrateful I am." LaRon got up from the table and turned to face the other diners. Then he began to speak in a loud voice.

"People, I just stood to let all of you and my gracious benefactor, know how grateful I am for the wonderful meal he just bought for me."

RJ was embarrassed. "Sit down. You are making a fool of yourself," he said.

"Oh no, sir. This is for you." LaRon continued, "I would like you all to give this fine man a hand clap for doing such a charitable deed, to a homeless, lazy good-for-nothing that just made him feel better about himself."

No one clapped, but many people began to whisper. LaRon didn't bother to sit and finish his food. RJ was utterly embarrassed.

"So this went well," said Tanya.

"Thank you for the food, and thank you for having a good heart, Ms. Tanya."

Making a sandwich of his omelet and toast, LaRon picked up his bags and left.

RJ was too embarrassed to look up at Tanya. He just said, "Let's go."

"I'm not leaving until I finish my food," said Tanya.

"That's just fine," remarked RJ sarcastically.

Chapter 3

S onny was warming up on the keyboard while waiting for the other guys in the group to arrive. He started playing the keyboard about a year ago and was doing quite well. The song he was working on was the song that Brother Winston had written and recorded at the same studio.

There was a little tweaking to do with some of the beats, but the rhythm was the same. He also added something to the hook. Everyone in the group was pleased with the sound and was working hard on getting the final touches so they could begin recording the final track.

While playing the melody, Sonny was reminded of Tanya and how much she resembled Alicia. *Maybe it's just a coincidence*, he thought.

Closing his eyes, he visualized Alicia, and then he meditated on Tanya. "No way can this be a coincidence."

He began thinking about their voices and the way each of them spoke his name. While he was in his mind thinking, his colleagues entered the studio. "Hey, Sonny, what's shaking?"

The abrupt greeting startled him. "Bustin! Come on, man, say something before you scream out my name."

His friends looked at one another and said in unison, "We did. We said hey."

"Very funny," remarked Sonny.

One of the guys was Sam Jackson, who was with Sonny the night Brother Winston died; he played drums for the band. The other was Daren Boyd, the bass player, and Lonnie Weatherspoon, the lead guitarist.

There was another band member, Sheila Boyd, Daren's sister. She played keyboard along with Sonny. Everyone was there except the sound person.

"So what are we going to work on today, Sonny?" asked Sheila.

"I'm hoping that we can finish this song and start recording it."

"You plan on recording it today?"

"Yeah, Sheila, I do. You don't have any plans for later, do you?"

"I do," said Sam. "I'm going to the Rib Ranch tonight about eight o'clock. You know I haven't been there since that one night. You know what night that was."

"You know what, Sam?" said Sonny. "I haven't been there since then myself."

The studio became quiet, and then the silence was broken by Sonny playing the introduction of the song. After a couple of bars, he began to speak.

"I've decided on what to call this song. We'll call it, *Heaven's Doors.*"

"That's tight," said Daren.

Lonnie responded, "Yeah, I like that."

"That sounds biblical," said Sam. "But I like it."

"What about you, Sheila?" asked Sonny.

Taking a moment before answering, Sheila responded, "You know, Sonny that is the perfect title. I really do like it."

Just then Malik, the sound man, arrived. Sonny presented him with the name of the song and he thought it was perfect.

"So it sounds like we have a consensus."

Everyone gave their approval a second time. "Bustin! Let's get started then," said Sonny.

After a few minutes of warming up their instruments, the band began to play. As the music played, Malik did the mixing.

He was an exceptional sound man and worked on tracks that were nominated for Grammys back in the nineties. Now he was interested in getting new and talented groups direction by lending his expertise.

The band recorded several tracks and listened back until they were all satisfied with what they had. Now it was time for Sonny to sing the lyrics.

Sonny wanted to get it right the first time because it was now late. When his cue came, he sang the song with Brother Winston in mind. Every word was sung with emotion and conviction. There were some changes made so that the song could become his, but the meaning remained.

The rest of the band was captivated. They knew that Sonny had skill, but he took it to another level.

After the song ended, there was silence for a span of about twenty seconds. Sheila was the first to break the silence. "Snap! That was off the chain. Boo!"

"I think we got a hit, Sonny," said Daren.

Lonnie just sat nodding his head with approval. Malik was tweaking something on the mixing board and didn't say much at first. Not until he listened to the song through headphones in segments did he respond.

He looked seriously at Sonny. "Man, you got something big here. I need to do some more mixing and fine-tuning, not much. It's pretty tight now."

He removed his headphones and played it back so that everyone could hear.

"Turn it up a little more," said Sonny.

They all listened quietly. Sheila began to sing a background harmony. Sonny looked over at her, then over at Daren. "You sing the same harmony, Daren."

Malik hit the record. "That's nice," he said.

After the song ended, Malik realized that he needed to mix in the background singing to enhance the song. So before they ended the night, he had Daren and Sheila to sing the background while he recorded them.

"That's it for tonight. I know we all have something else to do, so let's call it for now," said Sonny.

"I'll work on this more tonight," said Malik.

"Are you sure?"

"Yeah, Sonny, I'm sure. I want to have this ready by Monday when you come in."

"Make sure you lock up when you leave, and I'll see you all Monday." They all decided to go to the Rib Ranch, except Sheila. So after saying their good-byes, Sam Lonnie, Sonny, and Daren headed to the restaurant.

Sonny drove his own vehicle while the others rode together. It was quite surreal. He remembered that entire day that Brother Winston died. Driving through the intersection where he picked up his deceased friend, Sonny could visualize Brother Winston standing there, waving at passersby.

He would soon be at the restaurant where the tragedy took place. While sitting at a red light, his cell phone rang. He could see that it was a call from Las Vegas Nevada.

"Hello."

"Sonny, this is Malcolm Floyd."

"Yes, Malcolm."

"Have you had time to look me up?"

"Yes, I did."

"That's good. The reason I called you is because I wanted to know if you've made a decision yet, about the story."

"Not yet, but I'll let you know as soon as I decide either way."

"That sounds good. Please call me."

"I will, Malcolm."

"You have a good night, Sonny."

"You too, Malcolm."

The light turned green and Sonny made his way, which was only a block until he would arrive at the Rib Ranch.

When he got there, his colleagues were already out of their cars and waiting on him. They were discussing whether they would eat in or carry out.

"Why you guys standing out here?" asked Sonny.

"So do you want to eat here, or are you getting carryout?" asked Lonnie.

"It doesn't make me any difference," answered Sonny. "So what are you guys going to do?"

"Well, we decided to go over to Daren's house and watch some videos and eat there," Lonnie responded.

"That's cool. We can do that," said Sonny.

C.L. AUSTIN

They all went inside and walked up to the counter to place their orders. As Sonny took in the aroma of the place, the smell caused his mind to drift back to that night.

He could almost hear the commotion in the restaurant and see where Brother Winston lay on the floor grasping his chest. The sound of a ringing bell snapped him out of thoughts.

He ordered his plate of rib tips and was just about to leave with his friends, when of all the people to walk in came Tanya. She was wearing a pair of tight jeans and a loose-fitting, partially see-through blouse. Sonny also noticed that RJ was not with her.

"Ya'll go on ahead. I see somebody that I need to talk to."

"Are you going to come over?" asked Daren.

Sonny looked at Tanya, who had not noticed him yet. "I'm not sure. I'll call you if I do."

"That's cool. We'll see you Monday if not."

"Okay, I'll see you later."

Just as Sonny's friends left, he turned his attention over to Tanya, who was waiting to be seated. He approached her quietly. "Hello, future sister-in-law."

Tanya was surprised to see Sonny standing there. "Hey, Sonny. I didn't know that you were coming here tonight."

"Well, I didn't either. It was a last-minute thing."

"I've been wanting some of these ribs all day."

The waitress came over and addressed Sonny and Tanya. "Are there just two of you tonight?" she asked.

Looking over at Sonny, Tanya asked, "Are you leaving or staying?"

"I guess I can stay."

The waitress led them over to a booth at Tanya's request and seated them. She left and came back with water.

Sonny immediately took his glass and drunk it all down. "Man, that hit the spot."

"I hope so," said Tanya.

Sonny felt kind of awkward sitting there with Tanya, and she sensed his discomfort.

"So I wanted your brother to come along, but he seems to have an aversion to barbecue."

"I don't know why he does if that's the case. He eats Mom's barbecue whenever she cooks it."

"Well, I don't know. All I do know is that these are some good ribs in this place."

The waitress came back, and Tanya placed her order. She was very interested in getting to know Sonny, so she took advantage of the opportunity.

"So, Sonny, I hear that the Rib Ranch has quite a significant place in your heart."

"Yes, it does, kind of."

"So what do you mean by that, Sonny?"

Sonny was somewhat reluctant to go into any details about Brother Winston, so he said as little as possible. "Well, as you know, a very good friend of mine died right here in this restaurant." He paused and then asked, "Did RJ or anybody ever talk about Brother Winston?"

"Yes, Sonny. Your brother told me about him. He sounded like somebody you cared for very much."

"Yes, he was." Again Sonny became silent.

Suddenly, Tanya sneezed and it startled Sonny. The expression on Tanya's face resembled Alicia so much that Sonny was convinced that there was a connection between the two of them.

"Tanya, I need to ask you something that has been bothering me since I saw you at the house this morning."

"So what could that be, Sonny?"

Before Sonny could answer, the waitress brought Tanya's ribs and sat them on the table. Tanya took a deep smell of the sauce and the fries. "Oh, that smells so good." Taking her finger, she dipped it into the sauce to taste it. "Oh my goodness! It's sweet with just a little bit of heat. Oh, Sonny, you ought to taste this."

"I have some. I'll taste it later."

"No, you have to taste it now." She took a fry and smothered it in the sauce and reached over toward Sonny's mouth. "Here, try it."

Sonny opened his mouth and the fry was eased in. He bit off only half of it. "Bustin! That's good," he confirmed. He watched Tanya as she dipped the remainder of the fry into the sauce and ate it. Opening his carryout box, Sonny decided to eat there with her.

Between licking fingers and smacking on those savory and sweet ribs, Sonny was able to conjure up enough nerves to ask Tanya what's been eating at him.

"Tanya, do you have any siblings?"

She could not answer right away due to the gristle that she was sucking on. Sonny looked with amazement. He had never seen a woman tear into rib tips the way Tanya was.

Pausing for a brief moment to answer his question, Tanya spoke, "You know, Sonny, I do. But I haven't seen any of them for years." Picking up her napkin and wiping her hands, she added, "I was separated from them when I was very young."

Sonny became more intrigued at the possibility that Tanya could be related to Alicia. "Is there a chance that you have a sister whose last name is Highsmith?"

Tanya stopped what she was doing and placed her napkin beneath her plate of ribs. There was a deep questionable look on her face.

"Why, do you know someone by that name, Sonny?"

"Yes, I do. Her name is Alicia. She's about twenty-seven, and believe it or not, she looks a lot like you."

Tanya began to think about the days growing up as a child. It was a time in her life that she desperately tried to forget. However, Sonny seemed to have brought back to her a dark past that she would rather not talk about.

"No, Sonny, I don't know anybody by that name. I'm sure that she may resemble me in some way, but like they say, 'we all have a double somewhere.'"

Tanya's answer disappointed Sonny. Not that he was wrong, but that he knew in his heart that Tanya was not telling the truth.

"I guess you're right. I've been told many times that I look like somebody else."

"Yes, it happens."

"Yeah, it does happen." Sonny decided not to mention anything else about it.

The rest of the evening was quiet while they both ate their ribs. After Sonny finished with his, he waited until Tanya was done. She still had some left.

"I'm not even going to try to eat all of these tonight. I guess I'll take the rest home."

"Yeah, I'm ready to go myself. I'm pretty tired, and I have to get up early for church in the morning."

"That's right, Sonny. Are you going to sing tomorrow?"

"Yes, I am. I'm also going to direct the youth choir. I've been working with them since I've been home."

"I bet they're good, aren't they?"

"Yes, they are. They do a very good job."

As they stood and were leaving Sonny stopped to ask Tanya a question. "So tell me, Tanya. Are you planning on coming to church tomorrow?"

"Yes, I plan on being there," she answered.

"Bustin!" Tanya smiled, as they both left the restaurant.

Sonny walked Tanya to her car. Before they got there, Tanya engaged the remote lock and there was a double beep. The sound of the car security system being disengaged caused Sonny to stop just short of the passenger side door. As he was saying good-bye, Tanya reached out and gave him a hug.

Somewhat surprised by the gesture, Sonny slowly wrapped his arms around Tanya, and she gave him a light kiss on the cheek. "Thank you for staying there with me, Sonny," she said.

"You're welcome. It was my pleasure."

They simultaneously let go of their embrace, and Tanya quickly jumped into her car. Sonny didn't say anything else. He just turned and headed toward his vehicle. Before he got comfortable, Tanya drove by, blowing her horn. Sonny just waved and watched as she pulled out of the parking lot.

Bustin! What was that all about? he thought.

On his way home, he listened to the song he and his band had just recorded, replaying it several times before he arrived home.

Driving by the house to get to the driveway, he could see Martha was still awake and in her usual place in the den.

"Hi, Mom. You're up late tonight."

"Yes. I thought that I would wait up for you. I have something to talk to you about."

Sonny could sense the brevity in his mother's tone. He just had no idea what it was.

Taking a seat on the sofa, he asked, "So what could be so important that you had to wait so late to talk to me, Mom?"

"Well, Sonny, it's about you and Las Vegas. It seems to me that you have some unfinished business there."

"I wouldn't call it that."

"Well, what would you call it, Sonny? If your friend is alive, then I think you should go back there and see about her."

Sonny wasn't very interested in going back to Vegas for any reason, especially if it's possible that there could be danger awaiting his return.

"Mom, there is no way. I have too much going on here right now. I'm just not ready to go back there."

"Well, you should have thought about that when you went the first time. Listen, Sonny, I'm not saying you have to go anytime soon, but you really should go and see for yourself how she's doing. Just think about it, okay?"

Sonny knew that his mom was right. It's only right for him to know how Alicia is doing, or if she's even alive.

"Okay, Mom, I'll think about it, but right now do you mind that I go upstairs? I'm really tired. The group and I had a long rehearsal, and we went to the Rib Ranch afterward."

"Sonny, you haven't been back there since Jeremiah passed."

"I know, Mom." He then remembered that he saw Tanya there. "I ran into Tanya. She was there," he said.

"Was RJ with her?" questioned Martha.

"Actually, he wasn't. She was alone. Well, not really. I stayed with her to eat."

Martha was curious as to why RJ was not with his fiancée. "Did she say where he was?"

"You know, Mom. I didn't even ask, and she didn't volunteer that information."

"Humph," said Martha.

"Well, Mom, I'm going to turn in." Sonny leaned over and kissed his mother, saying, "Good night, Mom."

"Good night, Sonny."

Although Sonny was very tired, he decided that if he took a shower tonight, then he could sleep a little longer in the morning. He got undressed and stepped into the hot shower. As the water ran down his body relieving him of the stress of the day, he thought about Brother Winston. He even had a talk with his late mentor.

"Bro, what should I do? I am so confused about what's going on in my life."

After a moment of silence, he began to talk to the one person that could give him the answers that he needed. "Dear Lord, I really need you to speak to my heart. Tell me what it is that you want me to do."

Again there was silence, and then he heard a voice in his spirit. *Just wait. It will not be long. You will know what to do.*

"Bustin!" said Sonny. "I sure hope that was you, Lord."

After taking his shower and getting in bed, it was only a matter of seconds and he was asleep.

Tanya arrived at RJ's apartment to find that he wasn't there. She had a key, so she let herself in. Going to the kitchen and placing the leftover rib tips in the fridge, she decided to take a shower and get into something more comfortable.

Looking into her suitcase, she found a pair of silk pajama's and her makeup bag. She turned on the water in the shower and stood over the vanity looking into the mirror.

Standing there staring at herself, she moved her hand toward her face and rubbed a scar that was located on her left cheek. She began to remember how the scar got there.

Her father came home drunk one night in another one of his rampages. Whenever he came home this way, one of Tanya's elder sisters, Alicia, would take her into a closet and hide from him.

However, this night he found them, while he was looking for razor strap to beat their brother with. When he saw them hiding in the closet, he reached in and grabbed Tanya, and being pulled out by an arm, a zipper from a coat caught her on the face and she was cut.

He thought that Tanya's sister did it, and he began to beat her with the razor strap. When Tanya's eldest sister saw what her stepfather was doing, she took a knife from the kitchen and stabbed him. He was not fatally wounded, but he was injured enough that he was rushed to the hospital.

While standing there in the mirror, she also thought about Sonny asking her if she had any siblings. She began crying; she had not seen any of her sisters in nearly twenty years. Her sister Alicia was the one she missed the most. Ever since they were separated, and her foster parents who later became her adoptive parents moved out of the state, Tanya had no contact with her siblings.

She wanted so desperately to see Alicia. Until Sonny spoke her name at the Rib Ranch, Tanya did not even know if her sister was alive.

Chapter 4

It was after midnight when RJ made it home. He was expecting Tanya to be there but wasn't expecting her to be awake. As he entered the bedroom careful not to make too much noise, he quietly entered the bathroom to take a shower.

He turned on the water so that it could get hot and removed his clothes. A couple of minutes later, he put his hand into the running water to check the temperature. It was still cold.

"That's just great. She used all the hot water," he said.

He had no choice but to wait until morning to shower; however he knew that he couldn't sleep in the same bed with Tanya. Opting to sleep on the sofa, he took a blanket from the closet and retired to the living room all the while, not checking to see if Tanya was awake.

After getting himself comfortable he lay there thinking about his earlier activities. It wasn't something that he was proud of, but he wasn't going to let it bother him as he fell asleep in only a couple of minutes.

In the bedroom, Tanya was awakened by RJ fumbling around on the sofa. She wanted so desperately to get up and ask him why he was on the sofa instead of in his bed, but she didn't want to bother him.

He probably didn't want to awaken me, she thought. Convincing herself, she went back to sleep.

The next morning, Tanya was awakened by the water running in the shower. Realizing that it was Sunday morning, she arose from the bed and entered the bathroom.

RJ was just getting out with a towel wrapped around him. "Good morning," he said to Tanya.

"Good morning, RJ."

While Tanya was brushing her teeth, RJ asked her about her sleep.

"How did you sleep last night?"

"I slept well, even though I slept alone."

"Oh, I know. I came in late last night and didn't want to disturb you."

After rinsing her mouth, Tanya responded. "I figured that was the reason."

She remained quiet, waiting for an explanation of why he came home so late—an explanation that RJ was not willing to give.

At this point, Tanya felt as though RJ may be hiding something from her. "So are you going to tell me what kept you out so late last night, RJ?"

RJ became very casual about the question and just shrugged it off. "I was out with a friend having a drink and lost track of time. You know how it is."

"You lost track of time, huh? Well, I guess."

"What do you mean you guess? That's what happened." RJ didn't sound so convincing, but Tanya did not want to press the issue.

"Okay, RJ, it's fine. I know how those things can happen. You know, I used to hang out with my girlfriends, and on occasion, the same thing would happen."

RJ, feeling that he was off the hook, motioned to Tanya, "Come here, pretty woman, and give your big daddy a kiss."

"Big daddy, huh? I have only one big daddy, and that's my heavenly Father, but I'll give my soon-to-be-husband a big kiss."

She moved closer to RJ and wrapped her arms around him. The feel of her silk teddy and soft legs got him aroused. They were both getting heated up and were kissing passionately.

Suddenly Tanya stopped. "We can't do this before we go to church, RJ. Not only that, but I made a commitment to God, that I would abstain until we're married."

This revelation caught RJ by surprise, especially since he was so aroused. "What do you mean—'wait until we're married'? Shouldn't we talk about this first?"

"Well, RJ, we are talking about it. I've decided to wait. This has nothing to do with you. It's about how I feel about my relationship with God."

"Tanya!" RJ was very angry. "What in the—do you mean, it's not about me? Are you saying you can make this decision without me? If so, then that's just not right."

"Well, I'm sorry, RJ. The decision has been made, and, yes, when it comes to my spirituality, then I need to involve no one but God, and incidentally, you are not God."

Too angry to say anything else, RJ moped about the apartment until they were both ready for church.

"RJ, are we going to church in your car?"

"I think you ought to go in your own car, Tanya. Besides, you don't want anybody to think that we've been sleeping together."

"So is that how you're going to be, RJ?"

"Well, like you told me. It's not about you, it's about me. And I don't think we should ride to church together."

Tanya smiled and said, "Well, that's good too. I'll see you at church." She left the apartment and headed to church. RJ stayed behind.

He was just about to leave when his cell phone rang; it was Max. "Hello, there. No, she's gone. I had a great time. Yes, I'm about out the door. Okay, I'll call you later."

After talking to Max, RJ headed to church.

The parking lot hasn't looked so good in a long time. Since Sonny's return, he has kept it clean, and Pastor Brooks was very pleased. As the parking lot was quickly filling up with worshippers, Sonny was inside getting the choir together.

Pastor Brooks was in his office making some last-minute touches to his sermon and Martha was finishing up with the seniors' Sunday school class.

Tanya was just arriving at Mt. Sinai and was in a good place in her spirit. She was very excited to be back. She was more excited to hear Sonny sing again. When she pulled into the lot, she thought about the first time she ever heard Sonny. *That brother can sing. He's actually cute too.*

As she entered the church, she was met by Mother Brooks, who greeted her with a hug.

"Good morning, baby."

"Good morning, Mother Brooks."

Mother Brooks looked around as if she was looking for somebody. "Where's RJ, Tanya?"

"Oh, he's on his way."

"So you obviously don't want to talk about whatever is going on, but that's okay, baby. Everything will be just fine."

Tanya wondered how Mother Brooks knew that something was bothering her.

Recognizing the look on Tanya's face, Mother Brooks said, "Don't try to figure it out, baby. I've been around long enough and have seen enough to know when something isn't just right when I talk to people."

"Well, Mother Brooks, you certainly have the gift."

Martha smiled, saying, "Let's go get a seat. Service will be starting soon. And don't worry about RJ. He's just like his daddy in so many ways."

"I hope they are the good ways, Mother Brooks."

The two of them made their way to Martha's favorite pew and took their seats just as service began. Pastor was not yet out; however, there was a new associate minister who was conducting worship. Raising his hands, he called the congregants to worship; the congregation all stood up and repeated after the minister's opening worship statements.

They all remained standing while the choir director came to the front of the pulpit. To Tanya's amusement, it was Sonny.

He motioned the musicians and then the choir. They began swaying to the music as the musicians played the introduction. With one signal from Sonny, the choir began to sing a high-tempo praise song.

This was out of the ordinary in the past when RJ was the director, but since Sonny's return, he took over the music department as minister of music. RJ was concentrating on the business aspect of the church and Brooks cleaning.

The congregation was really enjoying the song, and the choir was being worked hard by Sonny. He brought out the best from them, and they always responded with enthusiastic singing.

After the song was over, the minister stepped up to the podium and opened his Bible. He flipped through the pages until he came to the passage that he would read.

He announced the passage to the congregation and waited a moment until he could no longer hear pages being turned. Just before reading, he noticed the door to the sanctuary opening, and in walked other worshippers, along with RJ.

It was only proper that the minister waited until all of the people were seated before he began to read. RJ was holding up the service. He was looking around and seemed to be agitated until he spotted Tanya sitting next to his mother.

An usher escorted him to where he wanted to sit, and he sat at the end of the pew near the outer aisle. Tanya looked over and saw him sitting there and gave a short wave with her fingers; he didn't return the greeting.

"Amen," said the minister. He continued, "Now that we are all seated, let us resume in worship." He began to read the passage.

The passage he read was Ecclesiastes 3:1-8. He read with clarity and feeling. After he completed his reading, he took his seat and quickly stood again as Pastor Brooks entered the pulpit.

The young preacher's etiquette intrigued Tanya. "Who is the new preacher?" she asked Martha.

"That's Reverend Joshua Lee. He joined us while you were away."

"He speaks very well. Did he attend seminary or something?"

"Yes, he recently graduated from Morehouse Theological Seminary and moved here to help pastor. You know, my husband is getting up there in age, so he wants to turn over the church to somebody else one day."

"That's very interesting, Mother Brooks. Well, I'm sure that Reverent Lee will do a great job."

"Yes, and he is doing very well. He can really preach."

"I can't wait to hear him, Mother Brooks."

Pastor Brooks could slightly hear the whispering coming from where Martha and Tanya were sitting and looked over at them.

"I guess that means we better be quiet," said Tanya.

After giving a formal welcome to any first-time visitors, Pastor Brooks turned the order of service over to the choir. Instead of taking the director's position, Sonny took the leader's stand while a young woman took over at director.

The congregation edged forward in their seats, to receive what Sonny had to deliver. Tanya was especially excited. She had not heard Sonny sing in quite a while.

The director motioned the musicians to start. After the first couple of notes, Sonny keyed in with the sound of magnificence. He sang a wonderful song that had the entire congregation captivated. Tanya was completely mesmerized; she and the entire congregation were pleased to hear Sonny.

The song didn't last as long as they usually did now that Sonny was a director; he did give a lot, but he made sure to keep some energy for directing. After the song ended, Pastor Brooks took to the podium and adjusted it to his liking. In his very distinct voice, he announced the passage of scripture that he would preach on.

"Today our scripture lesson is found in the poetic book of Ecclesiastes, the third chapter and verses one through eight. I want to thank Reverent Lee for reading that passage in our meditation reading earlier."

As the congregation all stood for the reading of the scripture, Tanya again looked over at RJ, who was not paying her any attention. He seemed to be occupied by something in his hand. She noticed that he smiled at whatever it was that he was looking at. Realizing that it was his cell phone, she knew that he was reading a text message. *Who could possibly be text messaging him during church?* she thought.

Pastor Brooks had begun reading and was aware that Tanya had been staring over at RJ. Mother Brooks noticed it as well and nudged Tanya on the arm. Tanya looked over at Mother Brooks and then up to the pulpit at the pastor.

"We are going to use as a subject, 'Good seed or bad seed, there will come a time for reaping.'"

The congregation said Amen and then took their seats. RJ quickly glanced over at Tanya, then back down to his cell phone to turn it off.

"Heavenly Father, we come thanking you for the word that you have given. We ask now that all are edified and your word magnified. Amen."

After the short prayer, Pastor Brooks readjusted his microphone and again began to speak. "In this poetic book of the Old Testament, King Solomon, son of David has concluded that in this life, all things are vanity. In the third chapter, he conveys to the reader that for everything under the sun, there is an appointed time.

"One of these appointed times is the time of reaping." There were a few amens from the church. Pastor continued, "With everything that we do in this life, there is a seed planted. This is a spiritual seed, and whatever the seed is, it will produce something. This planting process is called sowing."

"Amen."

"No matter what we sow, there will be a time that we will reap that which has been sown. Good or bad, there will be a time for reaping."

The entire church responded with a hearty amen.

Pastor continued preaching, but there were a couple of congregants who seemed to be preoccupied. RJ was not paying much attention to the sermon, because he was busy sending a text message. Sonny was watching Tanya, who seemed to be very much into the sermon.

There was something that was constantly on Sonny's mind. He knew that he needed to do something to find out about Alicia and was contemplating the possibility of going back to Las Vegas.

He also remembered what Mathias said to him; it could be dangerous going back.

The other thing that had him bugged was Tanya. There was something about her that he could not get a handle on. He felt that she must be related to Alicia, *but in what way?*

As the service continued, the pastor was making the first of his three points. "The first point I'd like to exalt is, what seed have you planted?"

He repeated, "What seed have you planted?"

Many in the church took notes, so he waited until he could see those who did raise their heads. "Remember, when we plant a seed, something must grow. In other words, there will be a manifestation of whatever you have sown. This we know. What we don't know is how or when it will happen."

"Amen."

Sonny was now paying full attention to the sermon, so was RJ. Pastor Brooks was really making some profound statements. After a while, no one was saying anything. The entire congregation somehow felt as if he was speaking to each one of them specifically.

Martha felt like her husband was prophesying to somebody, perhaps even to himself. RJ was trying not to see him being spoken to by denying any wrong in his life.

Sonny, however, had a revelation. He knew that he had to go back to Vegas, even if it was just to do a story on karaoke. Looking over toward Tanya, he caught her looking at him. She did not act as if she had just gotten caught staring. She kept her eyes on him. Sonny felt uncomfortable and looked down at his Bible.

I wonder what he's thinking about. He's got to know that I lied last night about not having a sister named Alicia, thought Tanya.

The sermon was now coming to a climatic end, and the church had been worked into a hallelujah frenzy. The pianist was playing chords that intensified the excitement.

Pastor Brooks was sweating profusely. He hadn't preached with such vigor in years. The congregation was fed from on high as they were convinced that this was a very special service.

After the preaching was over, Minister Lee extended the invitation for new converts. He was very convincing in his appeal; several teenagers and a few young adults came forward.

As they sat in chairs that were seated just below the podium, Sonny had taken the position at the microphone to lead another song. Instead of the choir standing alone, Sonny asked the entire church to stand as they all sang a familiar hymn.

This was usually what Sonny would do to calm the church down, so that those who came forth would not have to sit and wait too long. Many times the choir would sing longer as the Spirit would lead.

As the congregation sang along, Sonny looked about the church. He spotted RJ. He was not singing, but he had his eyes closed, holding his hymnal tightly in his arms.

Martha and Tanya were both crying—Martha about the new converts, and Tanya unknown. The rest of the church was mostly all singing and crying.

After the hymn was over, Minister Lee motioned everyone to be seated. Pastor Brooks who would normally speak to the new converts was too tired, and felt some discomfort in his throat, so he had his associate to do the duties.

After speaking to each person individually, they were all accepted into the church with a consensus "amen" from the congregation. Pastor stood to make some closing remarks and the benediction, and church was over.

People made their way up to the front of the church to shake the pastor's hand. Sonny made his way over to where his mother was sitting with Tanya. By the time he got there, RJ was standing there talking with Martha.

Sonny sat down and waited for his chance to speak to his mother, so Tanya sat next to him. "That was an awesome word pastor gave today," she said.

He kept looking straight ahead, not wanting to look into her eyes. "Yes, it was. It really touched a lot of people."

"It sure did. I quickly prayed and asked God to forgive me of whatever bad seed that I planted. You never know."

"You're right, Tanya. You never know."

"So, Sonny, what's on your agenda for the rest of the day?"

Sonny looked at Tanya and smiled. "You do mean after dinner with the family, don't you?"

"Oh yeah, how could I forget that?" remarked Tanya.

Martha and RJ finished whatever they were talking about, and she turned her attention to Sonny. "I'm so glad that you decided on the church singing the congregational hymn, instead of having the choir sing."

"Yes, I know. We would be still going at it."

Martha glanced over at Tanya, who was sitting very close to Sonny. Tanya stood saying to RJ, "So are you going directly to your mom's house?"

RJ gave her a look of contempt. "No, not directly. I have to meet with Max over at the restaurant, but I'll be there." He looked at his brother. "I'm sure Sonny here will keep you company until I arrive."

Sonny didn't find RJ's remark appropriate, so he totally ignored it. Tanya, on the other hand, was not so tolerant. "I'm sure Sonny will be great company. Tell Max that I said hello."

Smiling, RJ responded, "I will."

Martha was not sure as to what was going on, so she told them all, "I don't care what any of you have to do. I do know that I better see you all at dinner sometime today, is that clear?"

"Yes, ma'am," said Sonny. RJ didn't respond.

Martha repeated, "Is that clear, RJ?"

"I'll be there, Mom."

"I'll be there too, Mother Brooks, with or without RJ."

"That's good. Now one of you boys go see about your father. He looked pretty worn out after the sermon."

RJ headed the opposite way. "So where are you going?" asked Tanya.

"I told you that I have to meet with Max. What part of that didn't you understand?"

Sensing tension, Sonny said, "I'll go see about Dad."

RJ went on and left the church, leaving Tanya standing there with Martha. "What has gotten in to him?" said Tanya.

"Maybe he's getting nervous about the marriage, Tanya. I don't know, but he'll be all right."

Not so sure, Tanya remarked, "I don't know."

In Raleigh's office, Sonny was helping his dad gather some things together. "So where's your brother, Sonny?" asked Raleigh.

"He said he had somewhere to go. I think he mentioned something about somebody named Max."

"Is Tanya with him?"

"No, she's on her way to the house. Said she'd meet us there."

As the two were walking out of the door, Raleigh asked, "So tell me, Son. What do you think of Ms. Tanya?"

Thinking for a moment, Sonny answered, "She seems very nice. Of course, I really don't know her all that well."

"That's all right. I'm sure you two will get to know each other very well."

There was something in the tone in which Raleigh spoke that made Sonny curious.

"Why do you say, we'll get to know each other well, Dad?"

Raleigh became evasive. "Did I say that? I guess I meant there will be plenty of time for you two to get more acquainted."

At this point, Sonny had to come straight with his father. "So are you really saying that RJ doesn't spend much time with Tanya?"

65

Raleigh didn't respond as they were now in Martha's presence. Sonny decided not to query any more. Even if he had, he knew that Raleigh wouldn't disclose any more information about RJ.

"How are you feeling, baby?"

"I'm feeling just fine," answered Sonny.

"I'm not talking to you, boy. I'm talking to your dad."

"Oh bustin, my bad."

"I'm well. I'm just a little bit hungry," said Raleigh.

"Well, let's get home so I can warm the food. It should be ready by the time Tanya and RJ gets there."

"I thought Tanya was going straight to the house," said Sonny.

"She'll be there. She wanted to go to her apartment and change before coming over."

"So I guess I'll be right there behind you guys then," said Sonny.

"Okay then we'll see you shortly," said Martha.

On the way home, Raleigh had very little to say. Martha was aware that something was bothering him. "What's on your mind, Raleigh?"

Looking out of the window, taking a deep breath and exhaling slowly, Raleigh asked, "What is going on with RJ?"

"I don't know what you mean. Has he done something?"

"That's just it. I don't think he knows what he's doing. Why is he going to marry that girl? I don't think he really loves her."

This surprised Martha. She had not expected to hear those words come from Raleigh. She knew that he wasn't necessarily fond of Tanya but didn't know he felt that way about RJ's intentions.

"I'm sure RJ loves Tanya, Raleigh. Why would you say something like that?"

"Sonny told me that RJ is going to meet with Max before coming over to dinner, and Tanya is going to come alone."

"And what's wrong with that, Raleigh?"

Raleigh turned to look directly at Martha, saying, "Martha, do you know who Max is?"

"No, I don't. What does that have to do with anything?"

"I don't know. That's why I said what I did about RJ. He keeps everything so private. Did you know that he is considering going into the restaurant business?"

Martha stopped the car at a red light. Looking over at Raleigh, she responded, "No, I had no idea about that. Do you think he's intentionally keeping it from us?"

"I don't know what he's doing, Martha. I really don't." The light turned green and they proceeded; however, nothing else was talked about the rest of the way home.

Chapter 5

It was Sunday morning and Alicia's uncle DJ was at Wannabee trying to gather some items from his office. He had purchased Starz and was moving his office there. He had planned to convert Wannabee into a restaurant.

Pearl was concerned about DJ because when she inquired about where he had gotten all of the money he was spending, he told her it was winnings from the lottery.

She didn't question his answer because she was aware that he played the lottery regularly. Sometimes he would win several thousand dollars and not tell her about it until he made a purchase. However, he did all of a sudden come up with a lot of cash.

Pearl was at church when her cell phone began to vibrate. At the time, she was unable to get up from her seat thinking it was someone from the hospital, but when she looked, she saw it was a call from St. Louis.

She thought, *Who's calling me from there?* Since she didn't know who it was, she let it go to voice mail. She felt the vibration again indicating that a message had been left.

Service was over and as she was heading out of the church she was approached by a man dressed in a khaki colored cotton two piece suit. He was a white gentleman and acted very much like a cop.

"Hello, ma'am are you Pearl Walker?"

"Well, that depends on who's asking."

"Please excuse me." The man pulled out his badge. "I'm detective Riley from the Las Vegas police. If you remember I talked with you yesterday about your niece. So are you Pearl Walker?"

"Yes, Detective Riley, I'm Pearl Walker, how may I help you?"

"Well, Miss—may I call you Pearl?"

"Yes, that would be fine."

"Well, Miss Pearl, I need to ask you a few questions about your niece Alicia."

Pearl became alarmed and wanted to know if anything had happened. "What about Alicia, I was just with her last night did something happen to her?"

"No, no need to get excited, it's nothing like that at all."

Feeling a bit relieved, Pearl responded. "So what can be so important that you had to meet me here in front of this church?"

Wiping sweat from his brow, detective Riley answered. "Well, I've done my homework, so I knew you would be here at this time." He wiped his forehead again saying, "Can we go over to that diner across the street to get out of this hot sun."

"Sure we can go over there, but you have to make this quick, I have things to do."

Inside the diner the cool air conditioning was just what detective Riley needed. A waitress approached and led them to their seats. "Is this okay?" she asked.

"It's just fine," answered Riley. Then he added, "Can you bring us both a drink. What would you like to have Miss Pearl?"

"Sierra Mist, with little ice."

"I'll have a Coke and a menu."

"Okay, I'll be right back with your drinks and a menu."

Pearl looked up at the waitress and with a smile she asked, "What is your name young lady?"

"My name is Shareeka."

"Shareeka. That's a pretty name."

"Thank you, I'll be right back."

It had taken less than a minute and Shareeka was back with the drinks. She handed the detective his menu and waited a couple of seconds. "Do I need to come back in a couple minutes," she asked.

Quickly scanning the menu Riley handed it back to Shareeka. "I already know what I want; I just thought something else would entice me." Taking the menu, Shareeka asked, "So what will that be?"

"I'll have the meatloaf sandwich, mashed potatoes and gravy with a side of cooked spinach."

"That sounds great; I'll be right back with your lunch." When Shareeka was gone, Riley spoke to Pearl. "About your niece, it is really important that we get in touch with the young man that she was known to keep company with before the incident."

"Your mean Sonny," said Pearl.

"Yes, Sonny. We are positive that he may be able to help us solve this case. Is there any chance you may know how I can get in touch with him?"

Pearl was reluctant to get Sonny involved, she knew that he was getting on with his life and didn't need to be dragged back into the fray. "I don't know detective. Why should I give you any information about Sonny?"

"It's simple Miss Pearl, the only way we can protect your niece is to apprehend and prosecute the perpetrators. What happened here four months ago will not just go away. If we allow that scum to get away with murder and attempted murder, then they win. We can't allow our city to be turned over to the criminals. And just think about Alicia, she will one day recover and possibly leave the hospital; can you alone assure her safety?"

Pearl couldn't argue with that. As much as she did not like the idea of telling the detective Sonny's whereabouts, she knew that she had to.

"Okay detective. I'll tell you where he is. He lives in Saint Louis with his father. Do you need his address?"

Shareekah returned with the food. "Umm that smells good," he said. Saying, "Excuse me," he lowered his head and gave thanks for his meal. He picked up his fork and went for the meatloaf.

The taste of the onions and the crunchy top of the meatloaf covered in hot brown gravy really made his taste buds come alive. "Man-o-glory, this is delicious." Pearl just watched as Riley enjoyed his food.

"So what did you ask me Miss Pearl?

"I asked you, if you needed his address."

"Yes, that would be of great help. Do you have it?"

Pearl went into her purse to retrieve the address which she kept in her address book. Suddenly her phone vibrated again. This time she answered it because it was DJ calling.

"Hello."

"Are you going to be home soon?"

"Yes, I'll be there when I'm finished here at the diner across from the church."

"Are you having lunch there?"

"No, I'm actually talking to a detective Riley from the police department."

"Why? What does he want?"

"I'll tell you when I get home. Let me finish here so I can get home."

"Well, I'll see you later then."

"Okay I'll see you later."

After the conversation ended, Pearl found Sonny's address and gave it to the detective. "Thank you, Miss Pearl. You know what's funny. A private investigator has already gone to Saint Louis, in search of Sonny."

"So why did you ask me for his address then?"

"Well, the investigator hasn't gotten back with the department yet."

Pearl was beginning to get worried.

"Don't worry, Miss Pearl, we'll get to the bottom of all of this."

Pearl pushed away from the table. "I really have to go now. I just hope I've done the right thing."

"Yes, Miss Pearl, you have done the right thing. Remember it's about your niece's safety."

"You have a good day detective."

"You do likewise."

Pearl made her way back to the church parking lot and got into her car. Before leaving she checked the message that was left on her cell phone. To her surprise it was Sonny.

At home, Sonny was thinking about how to tell his father and mother, that he was planning on going back to Las Vegas. First he wanted to call Pearl. He remembered that she had given him the telephone number that he stored in his desk drawer.

She probably won't even recognize this number, he thought. He dialed the number and it rang several times until the voice mail picked it up. "Hello, you have reached Pearl. Please leave your name and number and I will call you back as soon as possible."

"Hello, Miss Pearl, This is Sonny. I'm sure you are probably in church so, I'll call you back later." He disconnected and placed the number back in the drawer.

Everyone was down stairs waiting for Martha to get the table prepared, Tanya had not yet arrived, and neither was RJ there. Sonny was changing into a pair of jeans when he heard the doorbell ring. Raleigh was in the bathroom and Martha could not stop what she was doing in the kitchen. The bell rang again. "Sonny can you get that please," she yelled from in the kitchen. She could have a very high pitched voice that traveled through the entire house, so Sonny heard.

He ran downstairs and opened the door. It was Tanya, who was standing there, and she did not expect the door to open so fast. "Bustin!" she said when she saw that it was Sonny. "What? said Sonny?" They both began to laugh.

"Is that Tanya?"

"Yes, ma'am it is."

"Good. Tanya can you come back here and give me a hand please," requested Martha.

Sonny let Tanya in and walked with her to the kitchen. "Hello, again, Mother Brooks."

"Hi, baby, can you grab some of those plates from the cabinet and set the table for me."

"Sure, I'll be glad to."

"Is there anything that I can help with Mom, asked Sonny?"

Before Martha could answer, Tanya responded. "Yes, you can help me by getting some silverware."

As Sonny and Tanya gathered up the things they needed to set the table, Martha asked Tanya, "Have you heard from RJ yet?"

"No, he didn't call me; so I guess he'll be here later like he said."

"I hope he doesn't take too long getting here," remarked Martha.

Sonny didn't say a word, as he was trying to remember which side the knives go on, Tanya noticed him. She went over to help him, "Forks go on the left side and the spoon and knives on the right. The knife is closest to the plate."

Graciously she set one place. "There just like that," she said.

Sonny watched as Tanya moved around the table with such grace. He was beginning to wonder if his brother even recognized just how beautiful she is. After the table was set, Raleigh who had been upstairs came down at Martha's request. He was not feeling very well, so he sat in the den waiting to be called for dinner.

Tanya and Martha was placing food on the table. There was smothered cabbage, Braised carrots, Johnny cakes, which Sonny just loved. There was green beans and green salad and the meat was a pork roast.

Raleigh's blood sugar was not stable, so Martha no longer made him any bludini kool-aid. He was now drinking iced tea with sugar substitute.

"Come on in Raleigh," called Martha.

Slowly rising from the recliner, he made his way to the dining room. Sonny could see that his father was not feeling well. He wouldn't mention it to him, because he knew that his dad would only deny that anything was ailing him.

Raleigh sat at the head seat and Martha sat on the other end. Sonny started to sit opposite of Tanya, but she beckoned him to sit next to her. "Isn't RJ coming? he asked Tanya."

"He'll be here, but its okay, sit down." Tanya was adamant.

Raleigh gave Martha an inquisitive look, before he gave thanks for the food. "Let us bow our heads to earth and lift our hearts to heaven." He began to pray. "Our Father, which is in heaven, we thank you for this abundance of food. We ask for your blessing upon it. In Jesus's name we ask it all amen."

They all began reaching for the closest dish and served themselves. Raleigh, who didn't have much of an appetite, began to drink his tea. Martha noticed that he didn't put any food on his plate.

"What's the matter, honey?" She asked.

Holding his glass close to his mouth, he mumbled, "Not hungry."

Sonny had gotten himself some cabbage and a slice of roast pork, and wanted some green beans, however they were situated on the far side of Tanya. Tanya noticed Sonny looking over at the beans. "Would like to have some of these beans Sonny?"

"Yes, I would."

Instead of passing them to Sonny, Tanya lifted Sonny's plate and served them to him.

"Say when, she said," as she scooped a spoonful unto his plate "That's good right there."

"Oh, have some more," she said, and scooped more on his plate. She then sat his plate back in front of him.

"Thank you, Tanya. That was nice of you."

Raleigh said nothing as he watched Tanya's display of kindness. Sonny didn't make much of it as he began to eat.

Just before he could devour a piece of meat, his cell phone rang. He had forgotten to put it on vibrate before coming to the table. Although he knew taking the call was against house rules, he saw that it was from Las Vegas. Excusing himself he rose from the table and went into the kitchen and out of the back door.

Just as he exited the back door RJ entered the front and made his way to the dining room. "Hello, everyone," he went over to Tanya and kissed her on the head. "Hello, baby," he said to her. "Hey," she responded.

The short greeting did not go unnoticed by anyone, especially Martha. Looking over at Tanya hoping to find an empty seat, RJ noticed a plate of food next to her. "Who's sitting there?" he asked. Not seeing Sonny anywhere and doing the math, he figured who it was.

He looked down at Tanya. Without saying a word he took a seat across from her and began serving himself.

Outside Sonny was on the call. "Hello, Miss Pearl. I'm glad you called me back."

"So how are things Sonny? It's been quite a while since I've seen you."

"Yeah, I know. You know, I take things one day at a time."

There was silence as both were trying to come up with a way to tell why each called. After a moment Sonny finally had the courage to ask. "Pearl, I need to know if Alicia is alive."

Pearl lowered her head then raised it saying, "Yes, Sonny, she is."

Sonny didn't know if he should be happy with that news, but he was certainly angry that this was intentionally kept from him. "So tell me, Pearl. Why didn't anybody let me know that Alicia wasn't dead? You don't have any idea how messed up I was over this. I've had to go to therapy and everything."

"I'm terribly sorry Sonny, but I was told by the police not to tell anybody, not even you. It was all for her safety, which is why I returned your call."

"What's going on is Alicia okay." Pearl could sense the tension in Sonny's tone.

"Yes, she's okay. She's in the hospital with twenty-four hour security."

"Why does she need security Pearl?"

"She may still be in danger. Whomever, did this to her is still out there."

Sonny was not sure what all of this meant. He needed to know more. "So you never told me why you called me."

"Well, Sonny, just a few minutes ago, I was approached by a Detective Riley, from the police department. He wanted to know if I knew where you were. I told him that I didn't want you to be involved, but he insisted, and that Alicia's safety is depended on him finding you."

"Well, did you tell him where I live?"

"Yes, I did. I hope you're not angry."

"No I'm not angry, Pearl. Actually, at this point I can tell you why I called. Friday night, I was also approached by someone, but he was a private investigator. He told that his name was Simon Jonas, but he went by Peter.

Wait a minute, he actually told me that his name was Mathias Blackmon. Yeah, that rascal gave me a false name at first. Anyway, he told me that Alicia was Alive, but I didn't know for sure. Not until you just told me.

Well, the reason I called you is because I'm coming back to Vegas."

Pearl was surprised to hear this. "Why are you coming back Sonny?"

"I really don't know why myself, perhaps I need to get some answers."

Before Pearl could respond, there was the sound of his mother's voice calling on him. Pearl, I have to go, I'll keep in touch with you."

"Okay Sonny, you do that. You take care of yourself okay."

"I promise you Pearl, I'll be careful.

"Good-bye, Sonny."

"Good-bye, Pearl."

Sonny put his phone away and hurried back into the dining room. Upon seeing RJ, he said, "Hey, bro, when did you get here?"

RJ didn't answer. Martha chimed in. "RJ did you hear your brother talking to you?"

"Yes, I heard. It's really none of his business to keep track of my time."

Sonny remained standing. "That's okay mama, he said."

RJ gave Sonny a peculiar look, saying, "Why don't you have a seat and finish eating."

Sonny was standing behind Tanya and had no intention of sitting next to her.

He picked up his plate and moved to the seat next to RJ on the other side of the table.

"What's the problem Sonny, you obviously were sitting next to her before I came. Why change now?"

At this point Martha had had enough. "You just stop it right now RJ You act as if you have a problem with your brother and Tanya. There is no need for that."

Under her breath, Tanya said, "I know that's right."

RJ heard. "What is that supposed to mean Tanya?"

"Nothing RJ, it means nothing at all."

"Is that right Sonny?" asked RJ.

"You know what, bro? I have my own problems. I don't have time for your trippin."

"So I'm trippin now?"

"Yes!" yelled Raleigh. "You both are tripping. Now it's my turn. Martha, I'm finished, I'm going to bed." He got up from the table having not eaten a thing and stormed upstairs."

Martha was very upset. "What is the matter with you boy?" RJ knew that she was talking to him. He didn't say a word. "I guess I'll join Raleigh upstairs, when I come back down, I would really like to not find you two fighting."

"You don't have to worry about me, Mom, I'm leaving. Let's go Tanya."

"What? Who do you think that I am RJ? I'm not your puppy; you cannot order me to do what you want, just because you're upset about something. What I would like to know is who spit in your kool-aid before you came here?"

"Aw snap!" said Sonny. RJ looked at him in disgust.

"You need to shut up boy."

"Hey, I'm outa here." Sonny then went upstairs.

"RJ," said Tanya. "I'm going to leave only because I don't want to say anything that will disrespect Mother Brooks, but I'm going to my own place tonight."

"Is that the way it's going to be Tanya?"

"Yes, that's the way it's going to be RJ."

He then stormed out of the front door without saying another word.

Tanya looked at the dining room and saw that it needed to be cleaned. "Mother Brooks, I'll clean the dining room before I leave."

"Will you do that for me, Tanya?"

"Yes, ma'am, I will. I don't have anything else to do but go home and if I do that, Then RJ will call me bugging me. I just don't feel up to that tonight."

"Thank you baby, but aren't you concerned about what got into RJ today?"

"Yes, I am, but he's got to deal with that by himself. I'm not going to be his verbal punching bag, not today or any day."

"Well, okay Tanya, I'm going to see about Raleigh, he's just not acting himself lately."

Martha departed while Tanya began clearing the table. Upstairs Sonny was contemplating going to Vegas and seeing Alicia. While he was thinking, he remembered Malcolm Floyd, the newspaper reporter, from the Las Vegas Sun.

"I need to give him a call." Searching for his cell phone he remembered that he left it downstairs in the kitchen. Tanya was in the kitchen placing some of the food in the fridge when Sonny entered.

77

"Hey, Tanya."

"Hey, Sonny."

"Did you happen to see a cell phone down here?" he asked.

"No I haven't. Did you leave it in the kitchen?"

"I thought I did." He began looking on the counters and in the drawers. Suddenly, he remembered where it was. "Ah I know where it is." He reached on top of the fridge and there it was, right where he placed it.

After finding his phone he headed out of the kitchen—Tanya called his name. "Sonny, can we talk for a minute?"

He turned back saying, "Yeah, what's up?" He then sat at the kitchen table.

Tanya sat across from him. "Sonny ever since I've come back RJ has been acting very peculiar."

Sonny chuckled.

"What's funny?" asked Tanya.

"Well, you said he's been acting peculiar ever since you've been back. To be honest Tanya, I've noticed RJ acting that way before you came back."

"Is that right?"

"Yes. He's been very distant. He hardly spends any time at the office and he doesn't seem to care that Dad is worried about him. It's very strange."

"Yes, it sounds like it. Do you think he's just working too hard Sonny?"

"Well, if he is that's his own fault. You do know about this restaurant that he is co-owner of don't you?"

Tanya became wary. "That's odd," she said.

"What's odd?"

"Yesterday, RJ told me that he was considering partnership in the restaurant. Now you are saying; he is part owner. Are you sure, Sonny?"

"Just as sure as I'm sitting here, in fact Dad told him that it would take away from his work at Brook's Janitorial, but he didn't listen."

"Wow. I can't believe this."

"You know what's even stranger; he has never introduced any of us to his partner all we know is his partner's name is Max."

"Yes, that's really strange Sonny. Why would he not bring this person around? Have any of you eaten at the restaurant?"

"Oh yes, a couple of times. Of course this was before he became partner, but not since."

"None of this makes any sense to me Sonny. I don't know what to think."

"Well, I don't know what to tell you Tanya. He's my brother and not even I know what to think about him sometimes." They both sort of laughed.

Sonny felt thirsty and asked Tanya if she saw any orange juice in the fridge. "Yes, there's some let me get it for you," she said.

"Thanks."

Taking a glass from the cupboard then pouring Sonny some juice Tanya again sat across from him. "Here you go, it's pretty cold."

"Yeah, just the way I like it." He took a long drink.

"So Sonny tell me, how are you really doing?"

Sonny was curious as to why she asked him that. "What do you mean Tanya?"

"I've noticed that you seem to be preoccupied a lot. Not only that but you also seem a bit anxious."

"Well, Tanya, to be honest, I really have been all of that." After taking another drink he felt it necessary to tell Tanya what's been on his mind.

"Tanya, I have something to tell you."

"Okay, go ahead I'm all yours." Sonny looked at her peculiarly as Tanya's expression never changed. *Bustin', he thought.*

"I have to go back to Vegas."

"What. Are you serious?"

"Yes, I am. There are some very important matters I need to take care of."

"What could that be, if you don't mind me asking."

"If I did mind, you already asked so I'll tell you." He drank the last of his juice, and then continued. "There's a young lady in the hospital that needs my help."

Tanya was curious. "Who is she?"

Sonny didn't want to tell Tanya who he thought Alicia was in relationship to her, so he hesitated. Tanya got up and poured him anther glass of juice, which he did not expect. "Oh, thank you again, Tanya, you didn't have to do that." He drank some. Incidentally he tipped his glass too high and juice ran down the corner of his mouth.

Tanya had in her hand a tea towel which she used to wipe the corner of his mouth. This triggered something in Sonny. He reached up and grabbed her hand saying,

"Alicia stop!"

Tanya immediately withdrew her hand saying, "What did you call me?"

Sonny realized that he just called Tanya, Alicia. "I'm sorry Tanya. You just remind me so much of Alicia. She's the person in the hospital."

At this point Tanya decided to let this skeleton out of the closet. Taking Sonny by the hand she said, "Sonny, I wasn't telling you the truth at the Rib Ranch last night. You asked me if I have a sister named Alicia. The answer is yes, I do have a sister named Alicia."

Sonny was intrigued. He listened intently while Tanya talked. "There are some things in my past that I would rather forget, but lately I have been coming to terms with my past, which means owning up to it.

When I was just a child, maybe four or five, I was taken along with my siblings into child protective custody. It's a long story and most of which I don't remember. Anyway, while there, I was split from my family and taken into foster care by a white couple. After several years, they adopted me.

I was so traumatized by the abuse that I suffered, that I actually forgot all about my siblings, except for one, Alicia. I have this scar on my face to remember her."

"So why didn't you tell me the truth at the restaurant, Tanya?"

"Like I said, I am just coming to grips with all of that, so when you asked me about Alicia, I went right back into denial." She became very dismayed.

Sonny sensed that she was having trouble with all of this, but he needed more explanations. "So when was the last time you seen your sister?"

"Like I said, I was about five years old. I didn't even know if she was alive until you mentioned her name." Tanya had an Idea. "Sonny you said that you're going back to Vegas, well I think that I need to come also."

"Are you sure, what about RJ, he's already trippin."

"I guess while I'm away he can figure out what he wants in his life."

"Bustin!"

RJ had finally arrived at his destination after driving around to cool down. He was upset at the way Tanya had spoken to him. He rang the doorbell and waited. A woman answered the door.

"Hey, what took you so long RJ," she said.

"I'm sorry; I had to do some cooling down. Dinner wasn't quite as pleasant as I hoped it would be. I couldn't wait to get out of there."

"You do look a little stressed, come on in and I'll fix you something." RJ went in and took a seat on the sofa. "What would you like; wine or stronger?"

"Stronger please," RJ answered. Within a couple of minutes and she was back with RJ's drink. He took a small sip from it. "Oh, that hit the spot."

Sitting next to RJ on the sofa, Maxine spoke about Tanya. "I can't believe your Fiancée would let you out of her sight."

"Well, Max, she's the one losing out." RJ wrapped his arms around Maxine and they began kissing passionately. Things began to get heated when suddenly Maxine gently pushed RJ away.

"What's the problem Max?"

Maxine looked deeply into RJ's eyes. She was contemplating on how to tell him what he needed to know.

"Maxine, whatever it is you can tell me," he said with compassion.

"RJ, I'm pregnant, and yes the baby is yours."

"Oh shit!"

Chapter 6

Back in Las Vegas, Pearl was just arriving home. DJ was there packing away some things into a safe that he brought from Wannabee. He didn't notice Pearl as she walked in.

Upon seeing her, he seemed anxious, because a couple of items he had not put away were things that he could not let Pearl see.

"What are you putting in the safe DJ?" She asked.

He hurried and closed the door and spun the lock. "Just Some important files I need to keep here." He turned to her and asked her about her day. "So what was church like today?"

"The usual; the choir sang, the Pastor preached. Actually it was good." Placing her purse on the kitchen table, Pearl felt that this was a good time to tell DJ about her visit from Detective Riley.

"When you called me, I was sitting in the diner with a Detective."

"What's his mane?"

"His name is Detective Riley."

"Well, what did he want?"

"He was actually asking me questions about Sonny. He wanted to know where he could be found."

"You didn't tell him anything did you?"

"Yes, I did. He told me that Sonny may be able to give him some information about what happened to Alicia. I really didn't want to say, but I felt that it was important besides, if it means finding those killers and keeping Alicia safe, I had to tell him all that I knew."

This wasn't what DJ wanted to hear. If they begin to dig too much into this he knew that the cops would be asking him questions. He had counted on this being a closed case since there were no witnesses.

He took a seat in the living room and turned on the football game. It didn't matter who was playing or what the score was, DJ wasn't into it. His mind wandered back to that night when Alicia was shot.

"Damn!" he said. Then he thought, *why did she follow him, she should not have been there. I didn't mean for her to get shot.* With his head down in his hands, DJ began to weep.

At the police station Detective Riley was compiling notes when the telephone rang. He answered, "Detective. Riley."

"Riley, this is Mathias."

"Well, it's about time you called. What do you have for me?"

"First of all, I found Sonny Brooks; second, he didn't know that Alicia is alive."

"Well, did you tell him, that she is?"

"Yes, I told him."

"What does he know?"

"As far as I can tell, he knows absolutely nothing. He seems to be totally oblivious to everything."

Riley was incredulous. "How could he not know about the drug dealing going on at the club?"

"Believe me Riley, he didn't know."

"Well, we'll have to keep working on this end. Tell me, do you think there's a chance he may return."

Mathias paused for a moment. He remembered reading something in the Vegas Sun about a story on Karaoke. "You know what, I'm willing to bet that he was contacted about the story that the paper is doing on Karaoke. I can't imagine Sonny being left out, he was the main attraction."

"Well, if that's what you think come on back, we'll take it up from here. I just hope he does return. I would like to have a talk with him myself."

"Okay Riley, I'll catch the next flight back to Vegas."

Chapter 7

Tanya arrived home just before dark and was wondering if RJ had called her at her apartment. She was hoping that he did since she had her cell phone turned off.

She checked her voice mail; it was full. She hit the playback button to listen. There were about fifteen calls in her voice mail and none were from RJ When she turned her cell phone on there were no calls at all.

Now she was suspicious. She called his cell and after only one ring it went straight to voice mail. Being a rational person, she refused to get angry or accuse him of something.

Instead of getting upset, she decided to take a shower and watch a movie. She undressed in her bedroom and put on a nightgown. She turned the shower on to let it get hot, while she washed the makeup off her face.

The scar again reminded her of Alicia. The thought of her sister being comatose, really bothered her to the point of tears. Even though she had not seen Alicia for over twenty years, she felt an attachment that has been missing for a long time.

Outlining the scar with her finger, Tanya pondered the idea of going to Las Vegas with Sonny to see her sister. Concluding in her mind that it would probably be good for her and Alicia, she knew that she had to find a way to let RJ know without him getting angry.

She realized that having never told him about a sister, coupled with the fact that she would be leaving with Sonny, she knew RJ would not be calm about the whole thing.

It wasn't very late, but she was exhausted from all that she had to take in from the day. *I guess I'll read a book before I go to sleep,* she thought.

She had actually begun reading a book about a week ago that she wanted to finish. Hunkering down on her sofa wrapped in a snuggly it wasn't long after that she fell asleep. While Tanya slept, she dreamt about her sister.

How happy she felt when Alicia would hold her hand while they walked to the corner pharmacy to get snacks. Tanya would always get a cherry flavored blow-pop. While Alicia's favorite was a bag of barbecue potato chips.

The joy, which the dream brought to her, could be felt in her sub conscience, as though it was real. There was no greater feeling than this; however the feeling would soon be disrupted. While sleeping, she could hear the telephone ring.

It actually rang a couple of times before she responded. Looking over at the table clock and seeing that it was 10:00 p.m., she wondered who it was calling her at this time of night.

The name on the caller ID let her know that it was RJ so she answered. "Hello."

"Hello, Tanya, were you sleeping?"

"Yes, I was."

"I'm sorry; I didn't know you would be asleep so early."

"You're right. I wouldn't be. I would be out with you somewhere but—well we know what happened with that don't we?"

"Now come on Tanya, we both know that you started the whole thing, but that's why I called. I don't want to argue about that."

"So why did you call RJ?"

"I just wanted to let you know that I'm all right. I mean-I haven't talked to you since I left Mom and Dad's house. I thought perhaps you were concerned about me."

"Well, I was. I called you several times but you never answered. All of my calls were picked up by your voice mail."

"Yes, I know. Somehow my cell phone got shut off and I didn't realize it until I was on my way home."

Tanya became curious as to where he may have been all of this time. "So where did you go after you left the house RJ?"

"You know how upset I was. I just drove around town. After a while of that I got hungry and went to a sports bar and got a bite to eat."

"So is that all you did for the last six or seven hours?"

"Well, yes. I did watch the ball game at the bar, but that's about it."

"So where are you now?"

"I'm at home, but believe me; I would rather be there with you."

"Is that right, and why should I even let you come over, besides I'm already in bed?"

"That's easy Tanya, because I love you and really want to make things up with you, that's why."

"I suppose that I'm convinced, but I don't think that is going to work tonight. I am really tired and need to get my sleep. So you just think about how wonderful it would feel lying next to me and just perhaps that will suffice."

"That is so wrong Tanya."

"Well, RJ that's about all it's going to be for tonight. I really need to get some sleep, so can I do that."

"What choice do I have?"

"You have choices RJ You could either say goodnight or you can keep talking while I hang up the phone—you choose."

"Goodnight Tanya."

"Goodnight RJ" As Tanya placed the phone back on the charger, she decided to just sleep the night right there on the sofa.

At his apartment, RJ's head was spinning. He had been devastated by the news given him by Max. His mind took him back to Max's house.

"How could you be pregnant Max?" RJ was furious.

"What do you mean how could I be pregnant. We had sex RJ, that's usually what happens when people don't exercise caution."

"Well, why weren't you on the pill or something. You know damned well that I'm engaged. What were you thinking?"

"You wait just one minute RJ Why do men always think that it is the woman's responsibility to use birth control? You are just as responsible as I am for this. I don't recall you ever putting on a condom. And as far as

being engaged; now it's a problem? It didn't seem to be a problem while you were getting wild with me in bed."

RJ started feeling that this relationship was now even more complicated. It was one thing to get romantically involved with a business partner, now this is another whole level of complication.

"Maxine are you sure that you're pregnant?"

"Yes, RJ, I am. I actually waited a whole month to tell you, because I wanted to be sure."

"So how far along are you?"

"I'm ten weeks, and just in case you think about it-I'm not getting an abortion."

Without saying a word, that is exactly what RJ was thinking.

"Look RJ, I was just as disappointed when I found out about this as you are now, but what can I do. There is no way that I'm going to terminate this pregnancy and since we are already in this partnership, we have to make this whole thing work for the good of the baby."

Those words infuriated RJ. "What do you mean we have to make this work for the good of the baby—I'm going to be married soon. What am I going to tell Tanya, and my family-oh my god. This is going to devastate them."

Maxine listened but said nothing while RJ went on about himself. When he finished saying all that he could think of, she spoke.

"RJ, I didn't know that you were so selfish. But I should have that's why we got into this relationship. At some point you have to stop being so selfish and start thinking about your actions, because there are always going to be consequences. Baby, you should have thought about getting married long before we started sleeping together. That part is yours. You handle that. But remember now you have another responsibility so figure out how to handle this."

RJ was perplexed; he didn't know what to do other than to call Tanya. He decided to leave and go home.

"RJ, I love you. Whatever you decide to do, I will always be here."

"Yeah, all right Max. Look, I have to go. I'll see you tomorrow."

Max watched RJ as he walked out of her house. She was also upset because she really wanted RJ to stay the night.

He was exhausted and needed to get some rest himself. He began to wonder when would be the right time to tell Tanya about Max. He also knows that Tanya doesn't know that Max is a woman.

Chapter 8

The sound of the alarm awakened Sonny from a good nights rest. He arose from the bed and slipped into his house slippers.

Oddly he sniffed into the air. *Humm,* he thought. Quickly he went to the bathroom to relieve himself and wash before going downstairs to investigate. Upon entering the kitchen it was confirmed that there was nothing cooking and nobody was there.

"I wonder where everybody is." This was very unusual for Martha; she would always be the first person up and in the kitchen cooking breakfast and having coffee.

Sonny looked out on the back porch and there was Raleigh, sitting in a lounging chair with his eyes closed. Sonny didn't want to disturb him so he went back inside still wondering where his mom could be.

As he was opening the fridge to get the orange juice he heard a car pull up the driveway. A couple of minutes later Martha entered the back door. "Good morning Sonny," she said.

"Good morning, Mom. Where did you have to go this early in the morning?"

"I went to the pharmacy for your dad. He hasn't been feeling well lately and he has this terrible cough and sore throat."

"Is he going to be all right," asked Sonny.

"I hope this syrup will do the job. I don't believe it's anything serious."

"You're probably right, Mom; it's probably just a cold or something."

Sonny finished his orange juice and headed back upstairs. Martha stopped him asking if he wanted any breakfast before going to work. "No, Mom, I really don't have time to eat but thanks anyway."

"Now Sonny how many times do I have to tell you; you should always eat something other than drinking orange juice."

"I know, I know. So if you can have some bacon ready by the time I come back down, I'll have a bacon sandwich, how's that."

"I guess that will have to do if that's all you want."

"Yes, ma'am." He ran upstairs to get ready for work.

From inside, Martha could hear Raleigh coughing. "Martha can you bring whatever it is you brought back from the pharmacy."

"Yes, here I come now." She turned over the bacon and lowered the heat to keep it from burning as she went out to bring Raleigh some cough syrup.

Handing him a spoon she opened the bottle and poured a spoonful. "Take all of this and come in so you can eat something."

Raleigh wasn't at all reluctant to take the medicine and swallowed it all quickly. "Oh, Jesus," he said grimacing. "If the cough doesn't kill me the medicine will."

In the kitchen, Sonny was making himself a bacon sandwich when Raleigh entered.

"Hey, Dad, how are you feeling this morning?"

"I suppose I'll make it, Son."

Sonny took a bite from his sandwich and with a full mouth said, "Time to meet the boys and clean something."

"When you see your Brother, have him to give me a call will you?"

"Sure Dad, I'll do that. Well, I'll see you all later today. I think I'm only going to work only until noon."

"Since you've been on salary, I don't think you've worked a full day at all have you Sonny?"

"Sure I have Dad. I actually make up the time working over."

"Now do you expect me to believe that your lazy behind works overtime. Get outa here before I fire you."

"Sorry, Dad, but you don't work anymore. You can't fire me." Sonny left the back door laughing. Raleigh was also laughing, consequently his coughing began.

Martha returned to the kitchen when she heard the coughing. "Baby are you okay?"

Hardly able to catch his breath, Raleigh answered, "Yes, yes that foolish son of yours made me laugh that's all."

"He is silly, but he's your son remember."

"Don't get started okay, said Raleigh. He finally got his cough under control.

On the way to work, Sonny's cell phone rang. Since he always placed it on the passenger side seat face up he could see who it was that was calling.

He recognized the Las Vegas area code. "I wonder who this could be calling me," he said.

He didn't check it out until he came to a stop light. He hit the call back and hoping that whoever called would answer. The phone rang a couple of times. "Hello, Mathias here."

"Hello, Mathias, this is Sonny Brooks."

"Yes, Sonny, glad you called back. I just called you."

"Mathias can I call you back I'm driving right now, but I'll call you as soon as I get to where I'm going."

"Sure Sonny, just call me back."

"Sure." Sonny hung up and when he made it to the office and got settled in he called Mathias.

"Sonny?"

"Yes, this is Sonny."

Mathias had something of importance to inform Sonny of. "So Sonny how have you been since I last saw you what about two days ago?"

Yeah, it's only been about two days, but I've been well; and you?"

"Oh, I can't complain."

"So Mathias is there something that you need from me?" Sonny queried.

"Yes, Sonny, I do have something to ask you. Have you thought about coming back to Vegas? Now it isn't all that important that you come, because I can always come there. We just feel that by you coming, our investigation may move along a little faster.

Sonny thought about the call that he received from Malcolm, now this call from Mathias. All of this has confirmed to him that he has made the right decision to make the trip back to Vegas.

"You know what Mathias, I have already decided to return; I just have to decide when.

"Well, Sonny, since you have decided to come back may I suggest that the sooner you come the better it will be for Alicia."

"If that's the case, I guess I can get there sometime this week."

"That's fine Sonny, just make sure you call me when you get to Vegas is that a deal."

"Yes, Mathias, I'll make it a point to call you as soon as I arrive."

"That's wonderful Sonny, You have a good rest of the day."

"Thank you and you do the same."

After talking to Mathias, Sonny had to meet with RJ and the rest of the staff to discuss the week's activities. He and RJ shared office space while an office was being constructed for RJ.

Just shortly after Sonny finished with his call RJ entered the office.

"Morning," he said. Sonny noticed the air of tension that rode in on his brother's shoulders.

"Good morning." After returning the greeting, he asked, "Are you feeling all right?"

"I'm good. Why are you asking?"

"I don't know, I'm just asking."

"Yes, I'm fine." After shuffling some papers together, RJ said, "Hey, I have some business to take care of this morning that's going to prevent me from attending the meeting."

Surprised, Sonny asked why. "So what is it you have to do? You know how important these meetings are."

Irritated by Sonny's response, RJ attacked. "Listen here boy, I'm not asking for your permission and don't you ever question me again!"

"Bustin! Damn. Bustin! What the hell is wrong with you dude?" RJ didn't say another word he just left the building.

The employees were now entering the building, a couple of them seen RJ leaving in what seemed to be in a hurry.

"Hey, Sonny, what's up with number one son?" That is what the guys often called RJ behind his back.

Sonny was still in a state of astonishment didn't answer right away. "Hey, Sonny, are you there?"

"Oh yeah, dawg, I'm sorry. You said you saw RJ leaving right."

"Yes. He looked like he was in a real hurry. Did something happen?"

Sonny wasn't sure what happened at all so he tried to brush it off. "Hey, you know RJ how can anyone tell what's up with him."

"You got that right dude, ol'boy be straight trippin."

Time was passing buy and Sonny had his own concerns to deal with. He had planned on telling RJ that he was going to take a leave of absence, but since RJ wasn't there Sonny decided to cancel the meeting and just hand out the work orders for the day.

When all of the crew members were present, Sonny let them know about his plans and assured them that he would tell RJ. He dispatched the crews and they went to their job sites, while he stayed back to finish up with some paperwork before leaving.

It was just before noon and he was about to leave when Tanya showed up at the office. He was surprised to see her.

"Hello, Tanya, what are you doing here taking an early lunch today?"

"No, not really, actually I called off today."

"You're not sick are you?"

"No, no, I'm doing just fine. I just needed to take care of some things."

After a moment of silence, Sonny spoke. "So if you are here to see RJ, he's not here."

"Yes, I figured he wasn't. I didn't see his car outside. When did he leave?"

"It was quite some time ago in a hurry and with a huge chip on his shoulders." Realizing that Tanya was still standing he asked her to have a seat. She took the seat on the opposite side of his desk.

"Tanya, I don't want to be nosy, but are you two fighting?"

"You really know how to get right to the point, don't you Sonny." Tanya lowered her head and began crying.

"I'm sorry Tanya, I should mind . . ."

"Oh no, Sonny, It's okay and you're right, kinda."

"What do you mean, kinda?"

"RJ's acting really strange, and he is blaming me for his behavior, I'm tired of it."

Sonny just sat and listened. Tanya continued. "Last night he didn't call me until after ten o'clock. I tried calling him but he say's that his cell phone was accidently cut off."

Sonny sort of grinned at that.

"What are you grinning about Sonny?"

"It's nothing. I just thought about something."

"No Sonny, it's not." Tanya was very upset. "Tell me what made you grin. What is RJ up to?"

"I promise you Tanya, I have no idea what he's up to or what he's doing. I was only thinking about how many times I've heard that excuse about the cell phone being turned off accidently."

Tanya regained her composure and felt that it was time to go. "Well, Sonny. I don't want to bog you down with my troubles so I'm going to leave."

Sonny decided that he would tell Tanya that he will be leaving soon. "I'm actually planning to leave as early as Wednesday. I spoke with someone in Las Vegas that will be expecting me."

When Tanya said that she would go with him, she didn't know how soon that would be. "So I guess that means I'll be going with you Sonny."

"Tanya, I'm okay with that, but do you think RJ is going to appreciate you leaving again with such short knowledge."

"Well, Sonny, to be quite honest, I really don't care if he doesn't appreciate me leaving. He doesn't seem to appreciate me being here as it is. I'll tell him where I'm going and whether he likes it or not, that will be his problem, not mine."

Sonny rose from his chair. "So you've decided then, you're going."

"Yes, Sonny, I'm going and don't worry about the air tickets, I'll book our flight today. I'll leave the return flight open, so we'll have time to do whatever we have to do while we're in Las Vegas."

Sonny stepped from around his desk to give Tanya a hug. Just as he embraced her, RJ walked into the office.

Quickly pulling away, Sonny stepped back around his desk, trying to not look suspicious. Tanya was the first to speak. "Hello, RJ, I was just leaving."

"When, after whatever that was you were doing with my little brother."

"Oh, that was nothing. Sonny was just giving me a hug as I was leaving, that's all.

RJ looked over at Sonny.

"That's all big brother," said Sonny.

"That's all," remarked RJ.

Sonny picked up his shoulder bag. "Well, I'm outie."

RJ was wondering where Sonny was going so early in the day. "Are you going to lunch already?"

"No I'm leaving, I've got plans."

"Plans, what is that supposed to mean?"

"Well, that means, I'm leaving work and will not be back for a while."

RJ didn't understand what Sonny was talking about. "Sonny what's going on here?"

Sonny reached into his shoulder bag and pulled out a letter that he was planning to leave at the office for RJ and handed it to him.

RJ read the letter. By his expression, Both Sonny and Tanya could see that he was not pleased by what he read. Never saying a word, he crumpled the paper into a ball and threw it into a trashcan.

"This is Bull-shit, Sonny."

"Well, Bro, call it what you want, that's the way it is."

RJ was very angry. "I thought you had enough of Vegas. Why would you want to go back there? That's the last place you should go back to, not to mention going alone."

After that was said, Sonny looked over at Tanya. RJ then looked at Tanya, who had this look which RJ could not quite read.

"What's going on Tanya? Did you know about this?"

"Yes, I know about it. I've known since yesterday."

RJ really hadn't asked Tanya why she was not dressed for work. He noticed that she was wearing jeans and a silk pullover.

"So Tanya did you go to work today?"

"No I didn't."

RJ decided that he wanted to spend some time with Tanya, perhaps do something that would calm his blood pressure.

"I don't have time to deal with Sonny right now, so why don't you and I go somewhere to eat."

"I don't think I'll have time for that RJ."

"What do you mean, you don't have time. What could you possibly have to do since you're not at work?"

"I'm planning on going on a trip, so I have to start packing."

"So where are you going?" He paused. It finally dawned on him. "Don't tell me."

Tanya then spoke. "Whatever it is you don't want me to tell you, I'm going to. Sonny and I are leaving Wednesday, going to Las Vegas."

Now RJ was furious. He would have stricken his brother, but he knew better. Sonny tried to explain. "Shut up, I don't want to hear a thing you have to say."

He turned to Tanya. "What is this all about Tanya?"

"The young woman that Sonny met in Las Vegas is my sister. She's in a coma and I have to see her."

RJ was speechless.

"Listen RJ, I don't expect you to understand, especially since I've never talked about my family to you. Believe me that when Sonny told me about her, I was surprised. What a coincidence I thought. But then, I suppose that this is more than a coincidence.

This is my opportunity to see my sister that I haven't seen in over twenty years."

RJ looked over at Sonny, who was standing halfway out of the door. Then he looked back to Tanya. He could see in her face that she was not going to change her mind.

"That's fine, just go. Do whatever you feel you have to do Tanya, just remember we are engaged to be married."

Tanya looked down at her ring. At this point she wasn't sure if she even wanted to be engaged. However, she kept her thoughts to herself. "Yes, RJ, I know. I'll be back when my work is done in Vegas."

Instead of a heart felt good-bye, RJ just held up his hand. "I'll see you later, Tanya."

On that note Sonny left, followed by Tanya, RJ stayed back at the office.

He felt somewhat relieved, because now with Tanya out of the way he could handle his other situation more easily. *I have to call Max,* he thought.

Outside Sonny and Tanya made plans to call one another to confirm flight times. "I'll call you as soon as I get the itinerary on the flights Sonny."

"Okay Tanya, Just call me on my cell."

"I sure will."

They both entered their own cars and headed their separate ways.

Sonny headed to the recording studio, while Tanya went back to her apartment to begin packing. She had no idea how long she would be there so she packed quite a lot. Before she finished she thought that she had better call her job and let her boss know about her plans.

The phone only rang one time before the receptionist picked up.

"Hello, First national bank of Saint Louis, how may I help you?"

"Hello, Terri, this is Tanya, is Bruce in?"

"I believe he is, let me connect you."

"Thanks." As she listened to muzak on the phone, Tanya thought about what she might tell Bruce. Bruce an easy man to work for was quite an exceptional boss. However; just returning from a training seminar and taking the day off was one thing, but now taking an indefinite leave of absence without any warning would probably not sit well with him.

It was only a short moment and he answered. "Hello, this is Bruce."

"Hello, Bruce, this is Tanya. How are you doing today?"

"I'm doing just fine Tanya, are things good with you?"

"Yes, thanks."

"How may I help you, Tanya?" This was going to be hard for her.

"Well, Bruce, I had something to come up in Las Vegas, Nevada, and I need to take some time off." She held her breath and clinched her teeth.

"What did you do Tanya? Did you leave some money there and you have to go try to get it back?"

"No Bruce, I don't even gamble. It's something a little more serious than that."

"Well, Tanya, being that you just returned back to work today, I can't see how I can authorize this with such a short notice." She anticipated that there may be a problem, but she was determined to get this approved.

"Listen Bruce, I have saved up about a month or longer in personal leave time, and was actually given an extra week, since I transferred here, and to be quite honest, I haven't taken anytime off at all since arriving. I really need to do this."

"You know Tanya, I totally understand. You have the time and we haven't really been too busy around here, so I don't think it will set us back if you go for a while. All I need you to do is fill out the time off request form and turn it in, I'll sign it."

Tanya was surprised at how little it took to convince Bruce to let her have the time off.

"Oh, thank you, Bruce, I'll get that taken care of today. I'll just have Terri to fax the form to me."

"Okay Tanya, make sure you get it in today. By the way when do you plan to leave?"

"I believe I'll be leaving Wednesday, if I can book a flight on such early notice."

"Well, good luck with that."

"Thank you again, Bruce. You have a good day."

Tanya quickly got on line to find a ticket for her and Sonny. After checking several discount ticket sites she was able to find something on Southwest that she thought Sonny would like so she sent him an e-mail with what she found.

Afterward, she called Terri at the office to have her send the fax with a time off request form. It had taken only a couple of minutes for the fax to come in and she promptly filled it out and sent it back. After taking care of that business, Tanya decided to pack. She thought little about RJ and what he thought about her leaving.

This was something that she felt strongly about and there was no way that he was going to talk her out of it.

Chapter 9

S onny didn't go home after he left the office. He decided to stop at the studio to let the band know that he's leaving. When he arrived, Malik was there doing something on the mixer. Sonny knew that he was working on the new song because it was playing.

"Hey, what's up Malik?"

Malik looked up from the mixing board and had this very peculiar smile. "Check this out man," he said.

He played the song back and Sonny was totally blown away by the sound. Malik had mixed all of the background vocals and tweaked some things. Sonny was very excited. "That's it!" said Sonny.

Malik didn't say a word; he just rocked his head to the beat. Sonny began to sing along with himself on the lead. Malik raised the volume just a bit as Sonny sang.

When it ended, Malik was convinced that Sonny loved what he had done. "There's much more that I can do with this Sonny. I think it's ready. All we have to do now is burn a few copies and shop them around.

Sonny was in agreement. "Bustin! This song is tight; man, you are the master for sure." Sonny sat down at the mixing table next to Malik placing his hand on Malik's shoulder.

"What's the matter, bro?" asked Malik.

Sonny removed his hand and rubbed his face. He was trying to find the right way to break the news. "I guess I'll just say it dawg," said Sonny. "I'm leaving, going back to Las Vegas."

Malik was taken aback by this. "What did you say?"

"You heard me right. I'm going back to Vegas."

"That's what I thought you said. My question is why?"

Sonny stood and walked over to the drum set and tapped a symbol. "I have unfinished business that I have to take care of."

"Damn Sonny! What about the business that you have here. I've worked all weekend trying to finish this track. Don't you realize what we have here? I'm telling you man this can be huge and you're telling me that you have unfinished business in Vegas. Man that's bull."

Sonny had a feeling that this would be the response, however his mind was made. "Malik, I don't expect you or anyone else to understand, hell, I haven't even told my father yet. Right now I don't have time to get into the reasons with you, because I have to get home and break the news there."

Sonny started out the door and paused when Malik called his name. "Sonny, aren't you going to tell the guys about this?"

Now he was beginning to feel the pressure and wanted desperately to not have to tell them himself. "I'm leaving Wednesday, so I'll tell them before I leave."

"Sure, you do that Sonny, You owe it to them."

"Yes, I know. I'll tell them don't worry."

Sonny had to get home and let his father know what's going on before RJ messes things up. He hurried as fast as he could but unfortunately, when he arrived RJ had already arrived.

"I pray to God that he didn't say anything to Dad yet" said Sonny getting out of the car. Inside RJ was in the living room with Martha. It appeared as though they had been discussing something of a serious nature when Sonny walked in.

RJ was sitting on the sofa next to Martha holding his head in his hands. Martha was just getting up from the lounger. "Hey, Mom, how are things today and why is everybody looking so down?"

Martha answered, "Well, Sonny, your brother has told me about your plans to leave, that alone is upsetting, but there's something that you need to know."

"What. Should I sit down to hear this? Is it serious?"

"I have to go upstairs so I'll let your brother tell you." Martha walked over to RJ saying, "don't be rude to him RJ okay." RJ just looked up at her and nodded. Martha then went over and kissed Sonny on the cheek. He was still standing, but as soon as Martha left the room to go upstairs he sat next to his brother.

"What's going on RJ? Is Mom, all right?" RJ didn't say anything for a moment as he was thinking whether he should tell Sonny the truth.

What Martha and RJ were discussing was about their father. For the last couple of days Raleigh has had a terrible cough that seemed to be getting worse. Martha had been trying desperately to get him to go to a doctor, but he refuses. She thinks it's something serious and is very concerned that it will get worse before it gets better.

RJ knowing what Sonny's plans are now has to tell him what's going on with their dad, but he's stalling.

"So Sonny are you sure that you want to go to back to Las Vegas?"

"Yes, I'm sure, but what's going on here? Mom asked you to tell me."

"It's nothing that serious Sonny; you know how emotional Mom can get."

"Don't tell me it's nothing RJ It must be something or else the two of you wouldn't have looked like you just left a funeral. I saw the look on your faces, so tell me what's going on."

RJ could see that Sonny was adamant and was not willing to except his weak explanation. "Okay Sonny, I'll tell you. Dad is not feeling very well and Mom is worried about him."

Sonny looked at RJ questionably. "So, and what else is there?"

"That's it," said RJ.

"That's it?"

"Yes. I told you that Mom was just being over sensitive."

"So where's Dad now RJ?"

"He's upstairs. I'm sure he's probably asleep."

Sonny was less than convinced of what his brother told him. "Okay if that's all then there shouldn't be a problem with me asking Mom if Dad is okay."

"No problem at all Sonny, do what you feel you have to do. Besides we all know that's what you're about anyway now don't we."

"Whatever, RJ."

Sonny went upstairs to check on Raleigh. He met Martha at the top of the stairs. "So Mom is Dad going to be all right?"

"Yes, Sonny, you know how stubborn your dad is, he'll be just fine."

"So is there anything that I can do to help. Are you going to be all right?"

"Yes, I'll be just fine. Look Sonny, there's no need to be concerned, I have everything under control. Besides, he's had this cough before, I'm sure it's just a cold, he'll get over it soon."

Feeling relieved that nothing seemed to be that serious, Sonny headed to his bedroom to begin packing. He decided that he would wait and tell his dad tomorrow after he's feeling better. While packing, he remembered that he had to let the band members know about his leaving.

He stopped what he was doing and sat at his computer. He wrote a short note and copied it to all of the guys. Before hitting send, he read it over. *Hello, I'm sorry that I have to tell you all this way, but I will be leaving soon on my way to Las Vegas. I'm not exactly sure when I'll be back. I heard the finished track and it sounds great Sonny.*

He realized how short it was, but he was hoping not to upset anyone with too much information. Before he could hit send, his cell phone rang. It was Tanya.

"Hello."

"Hello, Sonny it's Tanya."

"Hey, Tanya, are you doing okay?"

"Yes, I'm okay. I just wanted to tell you that I found a good price on the tickets. I decided that tomorrow morning would be the best time for us to go because all of the flights after tomorrow are booked to capacity. Is tomorrow too soon for you?"

Not really, it only means that I have less time to spend with my miserable big brother."

"That's good because I went ahead and purchased the tickets on my Visa."

"You didn't have to do that, I have money."

"Then you can pay me when we get to Las Vegas. Oh, before I forget, I also got a rental car."

"That should be just fine Tanya." There was a pause over the phone.

"Tanya, are you still there?"

"Yes, I'm here. I was just thinking. Have you seen RJ since earlier today?"

"Yes, I have. He's actually here now. Do you need to talk to him?"

"Not really. I just wanted to know if you've seen him."

"You really love RJ, don't you Tanya?"

"Yes, I do Sonny, and I make it very obvious, don't I?"

"No, no I hardly noticed at all." They both began to laugh.

"Well, Tanya I need to finish packing, but I'll see you tomorrow. So what time do we need to be at the airport?"

"Our flight leaves at seven thirty in the morning, so we should be there by six thirty."

"Bustin. That's early. Do you want me to pick you up or . . . ?"

"No. But thank you. I'll see if RJ can drop me off.

"Well then, Tanya, I'll see you tomorrow."

"Okay Sonny, I'll see you tomorrow, good night."

"Good night Tanya."

Feeling thirsty, Sonny craved for some orange juice. As he headed downstairs, he overheard RJ talking to somebody on the telephone. It sounded as though he was whispering. Sonny's intuition told him to tip lightly to keep from being noticed.

As he made his way to the bottom of the stairs he could hear RJ more clearly.

"So don't be upset Max, you know that I love you. I'll do all that I can to help you and the baby, just don't do anything drastic. I don't know exactly when she's leaving, but I'll have plenty of time to spend with you. She's going to Las Vegas with my brother. Yes, my brother. I don't know."

While Sonny eaves dropped on RJ's conversation he didn't know that RJ was making his way near the stairway. When RJ turned the corner, Sonny was busted.

"Bustin," he said.

RJ didn't say a word to Sonny right away. "Hey, something just came up; let me call you back later. Yes, I'll call you later. Bye." After getting rid of Maxine off the phone he turned his attention to Sonny.

"Were you eaves dropping on me?"

Guilty, Sonny answered, "Well, yes sort of."

"What do you mean sort of?"

"Well, what I mean is, I wasn't trying to until I heard you tell this person Max that you love them. So instead of you asking me questions maybe I should be asking you questions. Let's start with, who is Max, and are you going to be a daddy?"

RJ didn't appreciate Sonny asking him those questions. "What business is it of yours boy?"

"Oh, now I'm your boy. You know that's funny because all of the time you had us all thinking that Max was a boy. Now unless you're gay, I think Max is really a woman and maybe even a pregnant woman. So you tell me, what's up bro?"

RJ was livid. "You don't know a damned thing. What do you know? You haven't lived enough or experienced life outside of running off to Las Vegas. You're nothing but a sorry butt choirboy."

Sonny began to smile. "Did you know that in Las Vegas, they called me Choirboy too?"

"I don't care what they called you; you had no business listening in on my conversation."

"You're right RJ, I was wrong, but that doesn't answer the question, or should Tanya be asking you those questions."

"You keep Tanya out of this Sonny. It's none of yours or Tanya's business."

"I don't know maybe Tanya will be interested in knowing that Max is a woman. I'm sure she doesn't know either. In fact, I just finished talking to her, I have her phone number right . . ."

Before Sonny could complete his sentence, RJ out of rage grabbed the cell phone and through it to the floor and it broke in half."

"Bustin!"

That's right, busted. You are lucky that it's just your cell phone."

"What is that supposed to mean RJ? Are you threatening me?"

From upstairs, Martha could hear the arguing and she came hurriedly down to see what was going on. "What's going on with all of this fighting down here?"

She looked down and saw the broken cell phone. "Whose cell phone is that?"

"Its mine ma," said Sonny.

"Well, why is it on the floor and broken?"

"I guess you have to ask RJ about that." Martha looked at RJ "Did you do this to Sonny's phone RJ?"

"What difference does it make?" he remarked sarcastically.

"Don't get smart with me boy," snapped Martha. She continued, "Now what's going on down here?"

Sonny decided that he would begin. "Mom, did you know that Max, RJ's so-called business partner is a woman?"

Martha was surprised to hear this. She as well as Raleigh actually thought that Max was a man. "Is this right RJ is Max a woman?"

"Oh, that's not all. Tanya doesn't know either." Sonny was really making RJ angry.

"I've told you to stay out of this Sonny!"

"That's right because it's your business." Sonny was getting on a roll. "So RJ, you want to tell mama about the rest of your business, or do you want me to tell it?"

RJ felt it was time to divert the attention from him and put it onto Sonny. "Talking about business have you told Mom or Dad that you are going back to Las Vegas?"

Martha turned her attention to Sonny. "Is that right, Sonny?"

Before he could answer Raleigh's voice was heard from the top of the stairs. "So you decided to go back to Vegas, Sonny?"

Everyone looked up to see Raleigh coming downstairs. "I think we all need to have a talk in the living room," said Martha.

Sonny took the opportunity to go to the kitchen and get some orange juice. He picked up the pieces of his phone, which had not broken, but came apart top from bottom.

He connected the two parts and saw that it was still operational. RJ followed. He got himself a glass of water and went to the living room. From the living room Martha called out to Sonny, telling him to put some coffee on. After making coffee, Sonny joined the rest of the family.

Raleigh was feeling very weak, but he had to take control of his house. "What seems to be the problem here?"

There was silence for a moment, and then RJ spoke. "It seems that Sonny is minding everyone's matters except his own."

"You know RJ, why don't you tell Dad what's going on with you, and I'll tell him about myself, okay."

Raleigh gave them both a very stern gaze. "That sounds like a very good idea to me. You go first RJ."

"Well, Dad, there's really nothing to say other than, Sonny and Tanya are planning to go to Las Vegas together."

Martha was surprised. "Why on earth are you going to Las Vegas with Tanya, Sonny?"

Sonny couldn't believe that RJ manipulated the conversation. Before answering he glared at RJ.

"Well, Mom, as I have told you before, I have been in contact with Alicia's aunt Pearl as well as with a private investigator. I've been told that Alicia is alive and I have to go and see about her. Now as far as Tanya is concerned, you may not believe this, but Tanya and Alicia are sisters."

"You don't say. How in the world could this be Sonny?" asked Martha.

"It's a long story, Mom, I hope to tell you someday but right now, I think RJ has something to tell you, isn't that right RJ?"

Without much feeling, RJ remarked, "I have no idea what you're talking about."

"Oh, sure you do RJ remember the conversation that I overheard you having with Max. You said something about loving her and that when Tanya is gone you'll have plenty of time to spend with her. There was something else wasn't there. Oh, right, you mentioned something about a pregnancy. Yes, that's it. So go ahead tell Mom and Dad all about it RJ."

If eyes could kill, then Sonny would be dead seven times over. RJ was not about to disclose any information about Maxine. It was bad enough that he kept the fact of her gender from them, but this he really had to keep.

"Mom, I really don't have any idea what Sonny is talking about. Yes, he heard me talking to Max; however he no doubt heard everything that I said wrong. Listen Mom, Dad, I have to go it's getting late and I have an important meeting to attend in the morning that I need to prepare for."

RJ rose from his seat and headed toward the door. He paused, turned and said, "I hope you get yourself together Sonny, your imagination will get you in trouble one day."

Then he looked over to his parents. "I'm sorry for the disruption, it won't happen again." He then departed.

Sonny just sat on the sofa feeling as though he was broadsided by a Mack truck. As usual, RJ was able to maneuver his way out of some mess that he got started. This scene was all too familiar to Sonny.

Time and time again whenever he and RJ had a heated discussion and the parents were involved, RJ would ease out through the back door. The problem is that the door is always held open for him to slip out of. Sonny was beginning to wonder why his parents never seemed to reprimand RJ about his attitude.

The one thing that bothered him the most this time was that they never questioned him about Max or Tanya or anything that Sonny brought up. They just seemed to dismiss the whole thing.

After RJ had left the house, Raleigh wanted to know more about Sonny's leaving. "So Sonny, tell me again about you and Tanya going to Vegas together."

"Dad it's a long story, which I don't think you need to worry about. It's not like Tanya and I are going to become run away lovers."

"Well, I hope not," said Martha.

"Mom, she's going to see Alicia, I told you that. Since I had the talk with the investigator and then with the newspaper guy, I decided to go back there to see what loose ends that I need to tie." Sonny was becoming very emotional. "Look Mom and Dad, I really cared a lot about Alicia, but I didn't get to know her as well as I would have liked to. Now I have a chance to, and Tanya has a chance to see about her sister, whom she hasn't seen in almost twenty years."

Raleigh was not feeling very well; Martha could see it in his eyes. "Sonny, I have learned to let you and RJ both to make your own decisions all I care about is that you make the right decisions. I'm not sure about this one you're making Sonny."

Sonny stood to his feet and walked over to his dad and placed a hand on his shoulder. "Dad, I need to do this and I'm leaving tomorrow morning. I really don't want to talk about this anymore; I have to get up early so I'm going to bed. He kissed his mom and retired to his room.

Martha looked into her husband's eyes, "Honey, one day you're going to have to tell him the whole story, and you know what I'm talking about."

She stood to her feet and reached out her hand to Raleigh to help him up. He accepted her hand and rose to his feet saying, "I pray to God that that day never comes."

Upstairs, Sonny was packing a few more items while completely forgetting to send the message to his band members as the computer screen had gone to its screen saver mode. After packing, Sonny prepared to take a shower. He usually took his shower in the morning but he knew there wouldn't be any time for it then.

He was about to enter the bathroom when he heard his parents from inside their bedroom, it sounded as if they were arguing. He stopped to listen for a second, but was unable to hear clearly what they were saying so he continued into the bathroom to take his shower.

Had he stayed a second longer he would have seen his mom come out as she was going downstairs to get the medicine she had purchased for Raleigh. With the water running, Sonny could not hear the violent coughs coming from his dad. Martha was upset that he continued to refuse to go to a doctor, saying that it was just a cold and it would soon pass.

Alone In the bedroom, Raleigh rubbed his aching throat as he coughed. He felt something coming up from his throat. After coughing into a towel he looked into his towel. He thought it was mucous but was surprised to see that there was blood.

No way was he going to let Martha know about this. After stuffing the towel between the mattress and box spring, he looked into a nightstand mirror to make sure there was no blood around his mouth, just as Martha walked in.

"What are you doing?" she asked.

Raleigh placed the mirror back on the nightstand and answered, "Just cleaning my mouth."

"What was on your mouth?"

"Oh, just a little mucous, that's all. I told you that all I have is a cold Martha."

Coming around to Raleigh's side of the bed with a spoon, the medicine and a glass of water, Martha responded, "Well, whatever it is I still say you need to see a doctor."

Raleigh now realized that she was right. "Okay, I'll make an appointment tomorrow. Just maybe I'll be able to get in."

Martha agreed. "Well, I don't see why there would be a problem seeing the doctor tomorrow." She poured some of the syrup into the spoon and told Raleigh to, "Open wide."

Raleigh obeyed his wife and she gently inserted the spoon and he swallowed all of it.

"This mess really tastes awful," he said reaching for the glass of water. He drank all of it and sat the empty glass on the nightstand.

"I wish solving the problem between RJ and Sonny was as simple as a spoonful of medicine," said Martha. Raleigh didn't respond as he crawled between the sheets and laid his head gently on his pillow. Martha was disappointed by his lack of concern, but hid her feelings.

She leaned over her husband and kissed him on the cheek and got in bed and turned off the lamplight. Raleigh didn't go to sleep; he just laid there thinking about what could possibly be causing this condition he has.

When Sonny came out of the shower he stopped at his parents' door and placed his hand on it. He said a silent prayer for them, asking God to look over them as they slept. He finished and went into his room, stopped at the computer and sat down and wrote something on a sheet of paper. After finishing he climbed into bed. He sat up with his back against the headboard and began to pray for Alicia, and asked God for a safe flight to Las Vegas. He also said a prayer for RJ and Tanya. It wasn't long before he was fast asleep.

Chapter 10

In Las Vegas, DJ was busy at Wannabee trying to gather the last of his things. He was just about finished moving into his new office at Starz. Night had fallen and he was there alone. He wasn't expecting anyone to show up since it was not opened anymore, so he was surprised when he heard voices out in the lobby. Cautiously he went out to see who it might be.

Sitting at one of the tables was Rico, drinking a bottle of beer that was still in a brown paper bag. He was wearing an arm band covering the wound that he sustained during the shootout that killed Q and left Alicia wounded. DJ was not at all pleased to see him there.

"So I hear that you're moving into Q's old place DJ," said Rico as he took a long drink.

DJ didn't respond to Rico's comment. He was only concerned about why Rico was there. As DJ looked around he saw two other young black men that he didn't know. One of them looked like a hardened criminal, who surely did time in the joint. The other looked very young, probably not even twenty years old. They were all wearing their pants sagging with do-rags tied around their heads.

"What do you want with me Rico?"

DJ knew exactly what Rico wanted. Ever since the incident Rico has been in hiding until the flesh would healed, and the heat from the cops cooled down. During this time he had not received his cut from the drug money that was heisted from the scene of the shooting.

DJ was not pleased that Q was getting all of the nightclub business in the area which was putting a squeeze on places like Wannabee. Q had even approached DJ about buying Wannabee, which he was going to shutdown completely.

DJ was not about to sell out to Q. He had put too much time and all of his retirement money into his business; it was his dream, to own a nightclub. For years Wannabee was doing great until Q moved into town. He eliminated the former owner of Starz and poured hundreds of thousands of dollars into the remodeling of it.

Starz became a magnet for the nighttime crowd. Its success was the demise of many clubs in the area. Wannabee was the only club that hung on until the end, though barely. Q wanted to build an empire but DJ stood in his way, so he had planned to strong arm DJ to force him out of the business.

DJ, who wasn't a fool, discovered that Q was up to something, so he devised his own plan. He knew that there was a beef between Rico and Q, which was disclosed to him by Oliver, Q's janitor at Starz. Oliver had overheard Q talking about the drug deal and told DJ everything.

DJ knew that he could not implicate himself, so to get even with Q he filled Rico in on Q's plan. Rico laid in wait at the place where the deal would go down and ambushed Q and his drug man. Unfortunately, Alicia was caught up in the cross fire.

That same night, DJ met with a wounded Rico who gave him the briefcase with the money and the drugs. DJ was able to sell the drugs to another dealer,

Until now no one ever suspected that DJ had anything to do with the murders; no one except for Rico and here he is expecting to receive his piece of the deal.

Rico was trying to be nonchalant about not getting his cut, but for DJ to try and play him this way made him angry.

"You know damned well why I'm here! What's wrong with you man, you got amnesia or something?"

DJ realized that he was in a tight spot; because he never thought that Rico would come looking for him and the money was tied up in the purchase of Starz.

He tried to analyze the situation by observing the behavior of the two guys accompanying Rico. DJ kept a hand gun, but it was in the office. He had to think quickly.

"I have your money but not on me. I have to get it from the bank."

There was a small safe at Wannabee in the office which had about sixty-five thousand dollars in it. There was more but he had put most of it in a safe place.

DJ knew that he couldn't just put that kind of money in the bank without having to answer questions.

Rico also knew that this was the case. "Now see there you go again old man trying to play me for a fool. I've been in this game too long for some cat like you to try and play me." Rico rose up from his seat. The two other guys shifted their postures into a more threatening stance.

"Look DJ, I know there's got to be a safe around here. Why don't you just go to where it is and bring out the money and pay me."

"What makes you think that I have money here in this place?"

Rico reached into his pants and pulled out a nine millimeter handgun. "This does," he said pointing it at DJ.

"DJ was alarmed by the sight of the gun pointing at him. He tried to remain calm, but the tough looking guy, who Rico called big Mike, lunged toward DJ and grabbed him. DJ struggled but realized that this guy was much too strong for him to get loose from.

"So DJ, I guess you have to show me the money or else it could get really bad in here. Or maybe I should pay your cute little niece a visit. I hear that she's alive. I'm sure she could use some company. I still wonder what she was doing at Q's place that night."

"Let me go. Tell this punk to let go of me Rico." Big Mike didn't like being called a punk, so he punched DJ in the ribs very hard. The pain from the punch caused his knees to buckle, and he writhed in pain.

"I don't think big Mike appreciated you calling him names old man. Now before it gets really nasty in here tell me where the safe is."

Hardly able to speak, DJ said, "It's in the office."

"Good then. Let's get it open, so I can get what belongs to me and I'll leave you alone."

Big Mike let go of DJ who then led the way into his office. The safe was beneath his desk and it was left open because he was getting something out of it. His gun sat on a desk shelf next to the safe.

The younger guy named Craig stood on the side of the office where he could see underneath the desk. As DJ reached below the gun was spotted and the Craig yelled, "He's got a gun!"

Rico reacted by hitting DJ over the head with his gun, knocking him to the floor. Half conscious, DJ was able to reach for his gun and draw it out. When Rico spotted it, he fired a shot through DJ's head.

Rico looked beneath the desk and saw that the safe was wide open and full of cash and some other papers. He took only the money and the three of them quickly got out of there. While DJ laid there in a pool of blood, his cell phone began to ring as his life began to slip away.

From around a corner someone had been watching the whole ordeal take place. This was no passerby who just happened upon the nightclub where DJ laid dying. This man was purposely there and knew exactly what he wanted.

He carefully crept into the club and back into DJ's office. When he saw the club owner lying there he was upset to see that those thugs had killed him. He was also surprised to see that the safe was still open.

"There they are, just what I expected."

What he expected to find were the documents of ownership to the club which he planned to make good use of. Slowly the papers were removed from the safe and as he backed out he stumbled over DJ's body and grabbed the door of the safe to get his balance. After getting what he wanted he quickly got out of there.

It was getting late and Pearl was wondering what was taking her husband so long to get home from Wannabee. She never really checked up on him because it was not like DJ to come home early anyway. When his cell phone went to voice mail, she left a message and resigned to the idea that he was at some club or a casino.

Pearl had been spending a lot of time with Alicia, and there were signs that she was recovering, although she had not yet come out of her coma. Her head wound had completely healed, and there was only a light bandage to cover the incision.

No one knew exactly how much damage the bullet had done—which wouldn't be known until or whenever Alicia regained consciousness. Days and nights were all running together for Pearl. She was very tired at this point and retired to bed, oblivious to what had happened to her husband.

Chapter 11

After having a very tough night, RJ awakened early and was lying in bed thinking about how to handle the situation with Max. He wasn't really concerned about Tanya finding out about his dilemma since she would be in Las Vegas and was positive that his parents would not drop the bomb of his affairs on her.

Suddenly the phone rang, but he didn't answer it. Somehow he knew that it was Tanya calling him.

After a couple of rings, the answering machine picked it up. *Hello, you have reached Raleigh Brooks Jr. Please leave a message.*

"Good morning, RJ." It was Tanya. "I thought that I would call you early to let you know that I need a ride to the airport. I need to be there within the next hour. I figure that you're probably in the shower, so can you call me back as soon as you get this message."

She hung up and RJ just laid there. He had already made up his mind that he would not give her a ride. *She can get a taxi.*

Sonny was packing his toiletries and drinking his orange juice. After finishing in the bathroom, he went back to his bedroom to get dressed. He was between being excited and nervous at the same time.

He didn't know what to expect once he got to Vegas. However, he was excited about the idea of seeing Malcolm Floyd at the newspaper and doing the story on Karaoke.

As he was about to unplug his cell phone from its charger, he noticed that there was a voice mail. He thought, *I wonder if this is Tanya.* After entering his number, he listened to the message. *Hello, Sonny, and good morning. This is Tanya. I'm going to be a little bit late getting to the airport, but I'll still get there in plenty of time. I have your itinerary and will take care of the boarding passes once I arrive. I'll see you soon.* Then she added, *I can't wait to get to Las Vegas!* She sounded very excited.

He began looking for his wallet and moved some things around on the computer table until he found what he was looking for.

It was time to leave, and on his way downstairs, he stopped by his parents' room and listened to hear if anybody was awake. He didn't hear a sound, and he didn't want to awaken them.

He went downstairs, sat at the kitchen table, and wrote a note saying good-bye and that everything was going to be all right, and he signed it *Sonny.* He folded the note and hung it on the refrigerator using a magnet.

Making sure that he had everything, he left the house quietly closing the door behind him and locking it. Back upstairs in his bedroom, his computer had gone blank, so he didn't think to hit the send button, sending the message to his friends that he was going away.

Not only that, but he also laid his cell phone down on the computer table and covered it with the paper he had written on as he was searching for his wallet.

Sonny's drive along the interstate to the airport was peaceful, as there was very little traffic at this time in the morning. When he arrived there, he parked his 4 × 4 in the long-term parking lot and walked a short distance to the terminal.

The Lambert Saint Louis International Airport was in the middle of a huge remodeling project. There were already some new shops in the main lobby area, and more retail outlets, shops, and concourses were being added. Sonny decided to wait in the lobby for Tanya.

After about fifteen minutes, he thought that he would call her to see if she was at least on her way, but before he ever reached for his cell phone, he realized that he left it on the computer table back at home.

He didn't panic since there were phone booths placed near the entrance. Just as he was headed toward the phones, he saw Tanya entering the lobby.

Although it was early October, it was cool in the mornings and hotter as the days progressed. She was wearing a medium-weight brown jacket and loose-fitting beige slacks that looked very good on her.

Sonny made his way to her to help with the luggage that she was carrying. She had two pieces—a very large suitcase and a carry-on roller bag. Sonny did not have as much; he had just a carry-on.

"Hey, Tanya, let me help you with these." He took the heavier bag and helped her get it through the doorway.

"Is that all you have?" asked Tanya, looking down at Sonny's only piece.

"Yeah, I like to travel light. If I can't get it all in one bag, it stays."

"That's good for some, but a girl like me needs to bring all that can fit in these two bags."

"So why did you get a taxi? What happened to RJ?"

"I don't know. I called him this morning, but he didn't answer, so I decided not to wait until he called me back and called for a taxi." Sonny just shook his head in disapproval of his brother.

As the two of them walked through the terminal, Tanya stopped to look at the itinerary. "Our flight departs from concourse B, gate 8 at seven-thirty."

"What airline are we flying?" asked Sonny.

"Southwest," answered Tanya.

Making their way to the Southwest ticket counter, Tanya handed Sonny his confirmation printout while they stood in line. "Next please." Tanya stepped up to the counter and handed the lady her confirmation slip. Everything checked out fine, and Sonny stepped up and followed the same procedure. Tanya checked her large bag through, so all she had with her was her purse and the roller bag.

Going through the security check was the one thing about flying that Sonny disliked most. Fortunately, there were not many people in line, so it would be less painful for him. He hated waiting in long lines for anything. Even at the amusement parks, Sonny wouldn't get on any of the rides if it meant waiting for more than fifteen minutes. If he were hungry, that would be different; he would wait twenty minutes for food.

It didn't take long at all to get through security, and they were in the waiting area at the departing gate. Sonny's stomach growled loudly, and he placed his hand over it.

"Did you not have breakfast this morning, Sonny?" Tanya asked.

"No, I'm not really much on breakfast, which is kinda strange that I'm hungry."

"There's a coffee shop across the way."

Sonny looked in the direction Tanya was pointing and saw a Gloria Jean's coffee shop. "I guess I can get something over there. Would you like some coffee or something, Tanya?"

"Yes, I'll have a coffee with cream and sugar, please."

"Is that it? Don't you want a piece of cake or—"

"No, just coffee. I have some cookies in my purse."

Sonny reached for his bag, but Tanya caught his hand, holding it softly. "I'll watch this for you," she said.

For a moment, Sonny thought about Alicia and how she would offer her assistance by touching his hand the same way. Smiling, he said, "I'll be right back with your coffee."

Tanya watched Sonny as he walked, thinking how nice it would be if RJ was as kind as Sonny. Just the thought of RJ brought a bit of anger to her. How could he be so inconsiderate of her feelings? She thought about how distant he had been since she arrived.

Then she began to ask herself about his business partner. *Who is he?* she thought. Pondering on, Tanya decided that she would ask Sonny about everything she had been thinking about since the day of her arrival.

At the coffee shop, Sonny was looking over the menu that was on the wall. Most of what he saw was all types of coffees. He wasn't sure which one Tanya would like. He asked the barista if he could recommend a special blend.

"Is this for yourself or someone else?"

"It's for the young lady I'm with. She didn't tell me what kind she likes."

"Well then, I'll recommend a full-bodied coffee. Not too strong but it has enough flavor to awaken the senses. Something like this Kenya AA is a very fine coffee."

Not wanting to make too much of a deal out of buying coffee, Sonny decided on the recommendation and asked to leave room for cream.

"Will that be all for you today?"

"I'll have a bottle of orange juice, please."

Sonny paid for his purchase. As he was leaving, he asked the cashier where the cream was. She pointed to a table just behind him and there he added cream and grabbed a couple packs of sugar along with a stirrer.

Back at the waiting area, Tanya was already eating some of the cookies she brought.

"Here's your coffee." He handed her the cup and the sugar packets, then sat beside her.

"This is very hot," said Tanya.

"Be careful to not burn yourself."

Removing the cap from the cup so that she could add sugar, she noticed that Sonny put the exact amount of cream that she liked; it was the perfect color. "Smells good, Sonny. What kind is it?"

"Kenya AA. I guess it's supposed to be really good."

"Haven't you tried it?"

"No, I'm kind of a sometime coffee drinker."

Tanya added the sugar and began to look around for something to stir it with. "Oh, excuse me," said Sonny. He reached into the bag containing his orange juice and pulled out the stirrer and handed it to Tanya.

"Thank you."

"Um, this is very good," she said. "Here, taste some."

Again this gesture reminded him of Alicia. The first time he had ever drank coffee was the night after he had experienced another first time. His mind drifted back to that moment.

"What are you thinking about, Sonny?"

"Oh, it was nothing," he said.

"Don't you want to taste this coffee?"

"Sure, why not?"

Taking the cup from her hand, Sonny slowly placed the cup to his mouth and took a sip.

The heat from the coffee surprised him and he jerked, causing some of the coffee to spill out over his shirt.

"Bustin!" he shouted.

He was able to balance the cup so that more wouldn't spill and handed it back to Tanya.

"You okay, Sonny?"

"Yeah, I guess. Man, that coffee is hot."

Tanya laughed lightly as Sonny wiped his shirt. "So was the coffee good?"

"Yes, it was, Tanya, but I'll stick to my orange juice." Opening his bottle, he took a long drink.

Just as Sonny was finishing his juice and Tanya's coffee had cooled down enough to drink, the announcement for boarding flight 2814 to Las Vegas came over the PA.

"That's us," said Tanya.

The plane was completely full when boarding was complete, and since they were flying Southwest, Sonny and Tanya sat beside each other near the front of the plane.

Tanya wanted desperately to ask Sonny questions about RJ's behavior, but when they were in the air; Sonny wasted no time to fall asleep. Tanya felt very tired as well, so she let her seat back and closed her eyes, hoping to get some sleep.

Chapter 12

It was early Tuesday morning just after three o'clock. Pearl was awakened by a noise outside the house, coming from the back. When she turned over to awaken DJ, she realized that he wasn't in bed.

Immediately, she was concerned. Although it was not unusual for him to come in late some nights, this was beyond just being late.

Crawling quickly out of bed, the first thing she thought to do was check her cell phone. He wouldn't call the house phone after eleven o'clock in case Pearl was asleep; however, he would call her cell phone to leave a message.

There was no message. *Why didn't he call?* she thought.

She called his cell phone—no answer. She called his office at Wannabee—no answer there either. By this time, she had run out of numbers. All she could think of was that maybe something happened and he couldn't call her, *but what could be that critical that he couldn't call?*

At this point, she had no other resort than to call the police. She remembered that Captain Riley gave her his card. She searched her purse. After finding it, she called the station.

The phone rang only a couple of times. "Las Vegas Police Department Officer Adams here. How may I direct your call?"

A very anxious Pearl was hardly coherent as she was trying to explain her problem to the officer. "Ma'am, I need you to take a deep breath and slowdown."

Pearl took a moment to regain her breath, and not as fast, she repeated, "My husband is not answering his telephone. I think something's happened."

"Okay, ma'am, you said that your husband is not answering his phone and you think something has happened, is that correct?"

"Yes, I called both of his numbers and he's not answering. Oh, please, Jesus, don't let anything be wrong," she added.

"What is your name, ma'am?"

"My name is Pearl Walker. My husband is Dennis Jerome Walker. He goes by DJ."

"Okay, that's fine, Mrs. Walker now can you tell me when you last saw him and where he was going?"

"Yes, he left the house around nine-thirty this evening, and he was headed to his office."

There was a slight pause. Officer Adams then asked, "Can you tell me where his office is located, Mrs. Walker?"

"Wannabee's. You heard of that nightclub, haven't you?"

"Yes, I have. It's over on 72nd and Reno."

"Yes, that's it," answered Pearl. "Please, can you help me find him?" she added.

"Yes, Mrs. Walker, I'm sending a squad car out there right now."

"Oh, thank you very much, officer . . . What's your name again?"

"It's Adams, ma'am. Officer Adams. But before you hang up, I need your address, so I can send an officer to your house. We'll need to get more information just in case something comes up whatever it may be."

Pearl gave her address and hung up the phone. She was in such a bad state of mind that she poured herself a double shot of bourbon.

The dispatch went out and a car responded to it making its way to Wannabee. Two officers got out of the car at the corner of 72nd and Reno. When they approached the building, they could see that a light was on inside. It was very dark in the area; not even a marquee light was glowing.

One of the officers looked up at the sky. There was not a star to be seen, the moon was full, and the lights from the main boulevard reflecting from the haze in the sky could be seen. "This seems very strange," he said to his partner.

"Yes, it does," responded the other. However, the first cop had no idea what his partner was referring to. Apparently, he had made it to the front door and found it slightly ajar.

"Hey, quit you stargazing and get over here. This door is open." He easily withdrew his weapon. The other officer sensed the urgency and withdrew his.

Pushing the door open just a little wider, he yelled inside, "Police here anybody in there?" There was no answer.

They waited just a moment longer and then pushed the rest of the way in brandishing their weapons. "Is anybody here? This is the police."

With their weapons still in firing position, they began looking around the place. As they separated, one went down a hallway while the other went toward a light coming from a room.

Entering with caution and looked around, he saw a chair that was overturned and what appeared to be blood splattered on the wall behind a desk. He called to his partner.

"Hey, come here quick. I think I've found who we're looking for."

Before his partner arrived, he walked around the desk and found DJ lying in a pool of blood. The officer looked closer and saw that DJ's right hand was just inches away from is handgun.

When the other officer arrived and viewed the body, he called dispatch to report the find. It wasn't five minutes before sirens throughout the town could be heard, and no less than seven squad cars were at the scene.

While sleeping soundly, Detective Riley who was head of the homicide division was awakened by a phone call, which prompted him to rise up and make his way to the scene of the crime. He was not in a particularly good mood when he arrived. There were already officers there taping off the entire area outside of Wannabee. Inside where the body lay, forensic personnel were gathering clues and taking photos of possible evidence that could not be placed in a bag.

To Riley's surprise, the place had not been ransacked, so immediately a random robbery was ruled out as a motive. However, he noticed that the safe was opened, but at this point, why it was opened and if anything was taken from it could not be determined.

"Did the victim have a weapon or something?" asked Riley.

"Yes, Detective."

One of the officers pointed to the gun that was lying just inches from the victim's hand. "It doesn't look like he had a chance to defend his self," he said.

Riley had a forensic person to place the gun into a plastic bag. He took the bag and examined the gun, without removing it. "A thirty-eight. Too bad he couldn't get to it before he got shot."

"Riley, there's something else here," said a forensics person. Carrying a paper bag, he handed Riley a pair of plastic gloves. After sliding them on, Riley took the bag reached inside and removed a forty-ounce bottle of beer that was less than half-full.

"Well, this should lead us right to who's responsible for this homicide." He read the label on the bottle. "Olde English 800."

He handed it back to the cop, saying, "Make sure this place is thoroughly dusted for prints."

After more looking around, Riley told the uniform cops, "Well, there's nothing else I can do here until we get all the evidence we need to find whoever is responsible for this. We need to get someone to properly ID the victim. Can somebody do that before I leave?"

Apparently, Riley had no clue that the victim was related to Pearl Walker, whom he had previously spoke with at the restaurant about Alicia.

"Yes, Detective, there was a call just a few hours ago from a lady who said that she was worried why her husband had not shown up at home or even called. We had Adams to give her a call."

Back at the station, Adams was taking the call from the scene of the crime, letting him know where DJ lived based on the driver's license. After getting the information he needed, Adams made his way to DJ's home.

At home, Pearl was on her second drink; she heard a knock at the front door. With heart pounding, she was filled with fear and trepidation. Somehow knowing that this wasn't going to be what she wanted to hear, she opened the door reluctantly. There was an officer standing there.

"Mrs. Pearl Walker, I'm Officer Adams. I need you to come to the hospital and identify a man we believe is your husband."

Chapter 13

The sun was now making its way up over the horizon, causing a blinding light to shine through the windshield as Detective Riley made his way to the office. He was extremely tired. Lately, he had not been getting much sleep because of insomnia.

Stopping at a twenty-four-hour fast food restaurant to get a cup of coffee, he picked up a morning newspaper the headline was the homicide that had taken place last night. While he was ordering his breakfast, he had a call come in on his cell phone.

"Hello."

"Detective, this is Adams. We got a positive ID on last night's murder victim."

"Okay, do we know anything else?"

"Yes, we do. Apparently, he is the husband of Pearl Walker, which is the aunt of Alicia Highsmith."

Riley pondered for a minute. "I just met with Pearl a couple of days ago. I knew that she was married to a nightclub owner, but I didn't know it was this guy."

"Yes, Captain, they are related."

"How is she doing?"

"Not too well."

"I don't blame her." He paused for a moment and then asked, "Does she know anything?"

"I did ask, but she had no idea. She is still having trouble dealing with her niece."

While they continued talking, the cashier, a young white lady, waited; she scanned over the newspaper article.

When the phone call ended, she took his order and called it back to the cooks. "I'll bring your order out to you when it's ready. Just have a seat."

Picking up his receipt, Riley took a seat in the dining area. There weren't many people there, so his order of over-easy eggs with whole wheat toast and coffee was quickly prepared.

The cashier, who was doubling as a waitress, brought his breakfast over and sat it in front of him. "Sir," she said.

He looked up at her. "Yes, may I help you?"

Nervously she began to speak. "I have something to tell you. I think it may have something to do with the newspaper article."

Detective Riley became intrigued. "What about the article?"

The young lady was apprehensive, because now she wasn't sure if she should say anything.

"Go ahead. If you think you know something, you can tell me."

"Well, I've been here all night, and just about five this morning or four this morning, a couple, maybe three guys, came in here." She stopped.

"How many was it? asked Riley.

"I'm sure that it was three."

"What happened while they were here? Did they order food or what?"

"No, they just came in here as if they were running from somebody."

"What did they look like?"

"One of them was really big. One was kind of thin, and the other looked pretty young. He had a tattoo."

"Well, tell me what they were doing. Did you hear what they were talking about?"

"Yes, I did. They were talking about money. One of them had a stocking cap. I think it was a do-rag tied around something that looked like money. I tried not to look like I was being nosy, because these dudes actually scared me the way they came in. They were looking crazy."

Riley knew that this information could help, but before he could ask another question, a customer came in. "I'll be right back after I take this order," she said.

In the meantime, Riley devoured his eggs and toast.

Fortunately, her relief had already showed up. She came in through the back door. When she heard the entrance doorbell ring, she came to the counter. "Hey, Sheila, I didn't know you were here."

"I've been here for about five minutes."

"Can you take care of this customer for me, please? I'm going to take a break."

"Okay, Lisa, go ahead and take a break. I know you're probably tired."

"Thank you, Sheila. I'll be done soon." Lisa headed back over to Riley.

"So your name is Lisa?" he asked.

"Yes, I didn't want to tell you."

"That's all right, Lisa."

She took a seat next to him and noticed that his coffee cup was empty. She went to the back of the counter and got him another cup.

"Thank you," he said.

"So, Lisa, is there anything else you can tell me about these fellas who came in this morning?"

"Yes, I heard one of them say the name Rico."

That name alarmed the detective. He knew that Rico was short for Ricardo and he's been on the run since the shootings a couple of months ago.

"Thank you, Lisa. You've been a great help to me. Tell me something else. How long did they stay, and did they ever say anything to you?"

"You know what? It's very strange they never said a word to me. It was like I wasn't even here. After about ten minutes, they all left. I don't know if they got into a car or not. I didn't care to know. All that I know is that they were kind of scary looking."

"Well, Lisa, you certainly didn't have to say anything, and I appreciate all that you said. Thank you so much."

As Riley stood to leave, he pulled a twenty-dollar bill out of his pocket and handed it to her. "This should pay for the food and keep the change."

Smiling, Lisa said, "Thank you, and I hope you find the killers."

"We will. Trust me, we will."

Back in Saint Louis, Raleigh was not feeling well, but he managed to get out of bed. Martha had long been downstairs and was cooking a pot of oatmeal for breakfast. The coffee was already hot, and the smell of it traveled upstairs and awakened Raleigh's nostrils.

"That smells good," he said. So as best as he could gather himself together so that Martha would not notice his discomfort, he made it downstairs to the kitchen.

He felt soreness in his throat that had him concerned. Already deciding to visit the doctor today, Raleigh did not want to alarm his wife.

"Good morning, dear." Martha was pouring two cups of coffee when Raleigh entered the kitchen.

"How did you know I was on my way down? he asked.

"Call it women's intuition. Besides, I heard the toilet flush, so I had you timed."

Raleigh smiled and gave her a kiss, saying, "Good morning to you, baby."

"Before you sit down, there's a note on the fridge that you need to see."

"Who would leave a note on the fridge?"

"Who else," answered Martha?

Raleigh took the note from the fridge and read it. "So he couldn't say good-bye before he left?"

"We were probably asleep and he didn't want to awaken us."

Blowing his coffee before drinking it, Raleigh thought about what he had to do this morning.

"I'm going to see the doctor today. Maybe . . ." he began coughing. Martha noticed that it sounded worse than yesterday.

"I hope you can get in to see him before it gets too late in the afternoon. Maybe we should call his office to see when will be a good time for you to come in."

The oatmeal was done; Martha served up two large bowls and placed one in front of Raleigh. She then placed in front of him the butter and brown sugar.

Raleigh added a pat of butter and a spoonful of sugar to his oatmeal and began to stir it up. "Is there any milk?" he asked.

Before sitting, Martha got some milk. "Thank you," he said.

"So when are you going to call the doctor?" she asked.

"Soon after I finish eating, and reading the paper," he answered irritably.

"Why the attitude? I'm just concerned, Raleigh."

"I know you are. I just don't want to think about it right now. I'll call him soon enough."

"Well, all right then. You handle it."

Raleigh again began to cough; this time it was more profuse than before. He reached for a napkin to cover his mouth as Martha rose up to get him a glass of water. Looking into the napkin, there was blood just as there was last night.

Quickly Raleigh crumpled the napkin and stuck it beneath his thigh. "Here's some water," said Martha. She handed him the glass, and he drank just a couple of swallows.

"I'll go upstairs and get your cough medicine. Do you know where it is?" she asked.

After taking a drink of coffee, he answered, "It's on the nightstand on my side."

"I'll be right back down."

Martha made her way upstairs as Raleigh continued to try and eat his oatmeal. Several minutes had passed by before she returned with the cough syrup. But that wasn't all she had.

"What's this?" She was holding up a towel that had blood on it.

Raleigh felt his stomach turn and now could no longer hide what's been going on.

"That's okay. I'm taking you to the hospital emergency room."

Raleigh tried to protest, but to no avail. Martha had already made up her mind and wasn't going to move from it.

After Martha finished cleaning the kitchen, they got into their car and headed to Trinity Hospital. When they arrived, the emergency room was not very busy. There was a young man who was having heart palpitations, and he was rushed in immediately. With the exceptions of some sprained ankles, a burn wound, an elderly woman with dizziness, Raleigh appeared to be the most urgent.

He had given the intake nurse all of the information she needed and was sitting, waiting for his name to be called. A young African-American nurse came out. "Raleigh Brooks," she called.

"I'm Raleigh Brooks," he said.

The nurse smiled as she led both Raleigh and Martha back to an area where she told him to slip out of his clothes and put on a light blue gown.

The nurse introduced herself as Candace. She also told Martha that she could get her something to drink if she wanted it. Martha declined the offer.

"The doctor should be in here in a few minutes. There are about two people ahead of you. So just make yourself comfortable on the bed when you get changed, Mr. Brooks."

Candace paused for a moment before leaving, turned and spoke. "Aren't you Pastor Brooks at Mt. Sinai church?"

"Yes, I am. Why do you ask?"

"I know your son, Sonny. We went to school together. I haven't seen him in years. Is he still here in the city?"

Raleigh looked over at Martha, and she answered, "Yes, he still lives here, but he's sort of traveling right now."

"I would really like to see him again. Be sure you tell him that Candace Simmons said hello. I'm sure he'll remember me."

"Oh, he will, he will?" Martha responded.

"Yes. I had the biggest crush on him. We used to sit and have lunch together just about every day. He was so cute and could really sing. He used to sing Michael Jackson's songs all the time."

"He still does sing, and I'll be sure to let him know that we met you, Candace."

"Well, the doctor will be in here soon. He just went to the patient next door. You're next." She pulled the dividing curtain closed as she left.

"She sure is a nice young lady," said Martha. When she turned to Raleigh, he had undressed. "I didn't think she would ever leave," he said.

"She was just being social. Besides, she's a very nice girl."

Raleigh was now undressed and was trying to put on the robe. "Can you help me with this thing?" he asked.

"You're trying to put it on backward." Martha helped him get it on and tied it in the back. Raleigh was feeling very weak from the lack of oxygen, because he was having difficulty breathing.

He slumped back on the bed and sat back up quickly as he began to cough. Again blood came up. Martha was very upset by the sight of his blood and called for a nurse.

It wasn't long before both the nurse and the doctor came in. "What is the problem?" the doctor asked.

"My husband has been coughing up blood."

"How long has this been happening?" the doctor asked.

Martha gave her husband a look of contempt, answering, "I suppose since last night, or longer. I'm not sure." She kept her eyes on Raleigh.

"Yes, last night was when it started," he answered.

The doctor had the nurse to take Raleigh's vitals as he stepped out of the room. It was only for a second, and he returned with a notepad that he sat on a table.

"His blood pressure is a little low, and his pulse is high," commented the nurse.

While Raleigh was sitting up on the edge of the bed, the doctor began to check his heartbeat. Going through the usual steps, he had Raleigh to then lie down as he examined his organs. He then had Raleigh sit up to examine around his throat.

Raleigh grimaced when the doctor applied pressure. "All right," said the doctor. He wrote something on his pad. "There is a something there that I'm going to check out."

"What do you think the problem is?" asked Martha.

"I'm not quite sure yet, but it could be a number of things. I'm going to schedule some x-rays." He then sat on a stool and spoke to Martha who was also sitting.

"I'm going to have to admit Mr. Brooks so that we can take some tests. It doesn't make sense to send him home if he's coughing up blood."

"Jesus! There goes our savings," Raleigh smirked.

"You know we have insurance, Raleigh. Don't say that."

Again the doctor spoke. "I'll have the nurse to get some paperwork together for you to sign, and we'll find a bed for you. But in the meantime, just get comfortable, because it could take an hour or so before you're admitted."

While things were being put in place for Raleigh to be admitted, Martha decided that she would call her sons to let them know what was going on with their dad.

The first person she called was RJ. His phone rang several times, and then the voice mail picked up. After listening to his recording, she left a message. "RJ, this is your mom. I'm calling to let you know that your dad is being admitted into the hospital today. I'll give you as much detail that I can when I talk to you later. Bye-bye."

She then called Sonny. His phone rang as well until voice mail picked up. "Yep, yep, you reached Sonny. Leave a message, and I'll hit-choo back lay-ta."

Martha became a bit irritated with his recording but left a message anyway. "Sonny, this is your mom. I'm with your dad in the hospital, and he's being admitted for some tests. Please call me back, and I'll tell you more. Okay, love you."

Martha had no idea that Sonny had forgotten to bring his phone with him; it sat on his nightstand beneath some papers.

Before she could put her phone away, RJ returned her call. "Hello, RJ."

"Hello, Mom, I got your message. What's going on with Dad?"

"Well, we don't know right now, but all I can tell you is that he had been coughing up blood since last night. This morning, I found a bloody towel that he tried to hide from me."

"That's just like him, isn't it?"

"Yes, it is. Well, to his credit, he was going to see the doctor today anyway, until I found that towel and I made him come to the emergency room."

"Good for you. Is he going to be there long?"

"We don't know. He's got to take some tests. I hope it isn't serious, but all we can do is pray to God."

"Yeah, I hear you." After a moment of silence, RJ spoke again. "So have you called Sonny?"

"Yes, I called Sonny. But he didn't answer his phone." She added, "Did you know that he left this morning?"

"Yes, ma'am, I know. He and Tanya are on their way to Las Vegas."

"Did you take her to the airport this morning, RJ?"

"No, I didn't. I don't know how she got there actually."

Martha really wanted to know how RJ felt about her leaving but decided not to ask him. "Well, I'm sure they'll be all right. You just don't worry about it too much. Tanya loves you, and she just needs to get some time away to think things over."

"Well, okay, Mom, I have to get back to work right now." Actually, Max was calling him, and he wanted to talk to her.

"Okay, RJ, I'll let you know when Sonny calls and when I find out more about your dad. Remember to pray for him and those two in Vegas."

"Yeah, I will. Good-bye, Mom."

"Bye."

RJ answered Max's call. "Hello, Maxine."

"Oh, so it's Maxine now. What happened to baby and sweetie?"

"You act like there's nothing going on here. How am I supposed to feel when you put me off the way you did?"

"How am I supposed to act when you act like you don't want to have anything to do with me, since I'm pregnant?"

RJ knew that he had to smooth things out between the two of them to keep Maxine from becoming not just a mad black woman, but a pregnant mad black woman.

"Maxine, I'm sorry. I've been thinking about this whole ordeal. I know that I've been acting off the cuff, but I was afraid and not sure about things. You know the engagement and all."

Maxine just listened.

"Maxine, I don't think it's going to work out between me and Tanya."

Now Maxine spoke. "What do you mean it's not going to work out? What are you telling me, RJ?"

"Well, like I said. It's not going to work out. She's not the person that I thought she was. I guess since the time she cheated on me with this Alvin guy, I just haven't been able to feel the same about her. Lord knows that I've tried."

"So sleeping with me is trying, RJ?"

"What happened between you and I was different. I know that I was, or am engaged, but you just made me feel so much better about myself, especially while she was gone. Which, she's gone again."

"What do you mean she's gone again? Did she leave you, or did she just leave town?"

"She's left town, but she left very angry, and at this point, I'm ready to throw in the towel."

"Well, RJ, before you throw in the towel, there's something important I need to ask you, actually a couple of things."

RJ was curious; he didn't know what she was going to ask him. "So what is it, Max?"

"RJ, I need to know if you are going to be all in with the restaurant. I mean, you have been keeping me dangling, and I need the money to keep this place open, so are you in or out?

"Now think about it before you answer, because now the details have obviously changed. You need to know that I'm going to keep this child, so your decision could help you in the long run or hurt you. Either way, I'm going to get what I need for my child."

RJ was perplexed. He had no idea what Max was up to. "So what's the other thing I need to know, Max?"

"Well, RJ, does your fiancée know how you feel?"

"No, she doesn't."

"Well, I think she needs to know, RJ, because it's only fair that she does. I am willing to hang in there with you, but at this point, I have too much going on to play second. Where we go from here with the restaurant and our relationship all depends on you. Remember, I'm going to get what I need from you either way. So it's really up to you."

"That's kind of tough, Max. But I hear what you're saying. I need time to make some adjustments, but I'll certainly let you know."

"When are you going to let me know?"

"I don't know, Max. Tanya's out of town."

"Yes, you told me that. She's out of town with your very single brother."

Those words from Maxine bothered RJ. Consequently, he was beginning to feel a bit concerned about his brother and Tanya.

"I'll let you know as soon as I can, Max. That's all I can promise."

"Well, I'll be here, RJ. Call me." She disconnected.

"Damn! What have I gotten myself into? Damn!"

Chapter 14

The flight to Las Vegas went smoothly, not that Sonny noticed since he slept the entire way. Tanya was in and out of sleep but was awake just before the plane landed. She became anxious, thinking about the fact that she was going to see her sister for the first time after some twenty years.

Sonny was awakened by the flight attendant, telling him to raise his seat back into the straight-up position.

He looked over at Tanya, who was looking through the window. "Did you get any sleep?" he asked.

"I slept some, but not a whole lot."

"Man, I was tired. I crashed the minute we boarded."

"Yeah, I know. Good thing you didn't start snoring."

"I know that's right," Sonny replied.

As the plane taxied to the terminal, Sonny laid his head back. Tanya perceived that he had something on his mind. "What are you thinking about, Sonny?"

Raising his head to look at her, Sonny answered, "There are some things that I need to do as soon as we get off the plane."

As the plane came to a stop and the pilot turned off the fasten seat belt light, the passengers began getting out of their seats to get their carry-on bags from the overhead compartments.

Tanya stopped Sonny by placing her hand on his arm as he began to stand to get their things. "We have plenty of time, Sonny. Just wait until the people in front get off."

Sonny looked at her with submissive eyes, saying, "That's fine."

He then decided to call home to let them know that they had landed safely. Right away, without ever searching for it, he realized that he had forgotten his phone at home.

"Bustin!"

Knowing what that must have meant, Tanya asked Sonny, "Okay, what just happened?"

"You won't believe this, but I left my cell phone at home."

"How did you do that?" she asked.

"I'm sure that I left it on my nightstand. I must have covered it with something and didn't see it so, out of sight, out of mind."

"Well, don't worry. You can use mine."

"Thanks, but I still need to have my own. We're not going to be together the whole time, but we do need to keep in touch, don't you think?"

Tanya thought about that for a moment. "We don't really need to be separate that much either, do we? I mean, whatever you need to do, I can come along if you don't mind."

"I guess you could. Which brings me to ask, did you reserve a car?"

"I sure did, but I told you that already."

"Yes you did."

"Tanya, you really didn't have to do all of this. I mean, why?"

Tanya took Sonny by the hand and looked him in the eyes. "Listen, Sonny, I don't know what it is, but I feel very close to you. It feels so natural doing these things.

"Besides, you seem like you appreciate what I do, unlike your brother who acts like I'm supposed to do things for him. He treats me like I'm his personal secretary instead of his future wife."

"Bustin. I didn't expect all of that. I'm sorry I asked." Sonny smiled, then said. "I'm just joking. I know what you mean about RJ. He sometimes treats me like a stranger."

The line had diminished and Sonny got up to get the bags and they exited the plane. In the terminal, Sonny stopped. He had a de`ja`vu. He could see the first time he came to Las Vegas. He even felt the same way. His heart began to beat faster, and he became excited.

"What's the matter with you?" asked Tanya.

With sweat forming on his brow, Sonny could not believe how he was feeling. "I don't know, Tanya. All of a sudden I started feeling really strange, like something isn't right. I don't know what it is, but I feel crazy. Bustin!"

Tanya couldn't tell that he was not putting on. He looked very pale and flushed, which wasn't unusual. He always looked pale because of his light complexion.

She looked around the terminal for a place for them to sit. There was a Wolfgang Pucks near, so Tanya suggested that they go there to relax and get something to drink.

When they got seated, Tanya asked the waitress to get them lemon water. They decided to get their luggage later.

The waters were served, and the waitress asked if they needed something else. They both declined, although Sonny was just a little hungry.

"I can't eat anything right now, Tanya. I need to get a grip."

Tanya was amazed by the sudden change in Sonny's countenance. "Wow, I've never seen this happen to anybody before. What do you think the problem is?"

"I'm not sure, Tanya. But I do need to call Malcolm to let him know that I'm here."

"Sure you do, but not after you call your mom."

"Oh, right, I need to call home."

Tanya handed Sonny her cell phone, and he called home. The phone rang and rang until the answering machine picked up.

"Please leave a message."

The mailbox was full. He called his mom's cell phone. "*The Verizon number you have just called is not in service. Please call back later.*" His mom's phone was turned off.

"I can't get in touch with anybody. They're not answering the phone."

Since he didn't have his cell phone, he asked Tanya if he could call information. She approved.

"Directory assistance. this is Katy. What city and state, please?"

"Las Vegas, Nevada."

"What listing, please?"

"*Las Vegas Sun* press."

There was silence as the operator searched for the number. After a couple seconds, a recorder came on, "Here is your number, area code 702-605-6606. Stay on the line while you're connected. Thank you for using Verizon."

"*Las Vegas Sun* press. How may I connect our call?"

"Hello, I need to speak with a Malcolm Floyd, please."

"Hold one moment while I connect you."

"Hello, this is Malcolm. How may I help you?"

"Hello, Malcolm, this is Sonny. Sonny Brooks."

"Hello, Sonny, it's good hearing from you. How is everything?"

"I'm doing well. Thanks for asking. I'm actually in here in Vegas."

"Oh, great! So you decided to come and do the story that we talked about."

"Yes, I thought that I should do that and take care of some other business that I have."

Malcolm's tone became more somber. "Sonny, there's something that I need to tell you."

"Well, I'm here. What is it?"

"DJ Walker was found dead early this morning. It looks like he was murdered."

Sonny's gut burned inside; it felt like a hot dagger was just thrust into it. He was stunned by the news, and Tanya could see on his face that he heard something disappointing; however, she didn't say anything.

"Are you there, Sonny?" asked Malcolm.

"Yes, I—I'm here." Sonny could hardly speak. He managed to ask about Pearl. "How is Ms. Pearl?"

"I have no idea," answered Malcolm. There was a call coming in on his line. "Sonny, I have to talk to you later, so is this the number to reach you?"

"Yes, I guess so. For now it is."

"Okay, so I'll call you later."

"Yeah, I'll talk to you later. Bye." Sonny disconnected.

He sat there in a complete daze. Tanya looked on wondering what was said on the phone. "Tanya, you won't believe this."

"What is it, Sonny?"

He was now slumped down in his chair. "DJ Walker was found dead this morning."

Curious, yet concerned, Tanya asked, "Who is DJ Walker?"

"He is your uncle. He was your father's sister's husband."

"Okay," said Tanya, still not connected.

"You're not getting it, are you, Tanya? These are the people who raised your sister, Alicia."

"Oh my god!"

Chapter 15

After claiming their baggage, Sonny and Tanya headed to the car rental location, which was just a minute or two by shuttle from the terminal.

Tanya had reserved a full-sized car that had just enough trunk space, thanks to Sonny traveling lightly. "Bustin! Tanya, if I had just one more bag, there wouldn't be any room back here." Tanya didn't respond because she was thinking about meeting her aunt, whom she didn't know.

"So, Sonny, you said that this guy DJ is my aunt Pearl's husband, and he was found dead early this morning?"

Struggling to lift Tanya's luggage into the trunk, out of breath he answered, "Yes, that's right. He owned a nightclub where Alicia and I met."

After completing the loading, Sonny suggested that he should drive, since he was familiar with the area. "The first place we need to go to is Pearl's house to see how she's doing," said Sonny.

"Don't you think you ought to call there first to see if she's home?" Tanya handed Sonny her cell phone.

"I can't believe that I went off and left my phone at home."

"Don't worry about that now, Sonny. Just use mine while we're here."

Before taking off, Sonny started to dial Pearl's number but realized that he didn't remember it.

"What's the matter, Sonny?"

"Pearl's number is logged in my cell phone. I never remembered it."

"Well, then we just have to take a chance that she's at home. You do remember where she lives, don't you?"

"Yes, I know where she lives. I don't have Alzheimer's."

Sonny pulled out of the parking lot and entered the main highway. As they drove along, Tanya's phone rang. Tanya answered, "Hello."

It was Malcolm, who didn't realize that he was calling Tanya's phone. "I'm sorry I must have the wrong number."

"Don't hang up. You want to speak with Sonny?"

"Yes. This is Malcolm Floyd. Is he available?"

"Yes, he is. One second."

Tanya put the phone on speaker mode. "It's Malcolm Floyd. Go ahead and talk. It's on speaker," she told Sonny.

"Hello, Malcolm."

"Yes, Sonny, I'm sorry that I had to hang up earlier. I had an important call I had to take."

"I understand, Malcolm. So do you have any other information about what happened to DJ?"

"Yes, I do. In fact, that is what the call was about. Apparently, DJ was killed at approximately two o'clock this morning. The police are on the case, but they don't have any leads. Even if they did, they wouldn't say so, who really knows."

"So, Malcolm, what are they saying?"

"Well, I have an inside source that tells me, they believe that this murder is connected to the homicide that involved Alicia Highsmith and Quinton Brown. I just found out that Alicia has been placed under tight security until her case is solved, which now means Fort Knox type security with what has transpired."

"Bustin!"

"I don't know what 'bustin' means, but yes, bustin!" said Malcolm.

Sonny wanted to know about the story on karaoke that Malcolm talked about. "What do we do about the story, which is one reason why I came back here?"

"Yes, that's still on. I don't actually handle homicides or any other stories of serious nature. I just do events such as the arts and community interests of lesser importance.

So our story is still on, that is, if you're up to it."

Sonny looked over at Tanya to get her thoughts. She just hunched her shoulders with uncertainty.

"Well, Malcolm, I guess I will have to keep you posted. I really need to see how things are after this whole mess is cleared."

"Yes, I understand. Well, you take your time. I'm not going anywhere, but keep me informed when you've decided what to do."

"I will, Malcolm. I'll call as soon as things settle down. But can you do me a favor?"

"Yes, what is it?"

"Can you call me whenever you hear from your insider at the station about any developments?"

"Yes, my man, I'll do that. You can count on it."

"That's cool, Malcolm. Thank you. I'll be talking to you."

"Later."

"I sure hope Pearl is at home, Tanya. I need to know what's going on around here."

"I would also, Sonny. I'd also like to know that my sister is safe."

Sonny recognized the neighborhood that they were approaching. "We are just about there, Tanya."

Tanya began to get a bit anxious, thinking about what she would say to this woman that she doesn't even know or even remember from a child. They were now about two blocks from the house. Sonny looked over to Tanya, who was staring out of the window at the houses as they drove down the street.

"What you looking at, Tanya?"

"Nothing really," she answered, keeping her face toward the window.

"Well, since you're looking at nothing, you may as well look to your left, because we're here."

She looked out through the other side at the house across from where they parked. There was an SUV in the driveway that Sonny recognized as DJ's. It looked as if the front door of the house was open.

"Someone must be here," he said, getting out of the car.

He noticed that Tanya hadn't moved. She just sat there with her hands folded in her lap, twirling her thumbs.

"Tanya, if this is going to be too hard for you, then don't come in, okay?"

"No, Sonny, I was just praying. I don't know what to expect. I need God's help in this one."

"Yeah, I know what you mean."

Tanya got out of the car, and Sonny met her to hold the door open. She reached out and grabbed his hand.

This gesture made Sonny sweat. He felt a strange feeling in his gut as Tanya applied slight pressure to his hand, which she held on to as they crossed the street and walked up to the front door.

Just as they arrived, Pearl was standing there looking through the screen. Sonny quickly let go of Tanya's hand as he noticed Pearl's eyes were on their hands.

Opening the door, she greeted him. "Sonny, I'm so glad you could make it. Come in."

"Hello, Ms. Pearl," he said, entering the house.

Inside, it was very cool. The Las Vegas air was very hot outside. Tanya just followed not saying anything.

Before they sat down, Pearl gave Tanya a peculiar stare. She took a long look, tipping her head from side to side to get every profiled angle. Tanya felt very uncomfortable as Pearl gathered her visual information.

"Oh my Jesus," Pearl said. Then she went over and looked Tanya closely into the eyes. "Oh my Jesus," she repeated. "Don't tell me. Tanya, is that you?"

Tanya smiled.

"Oh my Jesus, it is! Tanya!" Pearl wrapped her arms around her niece and hugged her very tightly. She began to cry, which brought the tears that Tanya was holding pouring down her cheeks.

"Baby, I haven't seen you in over twenty years. You were just a little girl. How have you been?" Pulling back, Pearl took another long look into Tanya's face. "If you don't look like your momma—Oh, baby, sit down here. How have you been?"

Tanya looked over at Sonny, who had a huge smile on his face. He was relieved by the reception it really helped him to relax.

"Yes, Ms. Pearl, this is Tanya, and you won't believe this story of how we met."

"I'm sure it will be interesting, Sonny. I would love to hear about it, but tell me do you have time to go to the hospital with me? I'm going to visit Alicia. On the way there, I'll tell you about what happened to DJ."

"That's fine, but what about funeral arrangements? Have you taken care of any of that yet?"

"I'll do that tomorrow. It's just hard for me right now. I have so much on my plate; I need a day or two to get myself together."

"I understand just what you mean, Ms. Pearl."

Turning her attention back to Tanya, Pearl said, "There is so much you need to know, but one thing I want you to know right now. If I knew that your father was going to give you up for adoption, I would have taken you myself. I think family should always be together. We are to help one another in difficult times. What your father did was just not right, I'm so sorry."

Tanya actually had no idea what Pearl was talking about, but she knew it had something to do with her being adopted. "That's okay, Ms. Pearl—"

"Stop that right now, Tanya. I'm your aunt. Even though you may not know me, I'm still your aunt, your birth mother's sister. You can call me Aunt Pearl. That's who I am."

"Okay, Aunt Pearl, I'll remember that. But there's no need to apologize for something that you had no control over. Whatever happened doesn't matter now. I actually had a wonderful life. I had two parents that raised me very well. I'm not at all sorry for that."

Pearl took Tanya by her hands. "Thank you, Jesus, for taking care of my niece. Yes, Tanya, I can see that you were very well taken care of."

Pearl then became somber. "Your sister, Alicia, was well taken care of also, but she never quite got over the demons inside of her. Me and my husband DJ raised her best we could." Pearl wiped the tears from her eyes as she held tightly to Tanya's hand.

There was silence for a moment that was broken when Sonny spoke. "So, Ms. Pearl, you said that you were about to visit Alicia?"

"Oh yes, that's right. Let us go before I miss her lunch. I try to get there and have lunch with her."

This bit of information surprised Sonny. "What do you mean 'have lunch with her'?"

"Well, Sonny, Alicia is now responding. She's not speaking, but she opens her eyes on occasion, so she has come out of the coma. She's still not out of the woods, but she's eating intravenously."

"Bustin!"

Pearl laughed at Sonny. "I thought that I would never ever hear that word again. I'm so glad you came back, Sonny."

"Yeah, so am I."

They decided to go in separate cars to the hospital. They passed by many familiar places where Sonny and Alicia hung out at. There was one place that they passed by which brought chills to Sonny's body. It was the area where the murders had taken place.

Sonny's mind went back to that night when he saw Alicia's body lying on the ground and how he thought that she was dead. He could see his SUV in flames and the other bodies that were lying there. *What a frightening memory!* he thought.

"What are you thinking about, Sonny?" asked Tanya.

"Oh, nothing really. Just things from when I was last here in Vegas."

He quickly changed the subject. "So Pearl was really glad to see you."

"Yes, I'm surprised that she even recognized me. It's been so long ago, and I was a child when she last saw me."

"Well, Tanya, people don't really change the way they look all that much. Some may put on some weight or lose weight. They may go bald, like my dad, but the face usually stays the same."

"You know, Sonny, you're right. I guess that we really don't change the way we look, but other things may change."

"Yeah, like what?"

"Like the way one feels about another."

"Yes, it's like you think you know a person, then after some time together, you realize that there is more than meets the eyes."

"It's thinking that your elder brother is a butt-hole and when you get older, you realize that he really is a butt-hole."

Laughing, Tanya remarked, "No, Sonny, that's not what I'm saying at all. You are so silly."

"Well, it's true though now, isn't it? Tell the truth. It's true, right?"

"I'm not saying a word, Sonny." They both began to laugh.

Tanya placed her hand on Sonny's knee, saying, "You have no idea what I'm talking about."

What Tanya didn't know was that Sonny knew exactly what she was talking about, and her hand on his knee confirmed just what he knew. This was a very precarious position to be in for him. He believed in boundaries, but as much as he was fighting the notion, he was feeling the same way about her.

They were finally at the hospital. Pearl had driven into the visitor's lot, and Sonny followed. After parking, they met at the entrance.

"Sonny, we need to get special passes to go up to Alicia's room because there's security up there."

"Okay, where do we get the passes from?"

"Come on with me." They followed Pearl to the security office. There the officer was drinking coffee and reading a newspaper.

"Excuse me, Patrick," said Pearl.

The officer looked up. "Hello, Ms. Pearl, you going to see your niece today?"

"Yes, I am, and I have two visitors with me."

"Okay, just fill out these forms, and I'll get your badges for you."

"That's just fine, Patrick."

He handed Pearl three forms.

"So who do we have here with you today, Ms. Pearl?"

"Oh, this is my other niece, Tanya. She's Alicia's sister, and this young man is Sonny. He is a friend of mine."

The name Sonny made the security person to check his shift notes. He saw the name Sonny Brooks, but wasn't sure if this was the same person.

When the forms were filled out, he handed the badges to Pearl, who gave one each to Sonny and Tanya. "Enjoy your visit, Ms. Pearl."

"Thank you, Patrick. You have a good day."

"I will. Thank you."

As soon as they were gone, he checked the names on the forms again. There it was—Sonny Brooks. The guard immediately called the Las Vegas Police Department.

"This is Detective Riley speaking."

"This is Officer Patrick Simms at the hospital. I have some information for you."

"What is it, Officer Simms?"

"Sonny Brooks has just come to the hospital. He's with Pearl Walker and another young lady."

"How long have they been there?"

"Not more than five minutes. They're headed upstairs now."

"Thank you. I'll be there as fast as I can get there." Detective Riley hung up the phone.

Pearl, Tanya, and Sonny walked along the corridor to an area where not many people were allowed to enter. To get to where Alicia was, they had to go up an unmarked elevator. Inside the elevator, there were not any numbered floor buttons. There was just one button.

Pearl pushed the button and the elevator door closed and began to go up.

"Bustin. This is some top-secret, get-Smart James Bond action going here."

Tanya laughed. "Yes, this is very serious. They mean business protecting Alicia."

The elevator came to a stop. When the door opened, Sonny was surprised to see that the floor looked like every other floor except that it had only a few rooms. There was a nurses' station that they approached.

"Hi, Ms. Pearl, how you are doing today?" asked a young-looking white female nurse. She looked to be in her early thirties. When she looked up and saw Sonny, she couldn't believe her eyes.

"Hey, I know you. You are the guy they call choirboy. I used to go hear you sing all the time at Wannabee's. Where have you been? People are always talking about you."

Pearl interrupted, "I'm going to see Alicia. Can you bring him down when you're done asking him questions?"

"Sure will, Ms. Pearl." She turned her attention back to Sonny. "So are you still singing in those contests?"

"No, I haven't been in one of those since I left Vegas and went back to St. Louis."

"Well, if you didn't know there's going to be this karaoke contest at the college this weekend, you ought to go."

"I'm not sure about that. I actually have a group back home, and we are trying to cut this CD."

"Okay, but you really should try to be there. It's going to be off the chain for real."

"Sure. Tell me what room Alicia is in, please."

"Number 3, down that way."

Sonny followed where she pointed. In Alicia's room, Tanya was standing over her sister; she was crying. Sonny stood beside her and was near tears himself as he looked upon Alicia.

She had light bandages around her head as the wound was nearly healed. She was still on oxygen and had IVs connected to her. As she lay there asleep, Sonny could hear the sound of her voice as they talked and laughed. He even remembered their more intimate moments.

Suddenly he remembered that he was standing next to her sister who was pressed up against his side. Pearl just subtly watched them both. She got the impression that there might be something going on between the two of them.

"She looks so peaceful," said Tanya. "She still looks the same as I remember. Of course, there is a little swelling, but I still see her." Sonny placed his arm around Tanya.

"I remember that when we were kids, how she used to protect me from everything. I used to be scared of bugs, especially spiders. Alicia would come and catch them and take them outside. She never would kill them.

"She wouldn't hurt anything or anybody. I can't understand why somebody would do this to her. She was so caring."

Pearl listened to Tanya as she expressed her hurt and sadness. "Tanya, you didn't know how much Alicia really cared for others. She is a nurse herself. She got her degree in nursing and worked at this very hospital before she was injured. Apparently, she gave up her job because of her drug use."

Sonny listened to Pearl with regret. Somehow he felt responsible for her present condition. He knew that it was because of his money that he spent wildly that caused her to slip deeper into drugs than she was before they met. He felt that she quit her job because he was so caught up in the night life instead of trying to save her soul for the sake of Christ.

Now he wishes that he had never left his father's house when he did; there were so many things that he now regrets.

Suddenly there was a knock on the door that got all of their attention. The door slowly opened, and three uniformed cops and a man in a suit entered. Pearl recognized Detective Riley.

"Detective Riley, what's going on here?" asked Pearl.

"We need to take Sonny Brooks in for questioning. I need him to come with us."

"Bustin! "What did I do?"

"We'll talk to you at the station." Sonny came along without any fuss. Tanya was beside herself. She demanded an explanation, which she did not get.

"Don't worry, Sonny. I'll be here. Don't worry."

Sonny went quietly with the police officers and Detective Riley to the station where he would be questioned.

Chapter 16

Raleigh was taken to the room where he would be assigned to during the tests that were scheduled for him; Martha was with him. RJ had gone to the house to gather some of Raleigh's things that he would need. While he was searching his parents' bedroom for his dad's favorite house slippers, he heard a phone ringing.

He knew that it was Sonny's cell phone by the ring tone. Knowing that Sonny had forgotten to take it along on his trip, RJ refused to search for it to see who was trying to get in touch with Sonny. After finding the slippers, he walked past Sonny's bedroom and heard the ringing coming out from there. "Oh well," he said and kept on walking.

The caller left a message. "Yo, Sonny, it's Malik. I talked to the crew about you leaving, dude. They're not feeling you for not letting them know earlier. Also, I got the track finished. It's tight, man. Hit me back."

After the message was completed, the phone rang again. This time it went directly to voice mail. "Sonny, this is your mother. You really need to call me. Your dad is in the hospital . . ." Before she could finish, a prerecorded message interrupted, "The mailbox for this number is now full and can no longer accept any messages."

Martha was disappointed but didn't let it bother her too much because she was more concerned about Raleigh, who was taken to x-ray. She was wondering why Sonny had not answered her calls or returned her messages.

Moments later, RJ returned to the hospital with the items he went after. He brought everything except for Raleigh's pipe that he would smoke on occasions, mostly when he was uneasy about something that he couldn't control. Smoking a pipe would calm his nerves.

"RJ, I tried calling your brother again, but he just will not answer his phone."

"That's because he left it at the house in his bedroom," replied RJ.

"How do you know that, RJ?"

"I heard his phone ringing from his bedroom when I was there."

"Did you bring it with you?"

"No."

"What do you mean no, RJ?"

"I'm sorry, Mom. No, ma'am."

Martha was getting impatient. "RJ, you know exactly what I meant."

"Mom, if he forgot to bring his phone with him, that's his fault, not mine. Besides that, I heard it in his room, and I didn't feel like looking for it. I didn't know it was you calling him."

"That's okay, boy. One day you are going to need your brother for something. I just hope that he has just a little more compassion than you do when that day comes."

They were interrupted by a nurse who was coming to see if they needed anything and to tell them that Raleigh would soon return back to his room.

"No, baby, we are quite comfortable for now," said Martha. RJ, however, made a request. "Can we get some bottled water in here? I'm kind of thirsty."

Martha looked RJ in the face. "Please," she said.

When the nurse left the room to get some water, Martha turned her attention back to RJ. "By the way, what's going on between you and Tanya?"

RJ was not prepared to answer questions about Tanya at this moment. However, he knew that he better at least say something to put Martha at ease, even if it meant lying to her.

"Oh, it's nothing. Just the fact that she's doing a lot of traveling these days, and we hardly get a chance to see one another."

Martha being very intuitive responded with another question. "Why haven't we met your business partner at the restaurant? Is it because the two of you are more than just business partners?"

RJ was now caught between revealing the truth to his mom and running out of the hospital. "Mom, there is a lot that I have to tell you, but I don't think now is the best time. We have Dad to worry about, not me. I'll be fine."

"So there is something to what you and Sonny were arguing about the other night?"

"I'll explain it all to you later. Right now I have to go, but I promise you we'll talk about it."

"We'll talk? Okay. We'll talk about it later."

"Thank you for understanding, Mom. I'll see you later." Kissing his mom on the cheek, RJ made haste getting out of the hospital, believing he had freed himself from having to tell his mom about his relationship with Maxine.

Raleigh had now returned and was feeling very fatigued from all of the x-rays. He was laid in his bed, and Martha added an extra blanket over him that RJ brought from the house. "Here, this will keep you warm, because these hospitals will cause you to catch pneumonia from the cold."

After getting Raleigh snuggled in, the doctor entered the room. He had just gone over the x-rays. "Hello. Mrs. Brooks, is it?" he asked politely.

"Yes. Martha Brooks."

"Well, Mrs. Brooks, it's good that you got Mr. Brooks in when you did. There was some internal bleeding, which indicates that something isn't quite right. What the x-ray has revealed is that there is a tumor in his throat."

"Oh, Jesus," said Martha.

"Now we haven't determined anything for sure. We still need to take some more tests. I've scheduled a biopsy that will take place tomorrow morning. Don't worry about the bleeding. Basically that was caused by the heavy coughing, so we will give him something that will suppress his coughing.

"Now that won't fix anything, but it will give him a little relief so that he can sleep. He seems very tired. I presume that he's been up most of the night."

"Yes, he hasn't been sleeping well these last two nights."

"Yes, he's very tired," remarked the doctor. "I'm sure that you probably have to make some telephone calls to people at the church. You can make them from here if you like."

"I think I'll go home and call some people. Raleigh needs his rest, and I don't want to disturb him."

"Oh, that's fine, but you can call from here if you like."

"No, thank you. I really have to call from home. He needs to get some rest."

"Okay, then just check with the nurse to see what time the procedure is scheduled for tomorrow. You have a good rest of the day and try not to worry. We'll take care of your husband." The doctor left the room, closing the door behind him.

Martha went over to Raleigh who was asleep and said a prayer over him. "Dear Father, I know you can heal all sicknesses, but we are not claiming anything. I believe in what you have to say about this, that "no weapon formed against my husband shall prosper," so I am claiming that he is healed in Jesus's name. Amen." She kissed her husband and departed.

Before leaving the hospital, she stopped by the nurses' station to find out what time the biopsy is going to happen. Candace was pleasant and very helpful. She informed Martha the time would be seven in the morning. She also took Martha's number in case there would be any changes in Raleigh's health or any time change for the scheduled biopsy.

Martha arrived home and was feeling very much exhausted from the day spent in the hospital with Raleigh. Going into the kitchen to boil some water for hot tea, she remembered that she had to find Sonny's cell phone in case he decided call to it.

Before she could get halfway up the stairs, the house phone began to ring. Continuing on, she answered the upstairs phone. "Hello."

"Sister Martha, how are you doing?"

Martha recognized the voice of Betty Phillips, one of the mothers from the church. "Hello, Sister Betty, I'm doing well."

"Are you sure? I just saw Brother RJ. He told me that you were at the hospital with pastor today. I was hoping to catch you at home."

"Yes, I just walked in."

"So how's pastor doing? Is he—"

Martha interrupted, "Well, we don't know right now. He's going to have some tests done tomorrow."

"Well, what does—"

Martha again interrupted, "We are going to believe God's Word, Sister Betty."

"I know that's right, Martha. Let go and—"

"Sister Betty, we are going to say what the scripture actually says, so we'll be just fine."

"Well, praise the Lord then, Sister. Turn it over to Jesus, and—"

"He'll work it out?" Martha added.

"Yes, Sister Martha, he'll work it out praise God."

"Well, Sister Betty, thank you for calling and checking up on us."

"Oh, that's quite all right, Sister. Charity starts at home then—"

"God bless you, Sister. Have a good day. Bye-bye."

"Okay, bye now."

Finally off the phone, Martha couldn't help but laugh, because Sister Betty never attends Bible study and always quotes religious clichés. "Bless her heart," said Martha.

Sonny's bedroom was a mess. He usually kept it somewhat tidy, but for now, it was in disarray.

Martha looked all over his room for the cell phone but could not find it anywhere. She decided to search his desk. RJ said he heard it, so she wasn't going to end her search until she found it. Then it dawned on her to just call the number—she did.

It began to ring, but she still couldn't find it. With her ears in full attention, she followed the annoying ring tone of some hip-hop song until she came to his computer desk and found it beneath some papers.

Before lifting the papers, she instinctively read what he had written on the top page. She had to laugh aloud, as she read the note. "Don't forget your cell phone."

With Sonny's phone, Martha went to her room to make a few calls. She knew that the first person that needed to know about Raleigh was the chairman of the deacon's ministry, Brother McBride.

As she scrolled down her contact list, she hoped that Sister Betty hadn't called everybody in the church yet; she was notorious for spreading information before it was time. Not that she was a gossip; she just talked more than she needed to.

Deacon McBride's phone rang a couple of times and then he answered. "Hello."

"Hello, Deacon Mac. This is Martha."

"Oh yes, Martha. I'm sorry I didn't see your name on my phone."

"That's okay. How are you feeling today?" Martha was actually waiting to see if Sister Betty had said something to him.

"I'm doing just fine for an old man. I guess the Lord is still blessing me."

"I know that's right, Deacon Mac."

"So how's pastor, Sister Martha?"

"Well, Deacon Mac, I was calling to let you know that he's been admitted into the hospital today."

Surprised, Deacon Mac responded, "Oh my god! Is he all right? Well, I guess not if he's in the hospital. What's ailing him?"

"Well, he's scheduled to have some tests done, so right now we don't know."

"Was he sick or something or . . ."

"Yes, he was coughing up blood this morning and apparently last night also. You know how stubborn Raleigh is. He didn't tell me. I happened to find his handkerchief that he had been spitting on, and it had blood on it. So I made him come in this morning."

"Well, I'm sure everything will be all right. You know to put it in God's hands."

What the deacon just said made Martha realize she needed to get busy and start praying. "Well, Deacon Mac, I thought that you should hear from me before Sister Betty calls you since she knows already. RJ ran into her and told her about the pastor and she called me."

"All right, Sister Martha, I appreciate it, because let Betty tell it we'll be having his funeral tomorrow or in a couple of days. Lord knows I don't know how she gets things messed up the way she does."

Laughing, Martha said, "Deacon, you sure got that right."

"Okay, Martha, I'll let you go. I know you have a lot to deal with right now. I'll tell the other deacons myself, so don't worry about calling them. Will you keep me informed on how things are? Maybe I'll visit him this evening if it's all right."

"That should be okay. He was sleeping when I left, but by then, he should be awake. But call the hospital before you go. I gave them your name as someone they can release information to."

"Thank you very much, Martha. I appreciate that."

Martha knew that McBride was sincere with what he said. He was very instrumental in getting the church to think logically and not act hastily during Raleigh's impropriety. If she could trust anyone, it was Deacon McBride.

"Raleigh is at Trinity Hospital on the fourth floor. His nurse on duty is Candace."

"Thank you again, Sister Martha. I'll be praying for your strength and Raleigh's healing."

"God bless you, Deacon McBride. God bless you."

After the call ended, Martha reached for her bedside Bible and opened it where there had been some study notes tucked in. She had been watching on television a pastor teaching on divine healing and how to use the Word and faith to receive it.

She had a desire to raise her level of faith and prayer so that she could pray more effectively for others at the church's weekly prayer meetings. More of the people attending have also been studying the same teachings, and the prayer services have been getting positive results from those attending and those being prayed for.

Finding her scriptures to read and meditate on, Martha began to go into holy meditation and prayer with her Savior. She read over and over the promises of God concerning healing, and as she stood between the gaps for her husband, she claimed those promises and considered it done in Jesus's name.

For more than an hour, Martha stayed in communion with God in praise and worship, until she felt in her spirit that it was complete.

By this time, she was prostrate and on her face. Feeling totally exhausted, there was nothing more that she could say or do, not even get up from the floor.

She just lay there in complete surrender. None of the cares of this world entered her thoughts; she felt no discomfort, just peace. She knew that she was in the holy presence of the Lord.

Chapter 17

While Martha was feeling God's peace, RJ was feeling Maxine's wrath. Shortly after leaving the hospital and running into Sister Betty, RJ stopped at the restaurant to see if he could talk some sense into Maxine.

They were down in the stockroom having a heated discussion about what he said to her. "RJ, you told me that it wasn't going to work for you and Tanya. I just want to know if she knows this yet. Have you told her?"

"Max, I told you that she's out of town. You know this, remember? You reminded me that she's away with my brother."

"Listen, RJ, I don't know why you came here if you didn't have anything to tell me. You know, things have changed. Now I'm in control of this and you are at the end of my leash. I can either hold on or let go and let you run off like the lost dog that you are."

"Come now, Max. There's no need to talk to me that way. You act as if you're innocent in all of this. If you can remember, it was you who said that I should keep our relationship private until I could get rid of Tanya. Hell, I couldn't even tell my parents that Max is really Maxine. They actually thought you were a guy until last night."

Max was surprised by this revelation. "What do you mean, 'last night'?"

"Last night, Sonny overheard you and me talking, and he told my parents that you are actually Maxine."

"Well, that part was all of your doing. You could have told them who I was at least. Now I'm sure they have suspicions."

Max was standing against a stack of commercial-size canned vegetables. RJ noticed that the top box was not securely placed and looked as if would come down on top of Maxine. When he reached out to guide her away from the boxes, the natural tendency was to pull from him; because of their discussion, she didn't want RJ to touch her.

As she pulled away, she bumped the stack, and what RJ was trying to prevent happened as the top box came falling down, just missing Max.

The box crashed to the floor breaking open, and the large cans rolled out. Max was able to avoid any of the cans hitting her; however, RJ was struck on the ankle, and the force of the blow from the top edge of the can cut into his flesh.

"Oh shit!" He jumped and grabbed his foot falling off balance and into a free-standing shelf holding extra pans and skillets. Those went crashing to the floor, causing such a noise that everyone upstairs could hear. A couple of the wait staff came running down to investigate to find RJ rolling on the floor in pain and Maxine laughing so hard that she was crying.

"What's going on down here?" asked one of the guys. "Are you okay, sir? Is your foot okay?"

RJ sat up, pulled his sock down, and examined his ankle. He could see blood running down onto his foot. He removed his shoe and pulled his sock completely off, exposing a gash just below his ankle that would probably not require stitches.

"Do we need to call an ambulance, RJ?" asked Maxine.

While closely examining his wound, he concluded that it was only a shin tear and that it would be all right. He asked one of the waiters to get him a clean towel, which he used to apply pressure. In a matter of a couple of minutes, the bleeding stopped.

There was a first-aid kit in the kitchen which the waiter also brought down for RJ. There was some disinfectant and large Band-Aids in the kit that he used to dress his wound.

While he was attending to himself, Maxine just watched, not offering any help. "Thanks for helping, Max."

"I know you don't mean that, but you got what you deserved."

"I got what I deserved. What do you mean by that?"

Maxine was not about to go into any details about RJ's selfishness, but she did tell him how she felt. "RJ, you really should take a long look in the mirror and see exactly what others see.

"You put on this façade that makes you appear to be somebody special, somebody who seems to have it all together. You know what I'm beginning to see in you, RJ—a hypocrite."

"A hypocrite?"

"Yes, RJ, a hypocrite. What is this officer in the church as you like to call yourself doing? You are engaged to be married and about to become a father of another woman's child. That, honey, sounds like not only a hypocrite, but a pitiful individual who doesn't know right from wrong."

RJ became defensive hearing those remarks from Maxine. "Listen, Max, I'm not in this alone. You are just as responsible. Listen; there are two things that you need to know about me. The first is, I don't give a damned about what you think, and the second is this."

He thought for a moment about what he was about to say. "I've been thinking about what you said about me and my religion for some time now. I've come to the conclusion that I really don't believe any of that God stuff.

"This life was not mine by choice. My parents brought me up in the church, and for years, I've been living a lie trying to please everybody, while being left completely miserable. I even thought that I would get engaged to the woman my parents would approve of, but I don't love Tanya and never have. At first, there was something, but I guess that happens when sex is involved.

"So I have to disagree with you calling me a hypocrite. From the time that I was a child, I've witnessed things in the church, and in my own family that did nothing for me but made me doubt if there was really a god.

"I had to ask myself, if there is a god and these people are doing all this crazy stuff and so many bad things are happening, then why waste my time when it doesn't matter anyway.

"I may be a lot of things, but a hypocrite I'm not. What I am is nothing short of a fraud, a fake. My life is nothing but a façade. Now you tell me, is this the kind of man that you want to be the father of your child?"

Maxine was amazed by RJ's revelation. She never expected to hear such a thing from a man who seemed so sure of himself. She looked upon RJ with doubt about who he really was.

"RJ, there is one thing you left out that I said about you. You are pitiful. All that I have to say is it doesn't matter what type of man you are and whether you are ideal for a father. The fact is, what's done is done. I'm keeping my baby, and you are the father.

"I can't help how you feel about yourself. That's none of my concern, but you will take care of this child. So if you really want to start over in life, so that you can accept the choices that you've made for you, then you need to tell Tanya about this child."

RJ had nothing to combat Maxine with because he knew that she was right. He just didn't know what would become of him and how his parents would react to his feelings about the church, God, and his life. Most of all, he really cared for Maxine, but now he felt that he had lost her as well.

"Maxine, there's something that I really need to tell you."

"What's that?"

"I'm in love with you, and nothing would make me happier than raising a child with you."

"That's good to hear, RJ, but I think that I can raise the child on my own. I just need your help."

"What do you mean, Max?"

"I guess I didn't answer your question when you asked if you were the ideal man. Well, the answer is absolutely no. You're not the ideal man. Not just that, but I don't think I want you as a partner. While you have been trying to figure out how you could have fresh luscious fruit from my garden, I've been meeting with a couple of people who are interested in buying the restaurant, and we are just about to seal the deal.

"You know, RJ, the sad thing about all of this is I really wanted this for us, but you tried to play me and Tanya. Instead you played yourself. So although I appreciate the sentiment, no thank you."

RJ was devastated by Maxine's words of rejection. The pain of his ankle didn't feel so badly anymore now that his ego and manhood was wounded. He was speechless, which was something else he's never been.

"Max, I'm not sure what to say or do for that matter."

With a smirk, Maxine remarked, "Let me help you. Don't say a word. Just get up and leave. Don't even bother calling me. I'll call you when I need to let you know what I expect from you for the child when the time comes. Until then, you will probably hear from my lawyer."

RJ was now standing, favoring his right ankle. "Is that it? Just like that we're finished?"

"I wouldn't say totally finished, but yes, what we once had is over. But let me make a suggestion to you. Be honest to Tanya. She just may have more forgiveness than I do."

With that said, RJ limped his way up the stairs and out of the restaurant, bearing a scar that would soon heal and one that will take a while.

Chapter 18

The squad car that Sonny was loaded in arrived at the station just moments after he was picked up. Detective Riley rode in a separate car, and as they traveled, he thought about the string of events that was now challenging him.

He figured that there must be a connection between last night's shooting and the incident that had taken place a few months ago. But what does all of this have to do with Sonny Brooks? That was the piece he was hoping to find to complete the puzzle.

He arrived at the station just behind the squad car as the officers were taking Sonny in. Sonny appeared to be calm to Riley; there was no tugging or signs of resistance.

"I'll be right in," he called out to the officers as they entered the building.

Just before going inside, he stopped to observe his surroundings. "God, it seems like I live here."

He noticed that the grounds around the place really needed some attention. Young trees were dying; weeds were growing between the cracks in the walkway. And the hedges needed trimming badly.

Riley looked as bad as the unkempt shrubbery. Wearing the same clothes from the day before everything was wrinkled. He had a coffee stain on his shirt, and his facial hairs revealed that he hadn't shaved going on two days. What was worse was that he hasn't been sleeping well lately.

What he was really doing was thinking about the day he'd put down his badge and retired to be a gardener. "I think this is my last job. I'm tired of this crap."

Taking a deep breath, he continued on into the building and to the area where the officers were waiting with Sonny.

"Did any of you ask him anything yet?" asked Riley.

"No, we didn't, Detective," replied one of the officers.

"You better not have. I can't have you guys screwing things up. This is very important."

He looked over at Sonny, who was sitting quietly with his head down. "Hey, are you all right over there?" he asked.

Lifting his head slowly, Sonny replied, "Who, me?"

"Yes, you. You need some water or something?"

"No, sir. I'm good."

"You're good. All right then. Let's get to the reason why we brought you down here. First of all, my name is Detective Riley. Will you please state your name?"

"I'm Sonny. Sonny Brooks."

"Tell me something, Sonny Brooks. What do you know about the shootings that took place approximately four months ago involving the death of one Quinton Brown aka Q, and left the young lady Alicia Highsmith in the hospital. Now there were others who were killed, but I'm not interested in that right now. So can you tell me anything?"

"Well, Detective Riley, I wish that I knew. Believe me, I would tell you everything. But I don't know a thing."

"Isn't it true that you were working for Quinton Brown at his nightclub?"

"Yes, that's true. I won this singing contest, and the prize was going to be a recording contract with his studio. Well, that didn't happen right away, so he asked if I would help out at the club until he could tie some loose ends. I was the featured act during the huge opening night that was there at Starz."

Detective Riley wanted to know more about this supposed recording contract. "So did you ever get the contract signed or anything?"

Sonny didn't answer; he just shook his head no. Riley continued on with the questions. "There were four people who were killed that night. Two of them we figured had no business being there, but the other guy, Juan Martinez; we were able to find out, was a drug smuggler. The Florida cops had been trying to nail this guy for years. Somehow he was able to elude them until now."

Riley paused and rubbed his chin. "Funny thing they actually got their man when they weren't even involved. Anyway, Sonny, did you have involvement with Martinez?"

"No. I didn't even know him and never met him."

Riley became irritated. He wasn't getting anywhere with his investigation, because Sonny knew absolutely nothing.

Sonny had something to ask Riley. "Detective Riley, you came to the hospital and had me to come here with you. Do you have any reason to believe that I was involved with what happened? Look, sir, I lost everything that I had. My money was stolen from my hotel room, my vehicle was destroyed, and Alicia is lying in a hospital bed hanging on to what life that's still there. I'm sorry, but I have this suspicion of my own."

"You do, huh? What's that?"

"You know that I had nothing to do with the killings or selling drugs. You're hoping that I might say something that will implicate me. I'm not going to do that, because I don't know a thing."

Detective Riley could not rebut Sonny's comments. After speaking with Mathias, he was convinced that Sonny was nothing more than a victim of bad circumstances. However, Riley had to know for himself.

Through his years of police work and being a detective, he found that many people are more than they may appear to be. He hoped desperately that Sonny was one of those people.

"Sonny, I understand that the *Vegas Sun* is going to do a story about karaoke and you were asked to come and be a part of it. Before you do anything, are you aware that Dennis Walker, you know him as DJ, was killed last night?"

"Yes, I know." Sonny lowered his head again, troubled by what was going on.

"Sonny, we're going to take you back to the hospital. I'm finished here," said Detective Riley.

Sonny's head popped up. "Is that all, really?"

"That's all I need to know for now, Sonny. But know this. I'll be watching you, so keep your nose clean."

"Bustin! You're going to take me back to the hospital then?"

"Yes. Somebody get him out of here." Riley was frustrated and wanted to get this case solved. Just as the officer was about to leave with Sonny, another officer came in and said something into the ear of Detective Riley.

Riley listened intently, and Sonny could see the expression on Riley's face had changed from frustration to urgency. After the message was given, Riley told the officers to hurry with Sonny.

Riley was back in his office. On his desk was the fingerprint match that was on both the beer bottle that was left at the scene of last night's crime and the person whom the prints matched.

Riley could finally see that this investigation did have an ending. He got on the phone and called the chief of police to give him the findings. The chief then sent out an APB on the lookout for Ricardo (Rico) Fleming.

Back at the hospital, Alicia was connected to her feeding apparatus. Tanya looked on not completely sure what to think about all that was now happening to her sister, while Pearl was down in the cafeteria getting something to eat for her and Tanya.

Sonny had arrived back at the hospital and was on his way to Alicia's room. Not quite sure which direction to go, he was pleased to have met Pearl as she was on her way. "I am glad to run into you. I have no idea how to get back to Alicia's room." Noticing that Tanya was not with Pearl, he asked, "Where's Tanya?"

"She's with Alicia."

"So how is she doing?"

"She's about the same."

"I was really asking about Tanya, Ms. Pearl."

"Oh, I think she's doing okay. You know it's got to be hard on her. She hasn't seen her sister in a long time."

"Yeah, I know."

On their way back to Alicia's room, on the elevator, Pearl felt compelled to ask Sonny something personal. "So, Sonny, tell me what's going on between you and Tanya?"

Sonny was taken aback by the question. He hadn't even thought that there was anything between the two of them, but he felt that Pearl must have seen something.

"I don't really know what you mean, but if you're asking if we are involved romantically, there is absolutely nothing going on."

"Yes, Sonny, that's exactly what I'm talking about. I saw the way she looked at you. You may not know that she has feelings for you, but I can see it."

Sonny remained quiet and kept his eyes on the elevator floor indicator lights.

"Sonny, you can deny it all you want to. But there is something there. Now I don't know Tanya like I know you, so I'll just advise you to be very careful. I've seen these things turn into something not good."

Sonny nodded his head as though he understood what she was saying to him; however, he didn't think that Pearl needed to be worried about this. "Pearl, I'm okay with that, but you should be more concerned with DJ."

"You're right, Sonny. All day long I've been trying not to worry myself, but I know there are a lot of things that I have to do. I've called his family to let them know, so they'll take care of the funeral arrangements."

"Have they decided where the funeral is going to be held?" asked Sonny.

"Yes, they have. He's going to be taken back to North Carolina. That's his home town. Most of his family lives there in Charlotte."

"So when are they going to have that done?"

Feeling the pain of her loss, Pearl answered, "Hopefully, as soon as possible."

Sonny was beginning to feel the pain as well. No one was aware that DJ was partly responsible for Alicia being in the condition that she's in; consequently, his own death was a mystery.

Back in Alicia's room, Sonny hadn't thought about meeting with Malcolm from the newspaper until Tanya's cell phone began to ring.

"Hello, this is Tanya."

"Hello, I need to speak with Sonny. Is he available?"

"Yes, he is. Can you hold, please?" Placing to phone against her body, she said to Sonny, "I think it's the guy from the newspaper."

She handed him the phone. "Hello, this is Sonny."

"Hello, Sonny, Malcolm here. I have some great news for you. There is going to be this huge karaoke show tonight at the university. I think this would be a great opportunity for you to show your talent. Also, we can do a spread in the paper. I will have a photographer there to take pictures of the entire event with you being the main attraction. That is, if you're up to it."

"That sounds interesting Malcolm, but just hold a minute." He placed the phone down and spoke with Pearl and Tanya about the event.

Pearl and Tanya were encouraging Sonny to not let this opportunity pass. Pearl assured him that there was nothing that he could do and that everything was being taken care of.

"Sonny, you did mention that part of why you came here was to do the interview. You shouldn't leave your fans disappointed. Besides, I would love nothing more than to hear you sing," said Tanya.

It didn't take much to convince Sonny. "Malcolm, I'll do it."

"Fantastic, Sonny. I'll meet you at UNLV at about seven. The event will be at the recreation center. There will be signs to direct you there."

"Okay, Malcolm, I'll be there at seven."

"Okay, Sonny, I'll see you there."

When Malcolm was off the phone, Sonny looked over at Alicia. Pearl thought that she knew what he was thinking. "You two met at a karaoke show, Sonny."

"Yes, we did, Pearl. This all seems so strange. I just wish I knew who was responsible for this."

Chapter 19

Rico was trying to keep a low profile after he got wind of the news that the cops were looking for him in connection to the homicide.

He was holding out at an associate's house. He knew that nobody would ever think to look for him there.

Just around the corner was a liquor store, where he would decide to go to for beer. Against the advice from his accomplice, Rico defiantly took a chance on leaving the house.

He walked the couple of blocks to the store without any problem. When he arrived, he bumped into Craig, one of the guys that were with him when DJ was killed.

They spoke candidly about where Rico was hiding out which was heard by a patron. "I'm hanging out at 'Too-Short's house.'" After purchasing his beer, Rico noticed the customer staring at him.

"Hey, do you know me?" asked Rico.

The customer who was a black man, who looked to be in his forties—probably younger, but the alcohol was taking its toll—just shook his head and walked out of the store.

"I'm outta here, homes," said Rico to Craig.

"Keep low, man. You know Five-0 is looking for you."

"Yeah, man, I know. You keep low too, Craig."

"Bet."

They both departed, going separate ways. Rico made it back to Too-Short's house without being seen. When he entered the house, Too-Short was waiting there and didn't look happy.

"What's the matter with you?" asked Rico.

Walking over to a window and looking out, Too-Short was very irritated. "Did you see the cops out there just a minute ago?"

Rico was not aware of any cops anywhere in the area. He felt confident that none were anywhere around. "Man, what are you talking about?"

"No sooner than you left, I saw a squad car driving down the street. I told you not to bring attention to me or this house."

Apparently, Too-Short was getting nervous about Rico being there and was now about to let him know.

"Rico, I have far too much to lose. I can't have you taking chances on leaving here and leading the law back here. I think you have to go. Find somewhere else to lay low at."

"Where in the hell am I going to go, Too-Short? You know there's no place I can go."

"Now that's not my concern, Rico. You are the one who pulled the trigger. I told you to scare him. Hell, he was already a nervous wreck after putting that girl in harm's way. All you needed to do was what I told you to do, but you took it too far.

"So now you have to find somewhere else to go."

"Cool then. When do you want me to leave?"

"I want you to leave right now, Rico."

"Oh, hell, no, I can't leave now, Too-Short. The cops are out there. You told me you seen them."

Too-Short was standing near a desk and gently pulled out a handgun. "Well, Rico, I knew you would say that, so I guess that I have to encourage you a little bit." He pointed the pistol at Rico. "Get out now."

"Damn, man, I'll leave. You can put the pistol away."

"Not until you are down the street, Rico."

Rico threw up his hands. "Okay, man, I'm outta here. I thought we were cool."

"We are. I just have to take care of me until this blow's over—if it does."

"What do you mean 'if it does'?"

"I don't know, Rico. You know, like they say, what goes around comes around."

"Shh," remarked Rico as he walked out of the house.

It was now dark out, and Rico was very cautious keeping away from street lamps as he wandered down the street.

Meanwhile, the customer that was in the liquor store who was out to make a quick buck called the local crime-stopper hotline. "Yes, it was Ricardo. I saw him."

"Can you tell me where you saw him, sir," asked the phone operator.

"He was at a liquor store, but he said he was staying at some guy named Too-Short."

"Can you tell us anything else? Like what was he wearing?"

"He was wearing a red T-shirt and jeans. That's all I remember."

The operator gave the caller an identification number and told him if an arrest is made; he would receive up to one-thousand dollars.

After the call ended, a call was made to Detective Riley at the police station. All of the information was given, and several cars were dispatched to the area where Rico was last spotted.

It was nearing seven o'clock. Sonny and Tanya were at Pearl's house where they had showered and changed. Pearl convinced them that they needn't spend money for two hotel rooms when they could stay with her. She had two extra rooms. One was a guest room and the other was where Alicia slept when she lived with her aunt and uncle.

Sonny looked to be a bit anxious as Tanya noticed that he was walking in circles like he was lost. "What's the problem? You look preoccupied with something, Sonny?"

"Yeah, it's that obvious, huh?"

"Yes, it is. What is it?"

"It's the interview and being around so many people again. I've never really been all that comfortable around crowds. Even when I was here before, Alicia would help me to relax before going out on stage." Sonny sat on the sofa with his elbows on his knees and head in his hands. Tanya sat beside him.

"Well, Sonny, I'm not Alicia, but I know exactly what to do to help you to relax."

She smoothly reached her arm around his shoulders and placed her hand on his knee. When Sonny's attention went to her hand upon his knee, Tanya quickly poked her index finger into his ear. She began to tickle him with her finger which caused him to fall over.

She then began poking him in the ribs. This really made him squirm and laugh uncontrollably.

Tanya was relentless with her assault on Sonny's ribs. His breathless screams finally warranted Tanya's mercy, so she stopped.

"See there, that was sneaky and not fair," said Sonny. In one motion, without any warning, he sat up very fast and grabbed Tanya around her arms, holding them locked to her sides.

What Sonny meant to be a surprise to Tanya, Tanya surprised him by what she didn't do. She didn't struggle as Sonny expected but relaxed in his arms with her face turned directly in his. There they were face to face, breathing heavily, staring into each other's eyes.

How much she looks like Alicia! thought Sonny. *He doesn't look anything like RJ,* thought Tanya.

Don't do it, Sonny. You cannot kiss your brother's fiancée.

No, Tanya, he's your sister's . . . I'm engaged to his . . . It's not right. Tanya moved first and then Sonny. Their lips met for only a second, which seemed like an eternity. When their mouths parted, Tanya stayed very close to Sonny, looking deeply into his eyes.

Sonny loosened his embrace, freeing Tanya's arms, and she took a deep breath and exhaled softly into Sonny's nostrils. Her breath was fresh, and Sonny inhaled the fragrance.

"We need to get out of here, Sonny," Tanya said to break the bond between them.

Sonny looked at his watch and agreed. "Yes, it's time to go."

They got up from the sofa and made their way to the door, just as Pearl was entering. They looked at each other and began to laugh.

"What are you two laughing about? Is my blouse on backward or something?"

"No, Pearl, your blouse is just fine. We have to go if we're going to get to the campus on time," remarked Tanya.

Pearl looked around the room and noticed the sofa cushions were in disarray. She gave Sonny a look of suspicion. "It's not what you think, Pearl."

"And just what is that Sonny?" she replied.

"Nothing Pearl absolutely nothing. We're out of here." Tanya and Sonny began laughing again as they closed the door behind them.

"It better be nothing," said Pearl. Suddenly she thought of something.

"What time are you kids coming back tonight?"

Tanya deferred to Sonny. "I'm really not sure, Pearl."

Pearl reached into her purse for her keys and removed the house key. "Take this. I know I won't be awake when you get back."

In the car, Tanya was thinking about what occurred in the living room of Pearl's house. She was slightly smiling when Sonny looked over at her.

"I know exactly what you're smiling about. If Pearl would have come in just two minutes earlier, we were busted."

"Now that deserves a double bustin, Sonny."

"Bustin and bustin again."

"You're so crazy," said Tanya. She continued. "Sonny, what did happen in there?"

Sonny was not ready for that question, although he was wondering the very thing. "I guess we were both feeling vulnerable and our emotions just got the best of us, that's all."

"That sounds so matter-of-fact, Sonny. Is that what you think happened, that's all?"

"That's all, Tanya."

"Well, that's not what I think at all, Sonny."

"So what do you think happened in there?

"Well, we were engaged in something that we both knew was going to eventually happen. True, we are both vulnerable, but a kiss happens when two people are genuinely attracted to each other. I don't know exactly how you feel, Sonny, but I think that I'm attracted to you."

Sonny remained silent after Tanya explained what she thought and revealed her feelings. He didn't want to add any fuel to the fire that was burning in him or ignite a fire in Tanya. He had to draw a boundary somewhere, so he chose to draw it here, by not saying anything else about the matter.

The drive to campus wasn't a long drive, and they were nearing the main entrance. There were signs posted at the entrance that led them directly to the facility where the event was being held.

When they arrived, the parking lot was near capacity, but Sonny found a place to park not too far from the building.

They walked at a fair distant apart from one another, signifying they were together but not a couple. Sonny was okay with it; however, Tanya wished that they would at least be close enough to touch hands occasionally.

Approaching the building, there was a poster that immediately caught Sonny's attention. He believed it was a picture of him but wasn't sure until they got closer.

"Bustin!" he said when he saw the image.

"Oh my god," said Tanya. She continued as she read the poster. "Karaoke night featuring "Choirboy" Sonny Brooks." She began to laugh.

"What's funny, Tanya?"

Pointing up at the poster, Tanya responded, "This. Choirboy, are you kidding me?"

"They just insist on calling me 'choirboy.'"

"I think I'll call you choirboy too."

"That's not funny, Tanya. Not funny at all."

They continued on into the building and were met just inside by Malcolm. "Hello, Sonny, I see you found your way here."

"Ah man, it's already a mad house in here. I had no idea there would be so many people."

Malcolm looked over at Tanya, who was dressed in a black loose-fitting dress that draped lightly revealing the contour of her body. Having a low-cut neck, much of her bare chest was exposed while her breasts were tastefully playing peek-a-boo.

"So who might this be?" asked Malcolm with his eyes fixed upon Tanya.

Sonny couldn't help but notice Malcolm's fixation, which made him feel a bit protective.

Before he could introduce Tanya, she beat him to it. "I'm Tanya, Sonny's date for the night."

Sonny was astonished by the announcement of the date. He hadn't considered this outing as a date. In fact, he had no thoughts of it being anything more than Tanya just hanging out with him because she had nothing else to do.

After announcing that she was his date, Tanya then reached out and took Sonny by the hand, instead of offering it to Malcolm.

Sonny tried hard to not look surprised, which he did accomplish. Malcolm received the gesture and moved on. "So, Sonny, how did you like the poster outside?"

"I wanted to ask you about that. Was that your idea?"

"Yes, it was. I thought that maybe some of your fans would see it and attend tonight's event. By the look of it, I can say it worked."

Sonny looked around the building and remarked, "I guess it did work."

Malcolm went on to explain to Sonny how the night would go. "So the first thing we're going to do is have a presentation by the fraternity that's actually sponsoring this event. Have you ever been to a step show, Sonny?"

"No, I haven't, but I know my brother pledged with the Omega's."

"What about you, Tanya?"

"Yes, when I was in college but not since then. I didn't pledge."

Malcolm was a bit surprised, that neither was involved with any fraternity or sorority. "Well, I'm sure you both will enjoy the show. The next thing will be an open-mic interview with you, Sonny. I will—"

"Hold on a minute, Malcolm. An open-mic interview?"

"Yes, we will have the interview where your fans can hear what you have to say. Then there's going to be karaoke singing, and we hope that you will be a participant."

Sonny had a look of consternation. Tanya was concerned and asked, "What's the matter, Sonny?"

Sonny was unsure what it was that caused him to feel the way he was. He tried to explain. "It's not like I haven't sung in front of people since I left Vegas. I just haven't been in front of this kind of crowd since then. You know, church folk are a lot easier to sing in front of and—"

Tanya interrupted Sonny's babbling, "Oh, stop it, Sonny. You know what this is like. It's not like you have never done it. So there must be something else bothering you."

"I don't know what it is, Tanya. I'm just nervous about the whole thing." Turning to Malcolm, Sonny began saying, "I'm sorry for wasting your time, Malcolm. I can't do this."

Malcolm was not expecting this from Sonny. But he was experienced in getting people to do the very thing that made them nervous, especially interviews. He felt that he could convince Sonny also.

"Listen, Sonny, I understand how you must feel. There is a lot going on in your life right now that is more important than this interview, but you can do this. You came all the way from Saint Louis for this very thing. Not to mention Alicia. I know it must be weighing heavily on your heart, especially the death of DJ Walker.

"I think you would make them both proud by showing strength of character by giving this crowd all and more than what you gave them the first time you visited Las Vegas as a naive church boy from Saint Louis. I also believe that this beautiful young lady would be very disappointed if you don't perform for her."

Sonny took in every word and looked at Tanya. It was obvious to him by her body language that she agreed with Malcolm.

"Bustin! I guess I can't disappoint anybody."

Tanya just smiled.

"So you'll do it, Sonny?" asked Malcolm.

"Bustin! What choice do I have? I'll do it."

Malcolm was pleased. "Great, Sonny, and remember, your fans are expecting you to rock the house tonight."

"Sure, Malcolm, I'll rock the house."

Chapter 20

It was an unusually cool night in Vegas, and Rico was feeling every bit of it. He had finished the beer that he had purchased earlier and was now hungry and wanted more beer. The money that he took from DJ's safe was nearly all spent on drugs and alcohol.

Where he was at, there was a convenience store just a half-block away. He would make his way there.

He made sure that there were no cops on the street before he entered since the store was at an intersection. He waited a short while because there were customers inside. When they exited the store, he entered walking with his head down so that any cameras would not reveal his face. He saw only one employee, who was a young Mexican-American male.

As he walked down the aisles, he looked for small packaged food items. Finding some Vienna sausages and chicken salad in small cans, he quickly stuffed several cans into his pockets. His pants were big and sagged down below his buttocks, and his shirt hung below his waist.

He found a package of saltine crackers that he concealed in his hand as he entered the men's restroom and entered a commode room. While inside, he pulled the sausages out of his pockets and began eating them with the crackers.

He was in there for several minutes, so the clerk became curious. He looked around the store and didn't see Rico anywhere, so he assumed that he had left without him knowing.

About five minutes after Rico had gone into the bathroom; two cops pulled up to the store and came in.

One of them went to the soda cooler and the other was making himself a hot dog. Rico was just finishing his dinner and was making his way out from the restroom, when he saw one of the cops standing close by.

"F—" he said. He quickly moved back inside. He stayed there for about a minute, too afraid to even breathe. Suddenly the door swung open and in came one of the cops.

Trying to be nonchalant moved quickly to a urinal and turned his back to the cop. The officer seemed to not notice Rico as he made his way to the same commode that Rico hid in while eating his stolen food. Consequently, he left the empty cans there on the floor.

Seeing rubbish all over the floor, the officer turned to ask Rico about the trash. When he turned, he saw Rico leaving the restroom. Somehow this seemed to be suspicious behavior, but he let it slide.

The other officer was adding condiments to his hot dog when he just happened to see Rico in haste nearly running out of the store. "Did you know he was in here?" he asked the clerk.

"Naw, I thought he was gone, man."

The cop paid for his sandwich, and his partner approached him. "Hey, Steve, did you see that guy in the bathroom?"

"Yeah, I saw him. Why?"

"He just ran the hell out of here, and this guy here didn't even know that he was in the store."

"Is that right?"

The attendant handed the officer his change and said, "Yeah, man. I saw him come in, but I looked for him and I don't see him no more. I thought he was gone homes."

"There were some cans of sausages and some tuna or something on the bathroom floor," Said one of the cops.

"He must've taken them in there and ate it, I guess," said the clerk.

"Think we ought to check him out?"

"It's a slow night, why not." The two officers got into their cars and drove off.

Fate would have it that they went in the same direction that Rico was headed. "There he is."

They maintained their speed as they closed the distance between themselves and Rico. Deciding to cross over to the other side, Rico looked back to see how close the approaching car was. He recognized it as a police car and panicked. He took off running and cut through a parking lot.

The officers pursued him at a safe speed, watching closely where he might try to lose them. It was very dark out, and as Rico ran through the parking lot, his adrenaline was so high that it was blinding and he ran into a cement block which was holding a direction sign.

The force of the collision caused his face to smack into the sign pole, which also caused him to fall backward onto the ground. He was knocked complete unconscious.

"Oh sh!" said one of the cops as he witnessed the collision.

"Damn, that had to hurt like hell," he added.

They pulled up to Rico who lay there motionless, his face bloodied from what looked like a broken nose. One of the officers knelt over him and tried to bring him back into consciousness. He had to apply smelling sauce, which did the trick.

Rico jerked slightly, but he was still in a daze.

"Hey, what are you running from?"

Rico didn't answer. Soon it came to them who it was that they had just run down. They remembered seeing Rico's mug shot on the Internet as a suspect to the murder of DJ Walker.

"This is the man we've been looking for, and we found him knocked out by a 'one way' sign."

"Yeah, I guess he went the wrong way."

Although Rico was only half-conscious and face bloodied, the officers read him his rights and he was arrested, handcuffed, and taken to the station.

Slowly Rico gained more of his bearings as the squad car approached the station. Detective Riley was notified by radio that the suspect was in police custody. Therefore, he was there awaiting their arrival.

Rico could hardly sit up straight due to the pain in his head and the injury to his face. At the station, the officers were not very easy with him. As he was pulled out from the back seat, he hit his already aching nose on the upper doorjamb.

"Come on, man, my nose hit the car!" yelled Rico, reaching to sooth his nose with a light touch.

"Yo, I think my nose is broke!"

One of the officers commented, "Don't blame us for that. You're the one who ran into the one-way sign." Both officers began laughing.

"That shit ain't funny yo," complained Rico.

Inside the station, Riley was drinking coffee and smoking a cigarette. He had time to go home and get freshened up, so he felt a little more relaxed. Unfortunately for Rico, Detective Riley was at the end of his patience with the violence in his city, and Rico was about to feel his wrath.

Rico was brought into the interrogation room and was told to take a seat. Riley noticed the blood that was beginning to dry on his face.

"What happened to you?" he asked harshly.

"I think I broke my nose."

"How did it happen?"

"I don't know. Ask them." Rico pointed back at the arresting officers.

"What happened?" asked Riley.

One spoke. "We were pursuing him, and he ran through a parking lot and smashed into a signpost."

"You were pursuing him for what reason?"

"We had reason to believe that he was shoplifting in 7-Eleven store, and we wanted to ask him some questions. When we approached him as he was walking down the street, he spotted us and took off running. We didn't speed up because he ran through the parking lot."

"And so he ran through this lot and hit a signpost, is that right?"

"Yes, sir, that's correct."

Detective Riley went and stood near Rico. "Let me see that." He reached down taking Rico by the chin and examined his face.

"Yeah, it's broken, but you'll live." Somebody go and bring him a cold towel.

"Yes, sir."

Riley continued with Rico. "So were you in the 7-Eleven stealing?"

"I was hungry."

"You were hungry?"

"Yeah, man, I was hungry."

"So tell me your name."

"Ricardo."

"What's your full name?"

"Ricardo Fleming."

"You go by Rico, is that right?"

"Yeah."

"So, Ricardo Fleming, do you know that we have been looking for you?

"Yeah, I heard something like that."

"I'm sure you have. Do you know why?"

"No, I don't. What did I do?"

"We're not quite sure what you did. But we suspect that you were involved with a murder that took place over twenty-four hours ago. Tell me, Rico, what were you doing at Wannabee's at approximately 3:00 a.m.?"

Before Rico answered, the cop came back with a cold wet towel and a plastic bag with something in it. He handed Riley both items.

"I'm sorry, Rico. What were you doing there about that time?"

Rico knew that he was in trouble, but he wasn't going to say anything.

"I asked you a question, Mr. Fleming," said Riley angrily.

Rico held to his defiance. Now Riley was really mad.

From behind Rico, he took the towel, reached around, and pressed it onto Rico's broken nose and applied pressure.

Rico howled in agony. He kicked his feet and tried to stand, but Riley slammed him back into his seat.

"Listen here, you hood rat. You may think that you got away with something the other night, but just like the rat you are, you left your filthy droppings at the scene of the crime."

Riley removed a half-empty bottle of Olde English 800 beer from the plastic bag and placed it on the table in front of Rico.

"This crap will mess up your gut and your thinking if you drink too much of it," he said. He could sense that Rico recognized the bottle as he kept his face in the cold towel.

"It has your fingerprints all over it."

"Don't I get to make a phone call?" asked Rico.

"Sure you do, but not until we're finished with you."

Riley sat in the seat next to Rico and looked into his eyes. "Would you like to know something, Rico? I have a strong suspicion that you also had something to do with the murders that happened about four months ago.

"I have been investigating this working diligently day and night, trying to piece this thing together. Now I finally have the missing piece. We know that the gunman in the ambush was hit by a bullet but didn't get medical help. So if it's not too much of an inconvenience to you, I'd like for you to take your shirt off."

"I'm not taking off shit, man."

Riley, remaining calm rose from his seat and took Rico by his shirt collar. "We can do this the easy way or my way."

The two cops were still there, and they moved toward Rico. Knowing that this could get ugly, Rico said, "Okay yo. I'll take my shirt off."

He removed his shirt and exposed a scar that was left by something that penetrated the middle of his bicep.

"Man, that doesn't look good," said one of the cops.

"How did that happen, Rico?" Riley asked.

"Gang fight."

"How long ago?"

"I don't know."

"Well, it doesn't appear to be that old. I would say about four months ago. It would probably look better had you gotten medical attention. Why didn't you?"

Rico didn't answer.

"Listen, Rico. The sooner you talk to us, the easier this will be for you. I want to know if you had anything to do with the death of DJ Walker."

While putting his shirt back on, Rico spoke. "I want to make my phone call. I'm not saying nothing till I get my call."

Riley decided to let him make his call. A cop escorted Rico to a phone that he could use.

Rico dialed the number. Since all calls were collect, an operator put the call through. Rico was hoping that the call would be accepted. The call went through and there was an answer.

"Hello." A man's voice was on the other side and sounded very irritated.

"Yo, it's Rico.

The other party was silent.

"Yo, I need you to contact a lawyer for me."

"I knew they were going to get you," said the person on the other line. "I can't help you, Rico. I told you not to do anything stupid, but you don't listen. Now you're on your own."

"What am I supposed to do, Oliver?"

"Now you really pissed me off. I told you to never use my name. Go to hell, Rico, and while you're there, tell Q that it's all mine now." There was silence. Rico knew that the caller hung up.

He handed the phone back to the cop, and he was escorted back to the interrogation room.

"Did you make your call?" asked Riley.

"Yeah, I did."

"Did you call a lawyer?"

"I don't have one."

"After you see the judge, he'll assign you a public defender." Rico, with his head down, looked condemned.

"Take him to booking, and make sure he gets something for his nose."

Before he was taken away, Riley said, "Rico, you've come to the end of the road now. It's time to reap what you've sown. Oh, and before I forget, I also know that someone else was there. He left fingerprints."

Back at Too Short's place, Oliver aka Too Short was packing some things in a suitcase. He was going to get out of town as quickly as possible. The last thing that he could afford was to be implicated in this case.

Although he tipped off the cops and informed Rico about the deal that was going down on the night of the multiple homicides, he didn't have anything to do with killing anybody.

He was just a janitor at Starz and was tired of being pushed around. Now all of the spoils were in his hands. He had the deed to the nightclub and the money that was stolen from DJ and Q. While packing, he reminisced of the time he spent working for Q.

That arrogant, bastard! How could he think that he could play me the way he did? Oliver also remembered how he heard Q talk about setting up Sonny just in case something went wrong with his drug operations.

I couldn't let him do that to Sonny or Alicia. I had to stop Q before he got too big and destroy every young life around him. I just didn't know that DJ had set him up and got Alicia shot.

Oliver had to hurry, so he finished packing and was headed out to his car when he heard a knock on his door. He couldn't imagine anyone coming by, so he was hesitant. Again there was a knock and then someone saying, "It's the police we need to talk." They could see Oliver through the half-open window blinds.

Oliver started to turn away, but the quick-acting police kicked the door in and rushed him, knocking him to the floor. Once down, they put him in cuffs and arrested him.

"What did I do? You can't do this to me." Oliver struggled.

"You're under arrest for suspicion of murder." Afterward, his rights were read. Oliver knew that he was being taken for the death of DJ.

Chapter 21

Martha was at home getting ready for bed. She decided not to spend the night at the hospital with her husband, because she needed to get some rest, knowing that every hour or so, the nurse would come in to check on Raleigh and she would be awakened.

As she got comfortable in bed, her telephone rang. She kept it on the nightstand beside the bed. Seeing that it was RJ, she answered, "Hello."

"Hello, Mom, how are you doing?"

"I'm doing well. I'm in bed now, but I'm fine, Son. How are you?"

RJ wasn't doing very good because of his problem with Maxine. "I'll be all right I guess." His mom was oblivious to what that meant.

"Mom, I need to talk to you about something."

"Okay, what is it, Son?"

"Mom, I don't want you to be upset or angry about this, but I don't think that I'm going to marry Tanya."

Martha did not respond in any way as she listened. RJ was not prepared for the silence, which usually meant, keep talking.

"Well, Mom, Tanya and I are not alike at all, and I just don't think that I love her enough to be with her for the rest of my life. Besides, she's off with Sonny and—"

"Wait just a minute, Raleigh Jr." He knew that he was in trouble now. "What has this got to do with your brother?"

"Nothing really, Mom I just don't—"

She interrupted him again, "You don't what, trust her with him? Is that what it is?"

"Well, Mom, if you put it that way, yes, I don't trust them together. You saw the way she looked at him at dinner. She's always taking up for him, and I just don't like it."

"RJ, listen to yourself. You need to be honest with yourself, because you don't have me fooled at all. There must be something else going on that you're not telling me. Could it be this partner of yours?"

RJ remained quiet. Martha continued. "RJ, your father is in the hospital, and only the Lord knows his condition. Here you are telling me that you have doubts about Tanya because she's with your brother. I would have thought that you were worried about your father, which you failed to ask how he's doing."

"I don't know what's going on in your life anymore. You've become so private. There's reason why Tanya may find your brother more interesting, because you are so distant from everybody, even her. That's what I've noticed.

"Tell me this. Have you spoken to Tanya about how you feel? Does she know?"

"Not yet."

"Are you sure about this, RJ?"

"Yes, Mom. I think so."

"Then you ought to tell her as soon as she returns from Vegas."

"I will, Mom."

"RJ, why do I feel like there's something else going on here? Is there more that you're not telling me?"

"There is."

"Well, what is it, Son?"

"It's my partner, Maxine. She told me yesterday that she's pregnant."

"So is she pregnant by you?"

"That's what she told me."

Martha couldn't believe what she was hearing. "The apple doesn't fall far from the tree," she said.

"What is that supposed to mean?" asked RJ.

"Nothing, RJ. It means nothing at all."

RJ could sense the change of tone in his mother's voice. He had no idea just how much he had disappointed her.

"So, RJ, she said the child is yours. You haven't denied it yet, so I suppose it's true."

"Mom, I'm sorry I had to tell you this way."

"No, Son, don't apologize to me. It's Tanya you need to apologize to."

"She'll never forgive me. I can't tell her. Besides, Maxine and I are finished. She's sold the restaurant and is moving back to Louisiana. She doesn't want to have anything to do with me. I can't tell Tanya this. She'll leave me too."

"Wait a minute, boy! You just said that you don't want to marry her, so why not tell her?"

"Mom, I never said that I didn't want to be with her. I just don't want to marry her."

Martha was starting to lose it with RJ. "If that's not the most selfish thing that I have ever heard! You can't leave that poor girl hanging like that, RJ. What's wrong with you?

"Haven't you learned anything in your life about how to treat people? You can't go around sowing bad seeds. One day you will reap what you've sown, and the trouble is, you might sow one seed, but it comes back double. Boy, you better repent because I see harvest time approaching."

"Mom, there you go getting religious on me. I will handle this my way. I just thought that I'd let you know what's going on. I didn't expect to get preached at. I'll talk to you tomorrow. You have a good night, Mom." RJ disconnected.

Martha was very upset. *What in the world happened to her baby?* She wondered. One thing she did know was that, RJ was following the steps of his father and didn't know it. She wanted him to understand the mistake he's making, *but how would he learn when he's being so stubborn?*

She figured the only way he would see the light is to have the light shined upon him. Martha decided that as soon as Raleigh was able that she would tell him about his eldest son, so in turn, he could disclose the dark history of his own past. Hopefully, RJ after knowing the truth will change his ways.

Before going to sleep, she read a few chapters of her Bible and prayed to God that he would somehow intervene and show RJ the error of his ways.

Meanwhile, in Los Vegas, Sonny was at the event trying to get comfortable with the idea of being there with Tanya. She was acting as though they were really a couple, taking charge at times to get him a drink, make him a plate of appetizers, and even ate from the same plate.

It was now time for the interview as Malcolm was directing Sonny on where to stand so that the cameras for the local news station could get a good shot.

"Just stand here and look into that camera straight ahead when you talk. It's just that simple."

"Just that simple?" repeated Sonny.

Tanya was away; she had gone to the ladies' room, and while there, her cell phone rang. She answered it, and it was RJ.

"Hello, RJ. I'm glad you called."

"Yeah, I finally had time to get away from work and decided that I better explain what happened this morning."

"Oh, that's okay. There's no need to explain. I made it to the airport in plenty of time."

"So have you seen your sister yet?"

"Yes, I have. She's no longer in a coma, but doctors are still concerned that it may be a long time before she fully recovers."

"That must be tough on you. You know, not seeing her for so many years and when you finally do see her, she's in this condition."

"Yeah, it's hard." Tanya moved from the ladies' room and out into the hall where there was a lot of background noise.

"What's all that noise I hear, Tanya?"

"Oh, Sonny and I are at a huge dance party and karaoke event at the college."

RJ became suspicious. "You didn't tell me that you two were going to be hanging out at a dance party."

"Well, we really didn't know about the dance, but Sonny was previously asked to come because he is a featured guest. He's going to be interviewed, which will be shown on one of the local stations."

As she approached Sonny, the interview was just about to get started. Tanya wanted Sonny to know that his brother was on the phone.

"Hold a minute, RJ. Here's Sonny. Do you want to speak with him quickly?"

RJ answered yes, since he wanted to let Sonny know about their dad.

"Sonny, it's RJ." She reached the phone out to him.

Taking the phone, he placed his hand over one ear so that he could hear clearly. "Hey, bro, what's shaking?"

When RJ began to speak, the phone began breaking up, and Sonny could hardly make out what was being said.

"What did you say, you're breaking up?"

"Dad is . . . hop . . . day . . . esting." The phone was breaking up badly.

"Hey, RJ, I'll call you back later. My interview is about to start." RJ could barely hear what Sonny was saying. Sonny hung up the phone before RJ could give him the news.

RJ was not happy about the two of them being out like this together. Because of his own lack of trust in himself, RJ couldn't trust them.

The interview was beginning, and Malcolm was at the podium about to introduce Sonny. After taking care of the preliminaries, it was now time.

Malcolm had the full attention of the audience as he began to introduce Sonny.

"About a year ago, the city of Los Vegas, Nevada, was thrilled by one of the most amazing amateur singers to ever hit the karaoke circuit. He thrilled audiences everywhere he went, winning every contest he entered, even the big one that landed him a contract. However, four months ago, one night, tragedy struck our city. Four people were violently killed and one seriously injured. Tonight we have with us the star attraction which brought hundreds of people out to witness for the first time, the main attraction of that night performing with his newly formed band. On his return visit to Sin City, USA, we have all the way from Saint Louis Missouri, we all knew him as choirboy give a great welcoming applause to the sensational Sonny Brooks!"

The audience exploded. Sonny felt like he was finally back to where he belonged, in the spotlight. Tanya was surprised by the love and admiration that the people had for Sonny.

After several minutes of applause, Malcolm settled down the audience and began his interview. "So tell us, Sonny, how does it feel to be back into the spotlight?"

Sonny looked into the camera lens as he was directed and answered, "Bustin!"

The crowd repeated, "Bustin!"

Sonny was not expecting that response. Malcolm explained, "Everybody remembered that you always said 'bustin,' so it's been a catch phrase ever since."

"Bustin," remarked Sonny.

Again the audience echoed, "Bustin!"

Sonny laughed. So did Tanya, who was standing not far from the stage.

"So tell us, Sonny, what have you been doing over the last several months?"

"Well, back at home, I've been going to church and working at the family business."

"Well, I understand, Sonny, that you have been working on a very special project. Is it true that you are working with a former Grammy winning producer on a CD? Is that right?"

Sonny was curious as to how Malcolm knew about the recording. "Yes, that's right, but how did you know?"

Malcolm looked out into the audience and smiled saying, "He wants to know how a news reporter found out about his project. Now that's classic." The audience began to laugh. Sonny realized how foolish it was to ask.

Malcolm changed the interview to a more serious subject. "So, Sonny, it's no secret that the person who was very close to you was tragically killed a couple nights ago. Tell us what the late Dennis Jerome, DJ Walker, meant to you."

Sonny wasn't prepared to answer any questions about DJ, especially since he hasn't been buried yet.

"Well, you know, Malcolm, this is very hard for me to talk about, because I felt very close to DJ and not only him, but his wife Pearl and not to mention his niece Alicia, who is lying in the hospital now from what happened a while ago."

Sonny began to feel the pain of seeing Alicia lying in the bed totally helpless near a vegetative state. However, he mustered up the strength to speak clearly.

"DJ was very important not only to me, but to this community. He provided a platform for anybody who wanted to be a star for a night to show what they can do. When I walked into Wannabee's for the first time, I didn't know what I was doing there or where going there that night would lead me.

"Well, I was in for the ride of my life. I met some wonderful people and had lots of fun, but as you may not know, my life took a turn for the worse."

"So how could that have been, Sonny? You had seemingly everything going for you. People loved to hear you sing, you were winning lots of money, and most of all, you had a beautiful woman by your side."

"Malcolm, have you ever heard the saying, 'not everything that shines is gold'?"

"Well, that's what my life was like when I was here. All the bright lights, all of the popularity and money: man, I thought that I had it made.

"I had finally made it to the big stage, and I was going to bask in the glory of it all. Well, was I ever wrong! What I thought was golden was nothing but fool's gold. Yes, it shined like the real thing, but it was all deception.

"My life was actually spinning out of control. The fast life, drugs. What you all didn't know was that I was addicted to cocaine.

"Then the murders happened. My hotel room was ransacked, and all of my money was stolen. I was so caught up in the mayhem of this life that I never put my money into a bank where it would have been safe.

"It was all stolen, and I was left penniless and depressed. I had no car. My friends that I thought I had couldn't help me. I found myself at a homeless center. Somebody even stole my shoes when I was asleep out on the streets."

Malcolm was surprised by what he was hearing from Sonny. He wanted Sonny to add spark to the party, but his story was bringing something different. The young people in the audience were actually listening.

"Why do you feel the need to tell all of this to us right now, here, tonight, Sonny?" he asked.

"Because I made a promise to my savior, and Lord, Jesus that if I ever had the chance to tell people about the deception that my life fell into, I would do it no matter who liked it or not. The most important thing for me is to let young people know that life is all about the choices we make, and no matter what those choices are, there are consequences—some good, some bad. Mine turned out to be bad, but I thank my God right now that he turned what was meant for bad into good, because all of these people here tonight get to hear the truth of where I've been and the road I had to travel to get here."

Sonny then took the microphone away from Malcolm and walked to the edge of the stage looking out at the audience. The television cameras continued to run despite the disruption, but Sonny didn't care, as Sonny had the audience captivated with a different message.

He began to speak even more candidly to them. "Listen, people. You all think that I'm somebody who seems to have it made. The truth is that what I truly have is contentment, but it took tragedy to bring me to the realization that the grass isn't greener on the other side.

"I know that a lot of you come from good homes and some may be not so good. I come from a good home. Not a perfect home, but a good one with the same challenges that many of your homes are faced with.

"But trust me, you think that your life would be so much better when you leave home, perhaps it could be, I don't know, but don't be in a hurry to find out. Life can be tough for a young person who's never experienced independence.

"You may think that it's going to be a party every night, but that's the deception of the world. I left a near-perfect environment to come here in search of myself. I didn't realize that I already had what I needed—a loving family and friends at home who really cared for me. What I found was that living life in the fast lane is dangerous. I can't tell you why my life was spared, but I know that it was by the grace of God that he prevented me from being in the wrong place at the wrong time."

He looked over at Tanya who was watching him speak with so much passion. It looked as if she was crying. He turned back to the audience. "You guys really want to know something? I didn't come here because of the spotlight and karaoke. I came here because a dear friend of mine was nearly killed. In fact, I thought that she was dead. So I came back because of her. I also came back because her sister is here with me.

"I came back to make right the things that went wrong the first time I was here, and what that is, is to tell all of you that in life, fame and fortune isn't as promising as it looks, because in an instant, it can be gone.

"Relationships are what matters. A relationship with God through his son Jesus is the most important relationship anyone can have. I'm here to tell you that God wants to have a relationship with every one of you." Somehow the audience was still there listening to what Sonny had to say. Even Malcolm was paying attention.

"You all came to hear me sing some song that will put you in the mood, whatever that mood is, but I have a new song in my heart."

Sonny stopped talking and began singing. He sang a song that was very popular in the gospel music genre, by Marvin Sapp, which was also a major crossover hit.

He sang, "Never could have made it, never could have made it without you. I could have lost it all, but now I see, you're there for me. I never could have made it . . ." He continued to sing, ministering to all of the wandering souls out in the crowd. Many of the young people knew the song and began singing along.

His testimony reached the hearts of those kids who were straddling the fence in their relationship with God and with those who never had a relationship and were now seeing the light for the first time.

Women in the audience began to cry, but this had nothing to do with Sonny's singing. They were crying because of the truth in the words that he spoke and was now singing.

Tanya felt the unction to go out into the audience and began praying with some of the young women there. Present were other Christians, who after hearing what Sonny had to say followed

Tanya's lead, both male and female, and began praying for each other and leading many to the Lord in prayer.

What was taking place was the move of God in the most unlikely setting. What was meant to be a worldly dance party became a revival with many people being saved on the spot. This went on through the night, and it was all caught by video recorders and cell phones to be downloaded on YouTube.

The dance party turned revival, lasted into the early morning hour. When it finally ended and many people were filled with the Holy Spirit, Sonny was left with a feeling of peace in his spirit. He felt that this time he used his gift to the glory of God, and God was glorified.

Tanya was also feeling a sense of serenity. She had been worried about her sister Alicia ever since she arrived in Vegas, but after what had just taken place, her worries didn't seem so heavy.

When all of the people finally cleared the hall, Malcolm and Sonny had a talk. "Well, Sonny, you really surprised me. I had no idea that you were going to do this. I thought you were going to bring the house down, but you brought the fire of God down. I don't even know what I'm saying, but I know what I felt."

Sonny was not about to take credit for this, as he would have done not that long ago after he sang a song in church. "Well, Malcolm, to tell you the truth, I didn't know what I was going to do. But Jesus spoke to me and I listened, so he gets the credit for this."

"Sonny, all I know is that something happened here, and I'm sure it's going to be all over the Web. Looks like you did it again."

Sonny was curious. "Did what?" he asked.

"You came back to Vegas and excited the crowd."

At this point, he realized that Malcolm was oblivious to everything that happened. "Well, Malcolm, it's late or early, and I have to get some rest. It's been a long day and night."

"I just want to thank you again, Sonny, for coming and doing the interview. I'm sure we have lots to talk about later. So you two go and get some rest, and we'll be in touch."

"Okay, Malcolm, you take care. We'll talk later."

Malcolm shook Sonny's hand and gave both him and Tanya a hug, saying good-bye. He watched the two depart, but he had to stay back to make sure that all of the equipment was packed and loaded.

The drive back to Pearl's house was a quiet drive. Tanya leaned her head on the window as Sonny drove. He was too tired to talk. When they arrived, it was dark inside.

"She must be in bed," said Tanya.

"It doesn't matter. She gave me the key, remember?"

Sonny opened the door and they entered trying to keep quiet. "It sure is dark in here," said Tanya.

"I wander where the light is."

"No, don't turn the lights on. We don't want to alarm Pearl," said Tanya.

"Well, I'm tired. I need to sit down," said Sonny. Thinking he remembered where the sofa was, he felt his way around in the dark until his feet touched the bottom of the sofa.

"Here it is." He flopped down.

What he didn't know was that Pearl was lying on the sofa. She had not slept in her own bed for the last couple of days. Besides that, she was a very heavy sleeper. She never heard them as they came in. Sonny barely missed sitting on Pearl's head as his bottom side landed on the edge of her pillow.

"Ahhh!"

Sonny jumped up. "Bustin! I'm sorry, Ms. Pearl. I didn't know you were there."

"Yes, I'm here. What are you two walking around in the dark for?"

"We didn't want to wake you," answered Tanya.

"Is that right? Well, you did anyway."

Sonny apologized, "We're sorry, Pearl."

Pearl sat up and rose from the sofa. "That's all right. I need to get off that sofa anyway; I can hardly sleep on it. My back is aching." As she rubbed her back, she remembered what she had seen on the late-night news.

"Sonny, I saw you on television. It looked like something big was going on there at the college."

"Yes, there was an interview with me."

"But what happened, because all of a sudden, they switched to something else. They said something about technical difficulties."

"The station must have cut us off, because the cameras were running the whole time."

Pearl was curious. "Why would they do that?"

"Pearl," said Sonny. "I wish that I could tell you all that happened, but I can tell you this. Some people there had their lives changed and God moved in that place."

"It was awesome," said Tanya.

"Yeah, you might read about it in the paper tomorrow."

Pearl was tired and decided that she would get the rest of the story later, so she retired to her room. Sonny finally took a seat on the sofa and Tanya sat beside him.

They were both very tired; Tanya laid her head on Sonny's shoulder and rested her arm around his waist. Sonny didn't protest or resist. He did, however, stroke her hair with his hand.

Tanya snuggled closer, looking up into Sonny's eyes. As he looked at her, he couldn't help but see Alicia eye's looking back at him. He fought the urge to push away, because he was really feeling Tanya.

Softly he began to sing a lullaby. It was a sweet melodic song that made Tanya even more relaxed. She had never heard anybody sing so softly and beautifully; it was hypnotizing to her.

As Sonny sang, Tanya's now-heavy eyelids met bottom to top and the curtains into her soul were closed for the night. Sonny didn't bother to move. He just sat there, starring at Tanya as she slept in his arms.

Chapter 22

Oliver was struggling futilely as he was walked down the corridor of the police station to see Detective Riley. Riley was anticipating putting the missing pieces to this crime together, and now his main piece had arrived.

They did not bring him to Riley's office; instead he was brought to a larger office which had several desks with lots of papers and a computer on each. There were present other officers, some in uniforms and others in plain clothes.

While there, Oliver was placed in a seat and was told not to move. Riley was notified and was on his way.

There was some commotion coming from down the hall and was headed into the office. Four officers were struggling with two guys. Oliver recognized both of them. They were the two guys that made the hit on DJ.

"Damn," said Oliver.

Riley who was standing nearby, as he had just entered the room, asked Oliver, "Do you know these guys?" He looked up at Riley with a disgusting frown but didn't answer.

Soon after, the shady-looking character which made the call to the police about Rico entered the room and began discussing something with the two arresting officers.

After his discussion with them, he went over to Riley. He asked if he could have a talk with Rico.

"Yes, you can have a couple of minutes with him."

Rico was taken back to the interrogation room. When Rico saw the person whom he was to talk to, he recognized him as the guy in the convenience store that was being nosy. It turned out that this guy was Mathias, the private investigator. Again he was doing undercover work, because there was suspicion that Rico could have been hanging out in the area.

"Do you remember seeing me?" he asked Rico.

Rico looked at him. "Yeah, man, I remember."

"Well, I followed you to where you were hiding out. I didn't see you when you left the house, but somehow you got yourself caught. What I was able to do was get the police over to that house. Would you like to know who we have in custody?"

"Not really, but I know you gonna tell me anyway."

"That's right, I am gonna tell you anyway. We have Oliver and your two buddies."

Rico tried to remain unmoved by the information. He just slouched down in his seat.

Oliver continued, "I know the code on the streets. You don't snitch, but for you, my friend, it doesn't matter. But we do need your help. Now you'll get a lawyer and you'll go before the grand jury and you'll be arraigned and so on, blah, blah, blah. You know all of this, I'm sure.

"However, you can make things a lot easier on yourself if you cooperate. And by the way, the rest of your colleagues will get the same speech, but remember in these situations; only one will get the breaks—that is, the one who talks first and most."

After Mathias finished with Rico, Rico was taken back to his cell. The other guys were booked and questioned the same way, but Oliver was the only one who talked. It was discovered that Oliver was an ex-con who wasn't planning on doing any more time in the big house.

He told Riley about how he worked at the bar for Q and how Sonny was being set up to take the fall if ever anything was to go wrong. He also told how Alicia was caught in the cross fire because DJ was the one who told Rico and his gang about the drug deal.

"Yes, DJ had it out for Q. He didn't like how Q was taking over all of the business and selling drugs at the same time."

"So how did DJ find out about the drug deal?" asked Riley.

Oliver answered, "I told him. I overheard Q talking to his guy from Florida, and I told DJ. Then DJ asked me if I knew anyone who would carry out a hit on Q, and I told him about Rico.

"Rico had a beef with Q because Q was cutting him out of the business. All Rico wanted was a small piece, but Q was too greedy. He wanted it all for himself. He was building quite an empire using his nightclubs and this guy Sonny to bring in his customers.

"After I told DJ, I had nothing else to do with the rest that happened. You know, DJ was never the same after that night. His wife's niece getting shot and all she shouldn't have been there in the first place."

Riley still had to know why Oliver's fingerprints were on the safe. "So why you were at Wannabee's the night DJ was killed?"

"Because the building belonged to me. Q took it over because I was behind on taxes. I was renting it out to DJ, and then I got hooked on drugs and was using all of my money to buy drugs from Q. Eventually, I got in debt and he forced me to sign my building over to him, before DJ could buy it from me. This is why DJ had Q set up for the ambush.

"After that night, DJ continued his business at Wannabee's, and Starz was standing vacant. So DJ was going to move into Starz my building. I couldn't see another takeover of my place. So I had Rico and his buddies to go over and scare DJ into giving me the deed to the building.

"They were supposed to call me back to let me know if it worked, but they never did. I decided to go down there myself to have a talk with DJ, but when I got there, he was already dead. I saw that the safe was open, so I took the deed and insurance papers."

"So, Oliver, can you tell me where you got the money that we found in your luggage?"

"Rico handed it over to me. Apparently, DJ was holding the cash from the ambush. He had never given Rico his cut. So when Rico killed DJ he took this money. He gave me some of it for letting him lay low in my pad.

"One more thing," said Detective Riley. "Where were you going?"

"I was on my way to Oakland, California. I have family up that way."

"Well, I guess you have to change your plans."

Oliver appeared to be worried about the chance he may end back in jail. He was willing to do any and everything to keep that from happening.

"Listen, Detective, I don't want to go back to the pen. It wasn't a pleasant place. Just tell me what you want and you got it, but first I need to see my lawyer."

Riley realized that this case would be over soon, so he told Oliver just enough to get him relaxed about his probable testimony.

"You'll have time to call your lawyer, but for now, we have to keep you at least until daylight."

Oliver was taken to booking where he ran into Rico on his way back to the cell. They exchanged stares and Rico threatened him.

"You better keep your mouth shut, punk, or else!" Oliver didn't respond.

Big Mike and Craig were already in their cells as they were arrested for shoplifting. Mathias had them under surveillance while in disguise, and the cops apprehended them just outside the twenty-four-hour thrift center where they were stealing clothing.

Detective Riley was in a state of relief as he finally felt that this investigation had come to a near end. He knew that there was still work to do, but he was confident that there would be a conviction.

"Hey, Riley, what are you going to do now that we made an arrest? You know this will be over soon," asked Mathias.

"Well, my friend, I have some property in the south. I think it's about time for me to retire. But for now, I'm taking the rest of the day off. I need some rest. Good night."

Although it was nearing daybreak, Mathias returned the gesture, "Good night, Detective."

Chapter 23

Back in St Louis, RJ had given up on trying to contact Sonny to tell him about their dad. His attempts failed each time as his call went directly to Tanya's voice mail. He decided to leave a voice message with the information that Sonny had to have.

While in his apartment trying to figure out why so many things were going awry in his and his family's lives, he began to think about what he told Maxine out of anger. Although he was struggling in his faith, he really believed that there must be a higher power; he just wasn't sure who or what that may be.

He began to read his Bible, to try and find some answers. Remembering the time when his father was teaching on the life of King David, he turned to the Book of Second Samuel, chapter eleven and began reading.

As he read about David's affair with Bathsheba, he couldn't help but realize the similarities of David's family and his own. This he soon dismissed as coincidental. *It couldn't possibly be like my family*, he thought.

RJ read until he couldn't keep his eyes open any longer. He put his Bible down on the coffee table and stretched out on the couch. His apartment was not the typical bachelors' pad. He had a friend an interior decorator to make his place look exquisite.

Maxine enjoyed spending nights with RJ because it had so much space. Tanya also loved staying there on occasion. As he lay

201

there, thinking about how he messed things up with Tanya, and with Maxine, he also wondered about how much damage he must be doing to his family.

The last thing he ever wanted was to hurt his mom with the news of his promiscuity. He hurt inside really bad. Wrapping his arms around a pillow, he held it tightly, wishing it were Tanya. Soon he was asleep.

It was now day in Las Vegas; Sonny was feeling the pain in his body from sleeping sitting up with Tanya lying across his lap.

He looked at the clock on the wall; it was ten o'clock. It was yet very early for him, and it looked like a herd of cattle wouldn't awaken Tanya.

He had to get from beneath her so he could go and relieve himself in the bathroom. Slowly he lifted her head and tried to rise up. Tanya was much heavier than he expected, so he pushed harder to get her shoulders off his thighs.

It just so happened that when he pushed, he pushed too hard and Tanya was flipped over onto the floor.

"Oh, shoot!" he said as Tanya hit bottom.

Tanya awakened. "Sonny, why did you push me on the floor?"

She sat up rubbing her elbow which hit very hard. "I'm sorry, are you okay?"

"No, my elbow hurts, and I'm on the floor. What do you think?"

"I'm sorry, Tanya. I had to go to the bathroom."

Still sitting on the floor, Tanya asked, "Why didn't you just wake me up? I have to go myself, anyway."

She stood up and walked away. "Where are you going?" Sonny asked.

"Where do you think? I said I had to go to the bathroom."

When she turned away, Sonny quickly jumped up and tried to beat her there. He tripped over his shoes and fell back to the floor. Tanya then ran to the bathroom and shut the door.

While he waited for Tanya to come out, he heard what sounded like a cell phone alert. He searched for Tanya's phone and found it on the floor beneath the sofa. When he looked at it, he saw that RJ had left a message.

Knocking on the bathroom door, he let Tanya know that she had a message from his brother. "Can you hand it to me, please? The door isn't locked," she asked.

Hesitantly, Sonny opened the door and reached the cell phone through. He felt Tanya's hand as she took the phone. "Thank you," she said.

"Bustin, you need to spray, flush, and turn the fan on or light a match or something," he said.

"Forget you, Sonny. You play too much."

He walked away laughing.

Inside, Tanya listened to the voice mail. From the living room, Sonny heard the toilet flush and water running, so he hurried and stood near the doorway. "Hurry, Tanya, I'm about to go all over myself."

When the door opened, Tanya came out with a look of consternation. Sonny noticed her countenance. "What's the matter with you, Tanya?"

"I think you need to listen to this." She handed Sonny the phone.

He listened. "Sonny, this is RJ. I tried to tell you last night about Dad, but there was so much distortion in the lines. Anyway, Dad is in the hospital. He's undergone some tests to find out the problem.

"Apparently, he had been coughing up blood the last couple of days, but you know how Dad is. Mom found out early yesterday morning and rushed him to the emergency room. So he's been there since you left, but nobody could let you know because you left your cell phone at home." As the message replayed, Tanya could see his mood begin to change.

After the message ended, Sonny handed the phone back to Tanya. "Man, I have to get home."

Pearl was awakened by the talking in the hallway and came out to see what was going on. She saw Sonny looking worried and Tanya with her hand on his shoulder.

"Good morning, kids."

"Good morning, Pearl," said Tanya.

"Yeah, good morning, Pearl," said Sonny.

"What's the matter, Sonny?" Pearl asked.

Sonny looked at Pearl; she could tell that he was really bothered by something. "It's my dad. He's in the hospital."

"Oh, I'm sorry, Sonny. What's the problem?"

"I don't know. My brother said that my mom took him to the emergency room, because he was coughing up blood."

"Oh my god, Sonny, that doesn't sound too good."

"No, you're right. It doesn't."

"So what are you going to do? Do you have to leave right away?"

"I think that I should, but I'll have to get in touch with my mom and find out his condition first."

"Oh, I'm very sorry to hear that, Sonny. I'm sure it's going to be all right."

Sonny knew that she was only being kind, because quite frankly, she didn't know and neither did he.

"Yeah, I hope so."

Pearl patted Sonny on the shoulder and turned away saying, "Oh, goodness, I have to go to the bathroom."

Before Sonny could react, she was closing the door behind her and locking it.

"B—"

Tanya stopped him, "Bustin, right?"

"Yeah, Bustin."

After finally getting some relief, Sonny joined Tanya on the sofa where she was lying. "You look like you could get some more sleep too, Sonny," she commented.

"Yeah, you think. We got back at what time?"

"It was a long night."

"So, Tanya, tell me this. How is it that you can feel so comfortable sleeping on the couch with me, while you're engaged with my brother?"

Being caught completely off guard by his question, Tanya took a second to think about a good answer. "I guess because I feel comfortable around you. I don't think that there is anything wrong with that, do you?"

"I'm not really sure. It just seems awkward to me."

Tanya decided to mention to Sonny what she had thought of while on the plane, but as soon as she did, Sonny asked to use her phone to call his mom.

"Sonny, don't you think it's still a bit early to call her. She's probably been with your father most of the night."

Sonny hesitated and put the phone down and lowered his face into his hands. "God, I need to find out what the problem is with my dad," he said.

Tanya sat up and rubbed the back of his shoulders, trying to comfort him. "Just wait until midmorning to call her. I'm sure she'll tell you everything then, Sonny."

"I guess you're right, Tanya. I need to wait until she is up and about."

As he sat back on the sofa, Tanya turned and looked him in the face. It was a different sort of expression that Sonny hadn't seen on her before now.

"What's the matter with you, Tanya?"

Quickly, she decided not to mention the thing that was on her mind. "Oh, it's nothing."

"What do you mean nothing? Just a second ago, you looked like you had something serious on your mind, so don't tell me, 'Oh, nothing.'"

"Okay, Sonny, I'll tell you." She sat more straightly and looked more intently into Sonny's eyes.

"Sonny, I need to know what's going on with RJ and why he's been acting so strange toward me."

"You noticed that?"

"Stop, Sonny, I'm serious. You know what I'm talking about, don't you?"

"Yes, I've noticed a change in his behavior, but believe me, I don't know a thing that's going on with him. Have you asked RJ?"

"No. I haven't had time to talk to him since we've been here, and before we left together, he didn't seem to have any time for me. He seemed so caught up with his business partner at the restaurant."

Sonny thought he might help Tanya figure this thing out on her own. "So, Tanya, have you met his partner yet?"

"No, I have not."

"Don't you think that's kind of strange to not have met RJ's business partner?"

"I don't know, Sonny. Should it be?"

"Tanya, I think it's strange that you haven't asked to meet her, him, or them or . . . I mean."

205

"Exactly what do you mean, Sonny?" she asked him sternly.

Sonny just gave her a certain look. "Are you telling me that his partner is a woman?"

"I ain't saying nothing. I'm just saying. You know what I mean?"

"No. I don't know what you mean. But what I think you're saying is that RJ's business partner is a woman and I should have reason to be concerned about that. Is that right?"

"You didn't hear nothin' from me, okay?"

"That bastard!" She was angry. "Why would he keep that from me, Sonny?"

In her anger, she reached over and grabbed Sonny by his collar and began pulling it tight around his throat. He gasped for breath, she was really choking him.

"Sonny, you better tell me everything right now, or you will never say 'bustin' again."

He could feel by her grip that she was serious. He began straining the words, "Okay, I'll tell you, but please let go, I can't breathe."

Realizing that she may be hurting him, she let Sonny's throat and collar loose. Sonny began gasping for air while he gathered himself together. He looked up at her, and she had this look of bewilderment in her eyes.

"Bustin, I'm glad I'm not the one engaged to you. I feel sorry for my brother."

"Sonny, I'm waiting!"

"Okay okay, I'll tell you."

"Her name is Maxine, and he's been spending a lot of time with her, and that's all that I'm going to tell you, Tanya."

"What do you mean that's all?" She reached for him again, but he jumped from the sofa and made space between them.

"Look, Tanya, I may not care a whole lot for what RJ is doing, but that doesn't mean I'm going to tell what it is. Now I've told you enough. I'm going to have to face him myself, and remember he's still my brother."

Tanya lowered her head and began to cry. She had figured that RJ had been cheating all along but just couldn't face the truth of it. Now she was almost certain. Sonny began to feel bad about saying something at all.

"Look, Tanya, I'm sorry for all of this. I didn't want to say anything that would upset you."

"It's not your fault, Sonny. I made you tell me. I was wrong for getting you involved."

Sonny just stood quietly. He had something else to tell Tanya but decided that it should wait until later.

"May I sit down next to you, Tanya?" he requested nervously.

"Don't be silly, Sonny. You can sit."

They both just sat on the sofa for a while saying nothing until the house phone rang. It rang twice before Pearl, who was getting dressed, called out from her bedroom, "Somebody answer that."

Sonny answered, "Hello."

"Hello, this is Officer Adams at the Las Vegas Police department. Is Pearl Walker available, please?"

"Sure, she is. Can you hold?"

"Pearl, it's for you. It's the police department."

Tanya sat up straight, and Sonny held the phone until Pearl came in to get it.

"Hello, this is Pearl Walker."

"Mrs. Walker, this is Officer Adams. I'm calling to let you know that we have the suspect for your husband's murder in custody."

"Oh, thank you, Jesus," she said solemnly.

"There is nothing that we need you to do, and I assure you that justice will be served. Again I give my condolences."

"Thank you, Officer Adams. You have a good day." She hung up the phone.

"What was that all about, Pearl?" asked Sonny.

"They have the guy who killed DJ in custody."

"That's great, Pearl," said Tanya. "When is the trial?"

"Well, he didn't say, but it's all in God's hands now. I just pray for the strength to make it through."

"Amen," said Tanya.

Sonny noticed that Pearl was all dressed up to go somewhere, so he asked, "So what's on your agenda today? You're dressed very nicely."

"Oh, I'm going to meet with DJ's lawyer today. He says it's important for me to come and see him."

"Do you know what it's about?"

"Yes, I do know a little. He said something about insurance and other important documents."

"Well, I'm running late, so you two get cleaned up because I know you all slept in your clothes, and go ahead and get whatever you like out of the fridge to eat."

"Oh, thank you, Pearl. We'll make sure everything is clean before we leave," said Tanya.

"I expect nothing less, Tanya."

"Okay, Pearl, you have a good day."

In the meantime, Sonny was sitting on the sofa calling his mom. He couldn't wait any longer as he had to know the condition of his father.

He was glad to hear his mother's voice as she answered the call.

"Hello."

"Hello, Mom, it's me."

"Sonny, I'm glad you called. I've been trying to get hold of you for about two days now. How are you doing?"

"I'm good, Mom."

"And how's Tanya?"

"She's good also. Mom, how's Dad. RJ told me that he's in the hospital?"

"Well, Sonny, I'm not quite sure what the issue is, but he seems to be doing fine. I haven't talked to the doctor yet."

"You must be at the hospital now?"

"Yes, I am. I'm waiting to talk to the doctor." Just then the doctor entered the room. "Just hold on, Sonny. He's here now."

Sonny could hear the doctor talking in the background and tried desperately to hear what he was saying.

Martha spoke back to Sonny. "Son, I'll have to call you back later, okay?"

"What's going on? Can't you tell me what the doctor is saying?"

"I'll tell you later, Son. It'll be all right." She hung up the phone.

With Sonny off the phone, Martha told the doctor to go ahead and tell her about what the tests revealed.

"There was a lump in his throat which we did a biopsy on and found it to be malignant. It looks like its probably late stage II or early stage III throat cancer."

"Oh, Jesus—I didn't know."

"I understand, Mrs. Brooks, but the symptoms can be deceptive. It can start with a sore throat or constant coughing to a change in one's voice."

"You know when I think about it, his voice was beginning to sound kind of raspy, lately. I could tell that he was having a difficult time because he hasn't been preaching the same way. It's like he's been holding back."

"Of course, he was probably feeling some discomfort," the doctor commented.

"So what does this—what are you going to do?"

"It means that unless we can combat this, aggressively his cancer will quickly move to its third stage. We will give him radiation treatments, which will cause some discomfort in his throat."

"Will he be able to preach? He's our pastor."

"I'm sorry, but any strain will cause him pain. I'm afraid his preaching days are over at least for a while. It all depends on how he responds to treatment."

Martha asked the doctor if Raleigh knew this yet. "Yes, he does. I talked to him just before you came in. He should be still awake if you would like to go in."

"Sure, I would."

As the two entered Raleigh's room, he was getting his blood checked. The nurse was just finishing and gathered her things and left.

Before anyone said something, the doctor was paged, so he had to leave. "You two go ahead and talk things over. I have to get this."

"Okay, Doctor Anderson, and thank you for everything."

Now Martha was with Raleigh; she sat on the bed next to her husband, observing the bandage on his throat. "How do you feel, baby?" she asked.

"Tired," he said in a soft whisper.

"Listen, baby," said Martha, "I don't know how you feel about this, but I do know that your faith in God will make the difference."

Raleigh didn't say anything, as Martha spoke. "I want you to know that God has already provided you with healing. All you have to do is receive it and wait for it to happen. We will get through this."

Not wanting to strain himself, Raleigh whispered to Martha. "Do Sonny and RJ know about this?"

"I spoke to Sonny just a few minutes ago, but I didn't know the diagnosis yet. RJ called me last night, so he doesn't know either."

Martha began to wonder if she should tell Raleigh about RJ's problems. After considering it a minute, she opted to tell. "Raleigh, there's something that I need to tell you about RJ."

Raleigh looked on attentively. "When he and I talked last night, it was very disturbing. I don't know what to think about him or what he's gotten himself into.

"Apparently, he's been having relations other than business with this woman at the restaurant, which explains why he kept her identity from us."

"What do you mean?" asked Raleigh.

"Raleigh, RJ has gotten this Maxine pregnant."

Raleigh was shocked by what he heard. He tried to sit up higher but felt some pain. Martha helped him by sliding another pillow under his shoulders and doubled the pillow beneath his head.

She continued, "To make matters worse, he told me that he doesn't think that he's going to marry Tanya that he's not in love with her."

Raleigh shook his head in disbelief. "Is he crazy or something? What's gotten into that boy?"

At this point, Martha really didn't know where Raleigh's attitude was coming from. He of all people should be more merciful.

"Raleigh, maybe you should have a talk with him once you're able."

"Have a talk about what?"

Martha gazed deeply into her husband's eyes. She was thinking about the truth that had been hidden from their children all of their lives.

"You should tell both of your sons the truth about our family, Raleigh, especially now that it seems how RJ is headed down that same road that you once traveled, and remember, we were married."

Raleigh never wanted to have to disclose the whole scandalous affair with his sons, but he knew that if RJ listened, it would probably change the way he was living.

"Martha, I'm sorry."

"You're sorry about what?"

"I'm sorry about everything that I did. I know that what's happening now is the result of the seeds that I sowed so many years ago. I was such a young fool. I had everything that I could have wanted, but it wasn't enough for me. Now just like King David, I can say: My sins are forever before me."

Closing his eyes, he began to cry; one reason, it hurt him to talk and he couldn't say all that he wanted to. The other was, he loved his sons dearly, and he could see how his past has come to affect their lives.

"Yes, I'll have the conversation with them both. They need to know the truth."

Martha placed her hand on Raleigh's forehead and began to pray the prayer of faith. She prayed for his strength and thanked God for his healing. She also prayed for her sons, that they would not become bitter from what Raleigh would tell them.

Chapter 24

Sonny and Tanya were eating a late breakfast of eggs and sausage that Tanya had cooked. Sonny made a pot of coffee, which was very strong. Fortunately, Tanya liked her coffee that way.

"So, Sonny, are we going to leave today or tomorrow?"

"I would like to leave as soon as possible, but don't we have to give the airline a call?"

"Yes, once we decide on when we're leaving. I don't know how much time we need to give them."

Tanya rose from the table as she was finished eating, as was Sonny, and took his plate also and began to wash the dishes. Sonny helped her by putting away the things that they used.

When Pearl arrived at the lawyer's office, she entered the building and was greeted by a receptionist. "Who are you here to see, please?" she asked.

"I'm here to see Attorney Abercrombie."

"Do you have an appointment?"

"Yes, I do. My name is Pearl Walker."

"Oh yes, Mrs. Walker. He is expecting you. I'll just call him to let him know you're here."

After making the call to inform the attorney of his client, the receptionist turned her attention back to Pearl.

"The attorney will be out soon. Is there something that I can get you, maybe some water or coffee?"

"Oh no, thank you. I'll be fine, thanks."

"Okay, just have a seat in the waiting room, and he'll come out to get you."

"Thank you," said Pearl as she sat.

Noticing how plush the leather chairs were, Pearl wondered how DJ could afford such a lawyer. Admiring the décor convinced her that this was no low-fee attorney. After a brief wait, he came out to meet Pearl.

To her amazement, he was a black man. "Hello, Mrs. Walker, I'm Nathan Abercrombie. Pleased to finally meet you."

Pearl took his held-out hand. "Pleased to meet you too, Mr. Abercrombie."

"Oh, please call me Nate. Mister makes me feel old."

"Okay, I'll do that, Nate."

He led her into his office. Inside, it was beautiful. He had plaques and posters of football teams, along with all of his diplomas and certificates.

He had green plants that added a special touch to the office. His desk was huge and made of cherry wood.

"Please have a seat," he said to Pearl. Her seat was the same as the one in the lobby, which was very comfortable to sit in.

After some small talk, Attorney Abercrombie began discussing some of the things that he had to share with her. She was amazed by what she was told.

"Yes, Mrs. Walker, your late husband had an insurance policy worth five-hundred thousand dollars that was left to you."

"Oh my goodness, I had no idea he had a policy! I guess I really didn't know what he was doing with his money. He took care of everything when it came to paying bills and running the nightclub."

"Yes, Mrs. Walker, he took care of his business very well, but there is one other thing you must know."

Nathan rose from his seat and made sure that his door was completely shut. He then went into a closet and removed what appeared to be an old briefcase.

He placed it on his desk as Pearl watched. After removing some crumpled papers, he pulled out a bag and dumped the contents out on the table. What poured out of the bag startled Pearl. It was a large amount of cash.

"What is this?" she asked.

"Well, Mrs. Walker, this is money that your husband brought to me to hold for him."

Pearl's first thought was *why didn't DJ put the money into a bank?*

"I know what you're thinking, Mrs. Walker, and I'll tell you why there's this bag of money on my desk and not in a bank. Your husband came to me shortly after the murders that had taken place a few months ago. You know, the one involving Quinton Brown and also your niece." Pearl looked on saying nothing. "Well, he came to me and asked me to hold this bag for him. We had been doing business together for quite a while, so he felt safe coming to me with this.

"At first, I thought he had robbed a bank, but then he told me where the money came from."

"So where did it come from?" asked Pearl.

"Mrs. Walker, before I tell you that, I need to tell you that Dennis was looking out for you and his interest. What I'm about to tell you will definitely disturb you, but in the end, you will understand.

"This money came from the scene of the crime, when those people, including your niece, were shot down."

"Well, what did any of that have to do with my husband, and how did he get his hands on this money?"

"I'm going to tell you. After the shooting, a week or so after, he came to me with this bag. I wasn't going to take it until he explained to me why it was important that I did.

"Now here's the part that will upset you. Your husband had Quinton Brown and his connection in a drug deal set up by a local gang."

Pearl knew immediately what that meant. That DJ was partly responsible for Alicia being shot and ending up in the condition she's in.

"I can't believe this. He kept this from me all of this time. How could I have been so blind?"

"Don't blame yourself for not knowing what actually happened. The police didn't even know about this which is why he came to me.

"He couldn't tell you about the money, obviously, and he couldn't put in the bank because they already knew how much he was depositing each week. How was he going to explain the sudden rise in revenue in this economy?"

"So what did he bring the money to you for? You're an officer of the court. Aren't there legal issues involved?"

"Exactly. Why do you think I'm doing this secretly? Listen, there is nothing that you have to worry about, as long as you do as I say. But first, let me tell you why this money is here.

"Like I said earlier, this money is from the drug deal that went bad. DJ came to me in tears, totally distraught over what had occurred. He felt completely responsible for Alicia being shot and felt like he wanted to make good of what turned out be a disaster.

"He had one problem, though. How was he going to keep his secret from you, that he was the cause of Alicia being harmed? There was no way that he could ever tell you, instead we both came to the conclusion that this money would be used for any of Alicia's surviving siblings."

Pearl was having a hard time with what she was hearing, but she knew exactly who should get the money. She really didn't want any part of it.

"Well, Nathan, as you know, Alicia lived through the ordeal, but she'll never be what she used to be. The doctors informed me that there was just too much damage done to her brain."

"Oh, I'm sorry to hear that, Mrs. Walker."

"Well, I'm just glad that she's alive if not for Alicia, then for her sister."

Nathan was pleased to hear that there was a sibling. "So she does have a sister that's able to handle this kind of money and not do anything foolish with it?"

"Yes, Nathan, I'm sure her sister is very responsible. I believe she's in banking."

"Well, that's great. I'd like to meet her so that I can personally give her this money."

Pearl was now curious about how much money there was to give. "So, Nathan, exactly how much money is it anyway?"

"There's two hundred and seventy-five thousand dollars on this table."

Pearl nearly fainted. It took her a moment to get her composure, and then she reached out and picked up a bundle of one hundred-dollar bills.

"That's about two thousand dollars right there."

"Oh my god, what was DJ going to do with all of this money?" Pearl was incredulous.

"I really don't believe that he had any idea himself, Mrs. Walker, but I do know one thing: That could buy lots of cocaine."

"So, Nathan, if my husband got the money, what happened to the drugs?"

"Well, Mrs. Walker, your husband gave explicit orders, that I should never tell you that information. Given the circumstances, he chose what he thought best, over the alternative which I suggested."

"So what did you suggest, if I may ask?" Pearl queried.

"Let's just put it this way: It still found its way to the streets and I'll leave it at that."

Pearl was still holding the money and was about to put it down when Nathan spoke. "No, you keep that, Mrs. Walker."

Pearl refused vehemently, but Nathan insisted that she used it to help somebody else who may need it. After thinking about it a moment, she decided she knew who she would give it to.

After having their discussion about the money, Pearl was excited about getting home to let Tanya know about her wealth.

Back at Pearl's place, Tanya and Sonny were waiting for Pearl to return; also Sonny was waiting to hear back from his mom.

They were both asleep when Pearl entered the house. Sonny was immediately awakened by the door opening and closing. He was lying on the floor next to the sofa while Tanya was in Alicia's old bedroom.

"Hello, Pearl, how did it go at the attorney's office?" Sonny asked.

Pearl placed her purse on the coffee table, and as she walked into the kitchen, she said, "I need a drink. I know it's not quite noon here, but it is somewhere."

Sonny followed her into the kitchen. "We cleaned up after we ate just like we said."

Getting a cold beer out of the fridge, she asked, "Where's Tanya?"

"She's in the bedroom asleep. I'll get her."

"Yes, you do that. I have some bad and good news for both of you," said Pearl.

"Tanya, wake up. Pearl is back, and she wants to talk to both of us."

Still feeling fatigue from last night, Tanya gave no resistance as she slowly arose from the bed and followed Sonny.

"Hello, Pearl."

"Hello, baby. I have something to tell you. Have a seat."

Tanya sat at the table next to Sonny as Pearl remained standing and began to disclose the news. She told them everything concerning the insurance policy and all about how DJ was partly responsible for Alicia's condition.

Then she told them about the money. Tanya couldn't believe what she was hearing. Not knowing if she should feel angry or something else, all she knew was that she was going to receive a large amount of money, because of the tragic incident involving her sister.

At first, neither she nor Sonny believed Pearl's story about the money, not until Pearl pulled out the cash and they saw it for themselves.

"Bustin!"

"Oh my god! Where in the world?"

"I told you, Tanya. The attorney has all of the money, and he's waiting for you to come and get it."

There was something that seemed to be bothering Sonny. He wanted to know what happened to DJ and why he was killed.

"I don't understand why this happened to DJ, Pearl. Aren't you bothered by all of this?"

Pearl walked over to Sonny and reached out and gave him a hug. "Sonny, you know I loved DJ, and I was hurt terribly when I heard that he was dead. I didn't know what I was going to do.

"But having you two here has given me strength up until today. When I heard that he was partly responsible, I thought about the words my mother used to tell me years ago. She would say, 'Be careful about the seeds you plant because something must grow.'

"Those words were very sobering. I came to realize that the man I married twelve years ago was not who I really thought he was. He kept so much from me.

"Yes, I hurt, but life goes on, Sonny. Remember this; you have to live on even when something terrible happens to you or someone you love."

"Is it that easy, Pearl?" asked Sonny.

"No, Sonny, it isn't that easy. You take it one day at a time."

Sonny took a moment to reflect back to his late friend, Brother Winston. He knew that Pearl was right about that, because it was something that he had to do.

"One day at a time. Yes, that's it. One day at a time," he repeated.

Pearl had yet to meet with DJ's stepbrother who had flown down to make sure that all of the travel arrangements were in place for DJ's body. Pearl would fly to North Carolina with him where the funeral would take place.

Since Pearl had so much to do, Tanya and Sonny decided to drive their own car to the attorney's office as Pearl led the way.

Inside, Pearl introduced Tanya to Nathan. "This is my niece, Tanya, Alicia's sister."

Reaching out his hand to meet hers, Nathan greeted her, "It's a pleasure to meet you, Tanya."

Attorney Abercrombie wasted no time getting to business, telling Tanya everything. She could hardly believe what he was saying to her, especially when he told her how much money was in the bag. He assured her of the amount minus the two thousand that he gave to Pearl.

Wanting to make sure that Tanya was not going to do anything foolish, he wanted to know her plans on how she would secure the money and use it.

"Well, I'll get back to you on that, but I do need to go back to Saint Louis and talk about this with my fiancé."

"So you're getting married?" asked Nathan.

"Yes, I am. Is there a problem with that?"

"There could be a problem if the man you're going to marry is not able to understand about the money."

Tanya was interested by what Nathan just said. "What do you mean, if he doesn't understand? What is there to understand?"

"Tanya, you can never tell him about this money. And if you do, how do you explain that you just can't go spending it like the prodigal son that coupled with trying to explain where it came from in the first place?"

"Oh, I see now. I'll really have to think about that, don't I?"

"Yes, you'll have a lot to think about. Because you must know that you cannot travel with this money on a plane. So how do you intend on getting back to Saint Louis, on a bus or drive yourself? Either way will be dangerous."

Tanya was perplexed. She hasn't even touched the money yet, and it was already causing her a headache.

"Don't worry about it right now, Tanya. Take some time and really think about it and get back with me. In the meantime, whenever you need something, just call me."

They shook hands, and Nathan walked Pearl and Tanya out to the car where Sonny was waiting.

"Okay, don't forget to call me with your decision or if you need something. You both have a good day. Pearl, you have a safe trip to North Carolina." He turned and departed, entering the building.

"So how did it go?" asked Sonny as he got out of the car to talk to Tanya.

"It's true, Sonny. I work at a bank, but seeing all of that money and it's actually mine just blew me away."

"So where do you kids have to go right now?" asked Pearl.

"Nowhere at all," answered Sonny.

"Well, I'm going to the hospital to see Alicia and say good-bye. Do you want to come?"

Sonny answered, "Sure, I really wanted to go there sometime today anyway."

"That sounds like a good idea," Tanya added.

They went in separate cars and met at the hospital. They followed the same procedures as before to get to Tanya's room.

On the way to the elevator, they ran into Reverend Astin. He immediately recognized Sonny.

"Hello, Sonny Brooks," he said.

"Hey, Rev, what's happening?"

"Ah man, it's good seeing you. Where have you been since we first met?"

"I've been back home in Saint Louis and came back for an interview with the newspaper."

Reverend Astin smiled. "I saw you on YouTube this morning. Everybody on Facebook is talking about that party that turned into a revival. Man, it's getting tens of thousands of hits."

"Bustin! I had no idea that was going to happen."

Pearl interrupted, "Reverend, I was hoping to see you today."

"Yes, I was making my rounds here."

"Well I have something for you. I hope that you can use."

"Oh yeah, what's that?"

Pearl reached into her purse and pulled out the bundle of one hundred-dollar bills and handed it to Reverend Astin.

"It's about two thousand dollars," she said.

Reverend Astin didn't know what to say and knew better than to ask where it came from.

"I'm sure that you can find good use for this money, Reverend. Perhaps you can use it for your flower ministry."

"Well, thank you so very much, ma'am. I don't take these things lightly. I'll be sure to use it to the glory of God, just as it's meant to be used. You know, there are a lot of people that would be blessed if those with extra would give more often. Thank you and God will bless you."

As Reverend Astin walked off, Pearl asked Sonny, "Where do you know him from?"

"I met him the first time I came to Vegas. He was working at the men's store. Alicia and I were together."

Tanya could see something meaningful in Sonny's eyes whenever he spoke about Alicia. She was fully aware of their relationship, but she also had some feelings for Sonny that made her feel uncomfortable to think about.

They continued up to Alicia's room. Once there, they were glad to see Alicia awake; however, she was nonresponsive.

It would be the first time that she had actually laid eyes on Sonny since she last seen him at Starz.

Tanya and Pearl both wondered if Alicia would recognize Sonny. She didn't really show any signs either way toward anyone else. This would be a real indication if she would regain any cognizance.

When Sonny approached, he touched her lightly on the arm. She looked up at him with gazing eyes. Sonny could sense that she was looking straight through him.

He smiled at her, and she turned away as though she didn't see a thing. "Bustin!" he said, loud enough for everyone in the room to hear, even Alicia.

Something must have registered in her brain because as soon as she heard Sonny say "bustin," she turned back toward him. "Oh my god," said Tanya. Pearl looked on with cautious excitement.

"Hello, Alicia," said Sonny.

She looked like she wanted to smile, at least her eyes did; however, she turned away again. Sonny was saddened by this. "I thought she knew it was me," he said.

"I did too," said Tanya.

Pearl went over and rubbed Alicia's hair, which was growing back since the surgery, saying, "Well, the doctor warned us that we shouldn't get too optimistic about this. He said that she suffered a great deal, and if she does recover, it would only be minimally, and she would probably not remember anything from her past."

As Tanya listened to Pearl, she began to cry. Sonny placed his arm around her, holding her close. Nobody said a word while Tanya wept. Pearl continued to caress Alicia's hair and face, telling her that she would be away for only a short while.

That was when Tanya had a solution to her problem with the money that was left to her. "Pearl, I've decided what to do with the money, and I think it's going to work out for both of us, Alicia and me.

"While you're away in North Carolina, I'll stay here with Alicia as long as I have to, to take care of her."

"But what about your job?" asked Pearl.

"I'll call them and let them know what's going on. They'll understand. Besides, I can get a transfer if I have to."

Sonny then spoke. "That's a good idea, Tanya, but do you think that RJ will be okay with that?"

Tanya, who was now sitting, sat straight up in her chair and with much attitude said, "I don't give a damned what RJ is not okay with, Sonny."

"Oh, snap, Bustin, you go girl."

"Are you sure, Tanya? There isn't really a whole lot that you can do for Alicia, and she won't know that you're here anyway."

"You know what, Pearl? I don't care what those doctors have to say. The last I heard was that God and only God knows what lies ahead for any of us, so I'll confer with him. In the meantime, I'm going to stay here with my sister.

"When we were kids, she took care of me when I was sick, and even protected me from harm, so I owe her this. I'm going to stay."

While Tanya was speaking, her cell phone rang. Since Sonny was carrying it, he answered. By the number, he could see that it was his mom.

"Hello, this is Sonny."

"Hello, Sonny, this is your mom."

"Yes, ma'am."

"Sonny, I heard from the doctor, and your father has throat cancer. Now don't get upset, he'll be all right. He won't need surgery or anything like that."

"I'm glad that he doesn't need surgery, but I'm still concerned because we're talking about cancer."

"Yes, I know, Sonny. I'm concerned also. Anyway the other reason why I called is that your father wants you to come home as soon as you can. He wants to have a talk with you and RJ. Are you planning to be back soon?"

"Yes, Mom, I am. In fact, I was just talking to Tanya today about possibly leaving this week."

"Well, that's fine, Sonny. Wait a minute, will you? I think RJ is calling me." She changed over.

"Hello, Sonny, are you still there?"

"Yes, I'm here. Was that RJ?"

"Yes, it was I told him about your dad's diagnosis."

"How is he doing, Mom?"

"He's being RJ."

"Well, that could mean anything, Mom."

"Well, let me put it this way: he's not doing so well. So how's Tanya?"

"She's good. She's not coming back to Saint Louis with me. She's going to stay here with her sister, Alicia."

Martha was surprised to hear that. "It's probably best that she doesn't come home just now anyway."

"What do you mean by that, Mom?"

Martha became evasive. "It'll be all right, Sonny. These things have a way of playing itself out."

"I don't know what in the world you're talking about, Mom, but I guess I don't really care if it has something to do with RJ."

"Well, Sonny, you be safe and tell Tanya, we'll be praying for her, okay, Son?"

"Okay, Mom, I'll do that. I love you, and tell Dad the same for me."

"I will. Good-bye."

"Good-bye, Mom."

Sonny sat the phone down and looked at Tanya strangely. "What's the matter with you?" she asked.

"Nothing. It's what my mother said about you not coming back to Saint Louis with me."

"Well, what did she say?"

"She said it's probably best that you don't come back anyway."

"What could she have meant by that, Sonny?"

"I really don't know, Tanya. I really don't know."

Tanya stood and headed toward her sister. She sat next to her on the sofa and began to speak to her. "You know what, Alicia? You have a wonderful man. I really envy you. She then looked up at Sonny, who was standing there with his mouth hung open.

"You ought to see the silly look on his face, Alicia. It would make you laugh."

Sonny began to smile. At this point, he was really feeling Tanya, but he knew that it was taboo. How could he start something with her? She was engaged with his brother, and he already had something with her sister.

They all just sat around Alicia's bed sharing the good times they each had with Alicia, until it was time for Pearl to leave.

She said her good-byes to everyone and gave Alicia a kiss on the forehead. Tanya and Sonny stayed until visiting time was over, and they went back to Pearl's house.

They were both very tired and ready to retire. Tanya went to Alicia's old room, and Sonny opted for the sofa.

He was told by Pearl before she left that it was a sleeper, so he pulled out the bed and lay on it. He could hear Tanya in the bathroom taking a shower, and he began thinking about how beautiful she must look in there with water running down her sleek body.

Not wanting to be bothered by his imagination, he shook off the thought and tried to get some sleep.

He didn't want to sleep in his clothes, so he undressed, and since it was warm, he used only the top sheet to cover himself.

He was just about asleep when he felt one side of the sleeper bed sink down. He rose up just to see Tanya dressed in a silver nightgown, sliding in bed beside him beneath the sheets.

"Tanya."

"Sonny, I just don't want to be in bed alone tonight, so I hope that you don't mind."

Sonny didn't object.

He lay back down and turned his back toward Tanya with every intention not to let his flesh take over. As soon as he got situated on his pillow, he felt Tanya's long, slender, soft arm reaching around his shoulders and felt her body press gently up against his own.

He just lay there as still as he possibly could and felt relieved when he heard snoring coming from behind. Tanya had fallen asleep.

"Bustin!"

Back in Saint Louis, RJ was not handling the news about his dad very well. He had gone to a local bar to have a drink. While he was pouring down his third shot and was beginning to feel its effect, he decided to leave before he got drunk.

He drove home and made it there safely but was surprised to see a car parked in his other space. As he got closer to his parking spot, he noticed that the car belonged to Maxine, who was waiting inside for him to arrive.

He pulled up and parked; as he did, Maxine got out of her car and walked near the entrance to his apartment.

"Hello, RJ," she said.

"Hello, Max, what are you doing here? You are the last person that I expected to see at my door."

"I know, RJ. After our last meeting, I can understand why you would feel that way."

"So why are you here then?"

"RJ, I've been thinking about what I said. I really wasn't thinking when I said those things to you. We need to talk."

"Well, Maxine, you sounded pretty doggone clear to me then. What could we possibly have to talk about?" RJ then headed up the stairs to his apartment, and Maxine followed.

"Wait, RJ. I'm willing to let you back in."

RJ paused, turned, and asked, "Back in what?"

"I want to let you back into partnership with me at the restaurant."

"Is that what this is all about, Maxine? I thought you wanted to talk to me about our relationship, or perhaps the child, but you want me only for the restaurant. What happened to those other guys did they back out on you?"

Maxine didn't respond.

"Yes, that's it, isn't it? Your buddies backed out on you and now you come back here looking for me. I'll tell you what, Maxine. You can just get off my steps and get the steppin'."

As he turned away to go up the rest of the stairs, Maxine grabbed him by his shirt sleeve, pulling his arm toward her. RJ swung back to try and release her, but the force of his arm forced her backward, and she fell down the steps and was knocked unconscious when she hit bottom.

"Maxine!" RJ ran down to see about her.

He lifted her head to check her breathing. She was breathing however, there was blood coming from the back. "Oh, Jesus, what did I do?"

RJ began to panic as he dialed 911 on his cell phone.

When the EMTs arrived, RJ had covered her with his jacket and explained to them what happened.

While Maxine was being stabilized on the gurney, RJ spoke to the paramedics. "Is she going to be okay?"

One answered, saying, "She'll be just fine, although she has a small cut on the back of her head. We'll take her in, and she'll be thoroughly examined."

"Well, I just want you to know that it was an accident. She fell backward."

"We're not the cops, sir, but we do need to make a report. We'll get from her what happened also. I'm sure it was an accident."

"Oh yes, it was," said RJ. "But there's something else that you need to know."

"What's that?"

"She's pregnant, probably a couple of months."

"Thank you, sir. We'll be sure to check it out."

As the emergency vehicle pulled off with Maxine in the back, RJ entered his apartment, very upset about the whole ordeal. It was late, and he was too tired to even bother removing his clothes for bed, so he just flopped down on the living room sofa.

His mind would not let him sleep, so he decided to call Tanya. *I hope she's not sleeping*, he thought. *Better yet, I'll text her.*

Tanya, I miss seeing you. I hope things are well with your sister, and I'm anticipating you getting home soon. I love you, RJ. He pressed the send button.

The sound of Tanya's phone buzzing indicating a text message alarmed Sonny who was barely asleep. Tanya had long turned over and was in a deep sleep.

He picked up the phone from the end table next to the sofa and saw that it was from RJ After opening it, he read the message.

"Well, you just keep on waiting, Bro," he said softly. He placed the phone down and turned over and was now facing Tanya's backside.

He wanted so badly to reach out and touch her but didn't. He turned back over facing away from her and went to sleep.

Three Days Later

As Sonny waited to board the plane back to Saint Louis, he read the morning paper. The headline caught his attention: "Murder trial set for November 2011."

It would be the trial of suspected murder and troubled gang member thirty-five-year-old Ricardo Fleming. Also being tried for their involvement with the case is thirty-one-year-old Michael Clark and being charged as a juvenile, Craig Williams, all of Las Vegas, Nevada.

There was more about the case that Sonny read until the announcement to board came over the intercom.

CHOIR BOY II: A TIME TO REAP

He boarded the plane and sat near a window. Next to him sat a young lady who looked to be younger than Sonny.

"Hello," he said.

"Hello," she responded.

"Are you headed to Saint Louis, or is somewhere else your destination?" he asked.

"I'm actually headed to Pennsylvania."

"Do you live there?"

"Yes, I do, just outside of Pittsburg."

"So where's that?"

"Have you ever heard of McKeesport?"

"Not until now, but I'm sure it's a wonderful place."

The young lady laughed.

"What's funny?" asked Sonny.

"Oh, nothing, just what you said about McKeesport, being a wonderful place."

"It must be a wonderful place since you're going back, isn't that right?"

"Well, that's where most of my family lives."

"So my name is Sonny. Sonny Brooks. What's yours?"

"I'm Saundra Young. Pleased to meet you, Sonny."

"Pleased to meet you too, Saundra."

As the plane taxied down the runway, Sonny laid his head back and closed his eyes.

Saundra stole a quick peek at him. *He's cute*, she thought.

In his mind, Sonny thought about how attractive Saundra was. He felt her fumbling around below her seat. He opened his eyes and saw that she had a book. He looked at the cover which read, "Church boy."

"That looks like a good book, Saundra."

"It really is. It's about a young man who leaves home in search of his destiny after his best friend is killed in a gang fight."

"That's story seems familiar," Sonny remarked.

"How does it?"

"I actually left home once because my best friend died and I came to Vegas. You know they called me choirboy while I was here."

"Bustin!" said Saundra.

"Bustin!" Sonny began laughing.

Edwards Brothers, Inc.
Thorofare, NJ USA
September 27, 2011